PRAISE FOR SIMON GERVAIS

"In *Hunt Them Down*, Gervais has crafted an intelligent and thoughtful thriller that mixes family dynamics with explosive action . . . the possibilities are endless in this new series, and this will easily find an enthusiastic audience craving Hunt's next adventures."

—Associated Press

"[An] action-packed series launch from Gervais."

—*Publishers Weekly*

"Nonstop action meets relentless suspense . . . the blood flows knee deep in this one as Gervais uses his background as a drug investigator for the Royal Canadian Mounted Police to bring a gritty authenticity to his latest thriller."

—The Real Book Spy

"Gervais dishes out lavish suspense to keep a reader glued."

—*Authorlink*

"Superbly crafted and deceptively complex . . . this is thriller writing at its level best by a new voice not afraid to push the envelope beyond traditional storytelling norms."

—*Providence Journal*

"From the first page, *Hunt Them Down* is a stick of dynamite that Simon Gervais hands you, masterfully lights, and then dares you to put down before it explodes. Don't. It's worth a few fingers to read to the end."

—Matthew FitzSimmons, bestselling author of *The Short Drop*

"Your hunt for the next great adventure novel is over. If Jack Reacher started writing thrillers, he'd be Simon Gervais."
—Lee Goldberg, #1 *New York Times* bestselling author of *True Fiction*

"A huge thriller with intense action and emotion. *Hunt Them Down* had me squirming in my seat until the last masterfully crafted page!"
—Andrew Peterson, bestselling author of the Nathan McBride series

TIME
TO
HUNT

ALSO BY SIMON GERVAIS

PIERCE HUNT SERIES

MIKE WALTON SERIES

TIME
TO
HUNT

A PIERCE HUNT THRILLER

SIMON GERVAIS

Text copyright © 2020 by Simon Gervais
All rights reserved.

Published by Thomas & Mercer, Seattle

www.apub.com

Amazon, the Amazon logo, and Thomas & Mercer are trademarks of Amazon.com, Inc., or its affiliates.

ISBN-13: 9781542020824
ISBN-10: 1542020824

Cover design by Kirk DouPonce, DogEared Design

Printed in the United States of America

To Lisane, for allowing me to sleep on the couch for two weeks in a row.
To Flo and Gab, for understanding why Daddy couldn't go skiing with you.
To Louna, our family golden retriever, for all the walks we skipped.

PROLOGUE

Seventy-two hours ago . . .
Hotel Niles
Istanbul, Turkey

Charlie Henican woke abruptly, alarm bells going off in his head. He froze in the middle of a half-drawn breath and listened. Heavy footsteps were fast approaching. They were coming for him; of that he was sure. Somehow, someone had found out about him.

He dived for the loaded Glock hidden beneath the right-side pillow, but he was too late. They came in too hard. They came in too fast. They didn't leave him any chance.

There were six of them, all in black battle dress uniforms. No insignia of any kind. They took control of the room quickly and professionally. These men were soldiers, not amateurs. One man cleared the small bathroom while another stayed outside the room to provide security. The four others took position around Henican's bed, covering all angles. The men had automatic weapons, all pointed at him. Things weren't looking good.

"Your hands. Slowly," the leader said in nearly perfect English. "Don't make a scene. We don't want a mess. This is a family-owned hotel. I know one of the housekeepers."

It would indeed be a shame for one of the housekeepers to have to mop his blood off the nice wooden floor. Since Henican's arrival four nights prior, he had grown fond of the small hotel and its night staff, who always welcomed him back after his walks around the Grand Bazaar with apple tea and Turkish candies. Since dying in this room—as quaint and pretty as it was—wasn't part of his plan, he unwrapped his fingers from around the Glock and slowly withdrew his hand from under the pillow. The soldier on his right pounced on him the instant his two hands were visible. Henican was rolled onto his stomach. A knee, backed by the soldier's weight, dug into his spine, sending sharp jolts of pain up to his neck. The soldier shoved Henican's hands against his back and looped flex cuffs tightly around his wrists.

Another soldier grabbed Henican's Glock from under the pillow and removed the magazine before working the slide to eject the round already in the breech. Two soldiers gripped him by the elbows and lifted him up from the bed.

"Where are you taking me?" Henican asked as they led him outside the room. On both sides of the hallway, other guests, curious about the commotion, were starting to open their doors. Everything had happened so fast. Henican had been awake less than a minute.

"I want to speak to someone from the Canadian embassy," Henican said. "Now!"

With lightning speed, the leader turned around and punched him in the stomach, just above his navel. Henican gasped. Had the two soldiers not supported him, he would have fallen to his knees.

"We know who you are, Mr. Henican," the man hissed in his ear. "Despite what your passport says, you're no Canadian. You're an American assassin."

CHAPTER ONE

Now
Nassau
New Providence, Commonwealth of the Bahamas

Dorothy Triggs closed her eyes. The night breeze coming through the open sunroof of the Lincoln Aviator soothed her. This late, there was almost no traffic, and they were making good time toward the airport. She allowed herself a few precious seconds of respite, letting her mind roam free, and imagined herself basking in the sun on a deserted white sandy beach.

It would have been nice to spend a few leisurely days in the Bahamas. *Heck, even a few hours would be nice,* she thought. But she couldn't spare the time. Not now. Not with Charlie Henican missing his recent check-ins. As the deputy director of the Directorate of Operations—the clandestine arm of the Central Intelligence Agency—it was up to her to find a way to reestablish contact with Henican or, at the very least, find out what had happened to him.

Her first attempts had been met with frustration and grief. None of the agency's contacts in the region had come up with any actionable intelligence on Henican's whereabouts. Turkey was a complicated country whose allegiances switched almost weekly. The geopolitical situation was even more complex now that Turkish dependence on Russian gas and nuclear energy know-how was at an all-time high.

The TurkStream—a natural gas pipeline originating in Russia that had cost more than €11 billion—was finally operational. And the Turkish president had threatened to shutter an American early-warning missile defense system at Incirlik Air Base. Triggs had openly questioned Turkey's commitment to the Western alliance with President Joshua Reilly during their last meeting. Reilly had only partially agreed with her assessment and had explicitly forbidden her to run any covert operations in Turkey.

"Diplomatic relations with Turkey are dicey enough as they are, Dorothy," Reilly had warned her. "Don't you go over there without telling me first."

By sending Charlie Henican to Turkey, she had disobeyed a direct order from her commander in chief. That wasn't something she had done lightly, but to get to the Venezuelan narco-terrorist Jorge Ramirez, she'd been ready to shove a lot of chips to the middle of the table. Ramirez had been behind the distribution of a new, ultra-addictive synthetic amphetamine pill that had killed young American athletes and devastated countless families. As if that weren't bad enough, Ramirez had recently acquired highly sensitive intelligence detrimental to the national security of the United States.

And to me, Triggs thought. What she had done and tolerated in order to oust the former Venezuelan president and replace him with Colonel Arteaga—someone the CIA had at least some degree of control over—wouldn't be seen with a kind eye by the American public.

To keep congressional hearings at bay and safeguard all the progress they'd made in Venezuela, Ramirez had to be stopped. He had to be put down.

Permanently.

It was why she'd sent Henican to Turkey after Ramirez and why she was in the Bahamas now. To secure the help of Pierce Hunt. With him, she could offer the president complete deniability. If, God forbid, everything failed and Hunt was captured or killed, she could use the ex–DEA agent's reckless past against him to distance herself, the president, and the United States government from anything that happened in Turkey.

"What do you think Hunt will do?"

Seated next to her in the back seat of the Aviator was her son, Max. He pecked on his laptop keys in his signature two-fingered way as he spoke.

"He has no choice," Triggs replied. "He owes Henican too much. Don't you agree?"

"I'm afraid so," Max replied dryly.

Hunt, a former Army Ranger, was the ultimate operator. He didn't need to be babysat, and he wasn't in the game for the money—unlike most of her assets in Turkey. With his unfailing loyalty to his friends, Triggs knew he was the right man to go after Charlie Henican. The fact that Hunt had crossed paths with Jorge Ramirez before was also a major plus.

The problem was that Hunt technically worked for Tom Hauer, and the administrator of the DEA wasn't known to share his resources. Hunt wasn't a full-time DEA agent anymore, but he and his friend Simon Carter were valuable assets to hold in reserve, so Hauer kept them on retainer. They'd partnered with the CIA on an operation four months ago—the one that had led to Jorge Ramirez's escape—but Hunt had nevertheless impressed Triggs and her colleagues.

It had been a gamble to take a day and fly unannounced to the Bahamas to meet with Hunt, but the meeting had gone as well as she could have hoped.

After a moment, Max stopped typing, closed his laptop, and set it aside. He looked over at her.

"What is it?" she asked, sounding a bit impatient. She knew her son. Something was bothering him.

"Why send Hunt?" Max asked. "He isn't one of us. He doesn't know how we operate. I could go to Turkey. I have contacts there."

Triggs looked at her son. Max had been an infantry officer before joining the CIA thirteen years ago. He had spent ten of those years as an operative under nonofficial cover—NOC—in Turkey. His intelligence work had helped shape the past White House administration's foreign policy in the Middle East and in Asia. Then something bad had happened. Something terrible. His pregnant wife, Zehra, a local teacher he had met through a friend, had been killed in a mass shooting at a nightclub by a gunman associated with ISIS. Max had wanted to go after the perpetrator—a demand Triggs had flatly refused. Max had lost his mind, ditched the cover he had built for himself, and without informing his CIA handler—or his mother—gone after the perpetrator and his affiliates. A month later, Max had shown up at her Langley office. She'd never asked him what he had done during his thirty-day off-the-grid ordeal, but she had a pretty good idea from the number of dead Turkish citizens linked to ISIS who'd popped up in and around Istanbul. Since his return, he had served two years as an instructor at the Farm—the CIA training academy—and one year as her right-hand man at the Directorate of Operations. Max was well liked by his peers and by almost everyone on the seventh floor at Langley. By keeping him close to her and involving him in the decision-making process of her directorate, she hoped he'd stick around and take her place at the top when it was time for her to retire.

"Hunt's expendable, my dear. You're not."

Max grunted, clearly not satisfied with her answer. "At least pair him with another operator," he suggested, reopening his laptop. "One of ours."

"You have someone in mind?"

Max rubbed his chin thoughtfully, but Triggs wasn't duped. Her son already knew who he wanted Hunt to be paired up with. Max was manipulating her, and that made her incredibly proud. The ability to manipulate people was an important asset in the spy business, and that was even truer at the strategic level Max was now working in. Her son

6

was good at it, but she had been playing the game for much longer than he had. Max still had lots to learn.

"What about Harriet Jacobs?" Max asked. "She's a great operator, and she's good friends with Henican."

Triggs shook her head. "She's on an operation in Malaysia."

"Not anymore," Max replied. "I pulled her out."

"Did you now?" She raised an eyebrow.

Max glared at her. "You already knew, didn't you?"

"I'm the deputy director of the Directorate of Operations of the CIA, Max. It's my job to know at all times where my clandestine operators are and what they're doing. Wouldn't you agree?"

Her son flashed her an insincere smile. "Of course."

With the back of her hand, she slapped him on the shoulder. "You better, because in a few years, you'll be DDO," she said.

"So you think that partnering her and Hunt is a good idea, then?" Max asked.

"Absolutely. I've heard that Turkey's Aegean coast is a happy choice for honeymooners. And so is Istanbul."

Max laughed out loud. A rare occurrence nowadays. Her son had a wonderful, deep-throated laugh that reminded her more than a little of his father's, a navy pilot who had perished at sea during a training exercise a decade ago.

"What's so funny?" Triggs asked.

"Did you forget about Hunt's girlfriend? Not sure Anna Garcia will love the idea of that particular cover story."

"She'll understand," she replied, more or less convincingly.

"Should I set it up? Send Harriet Jacobs a warning order?" Max asked.

"Isn't that what you've been doing all along? Show me what you have." Triggs pulled Max's laptop toward her.

It took Triggs longer than she expected to go through the file Max had prepared. Her son had once again surprised her. The document was detailed, precise, and thorough. He had designed an entire overseas operation, including a financial analysis of the cost involved and numerous contingency and disaster-recovery plans. He'd even added a list of potential support personnel who could increase mission success probabilities.

"Great work, Max," Triggs said. "And good idea to pick Barry Pike and Colleen Crawford for support. They've worked with Hunt in the past."

She took a minute to think about it. Sending Hunt and Jacobs to Turkey, supported by a small team that Hunt had already worked with and trusted, made sense. She'd have to keep working her regional contacts for additional intelligence, but at least she'd have people she could depend upon on the ground, ready to act.

"All right," she finally said. "Approve transportation to Langley. Time is of the essence, but I want to brief them all personally."

CHAPTER TWO

Palm Cay Marina
New Providence, Commonwealth of the Bahamas

Pierce Hunt rushed past Anna Garcia, gun still in hand, and climbed the steps to the second floor two at a time. He'd almost shot Dorothy Triggs when she'd shown up unannounced in his living room.

Almost.

"Would you calm down for a second?" Anna called after him. "Please."

Hunt wasn't ready to calm down just yet. Triggs's unexpected visit had ruined the perfectly fine day he'd spent fishing with his sixteen-year-old daughter, Leila, on his new-to-him Cobia 296.

Why the hell hadn't Triggs alerted him beforehand?

Because she knew you'd refuse to see her, Hunt thought, answering his own question. Her son, Max, though, had looked as annoyed with his mother as Hunt had been. Max hadn't seemed thrilled to be there, either, but Hunt hadn't had much time to form an opinion about him since he'd remained quiet through the conversation.

"Pierce!" Anna shouted, her voice finally breaking through his thoughts. "What are you doing?"

"I'm getting my go bag," he said, opening the closet door. He pushed some clothes aside to reveal a fireproof safe embedded in a wall.

He set the gun on top of it and entered a five-digit code, and the safe opened.

"You can't be serious. It's past midnight. Can we talk about this?" Anna wasn't asking, and Hunt knew better than to ignore her.

He removed his go bag from the safe and turned to face her.

She was leaning against the doorframe of the master bedroom, her arms crossed, watching him defiantly with unflinching emerald-green eyes. Despite the chaos in his head and the urgency of the situation, Hunt was once again struck by Anna's lustrous beauty, which seemed to be accentuated by her emotional upset. She had the body of a professional dancer, her figure slim but curvaceous. Her skin was tanned brown and smooth, and her loose dark hair fell down past her shoulders.

"I just want to talk for a minute," she said kindly, taking a step toward him. "That's all."

Hunt studied her expression for a moment. Anna's lips curved into a smile. She took another step. She was close enough that Hunt could feel the heat of her body. His heart contracted.

"I have to go," he said, his voice apologetic. "Charlie . . . he would come for me."

Something in the set of Anna's posture and the light in her eyes told him she already knew that there was no way he would sit on his ass and simply hope for the best while his friend was downrange and badly in need of assistance.

Not after Gaza.

In 2007, Hunt and Henican had been part of a small task force of Rangers and Delta Force operators sent to Gaza to provide training and assistance to the Palestinian security forces in their struggle against Hamas terrorists. When two of Hunt's men had been killed and another had been taken prisoner, Hunt and Henican had mounted a rescue operation, despite being formally ordered not to intervene. They'd succeeded in getting their man back, but very few people knew the entire story of the operation, and even fewer knew how much of his soul Hunt had left in Gaza. Charlie Henican was one of those few.

"I know this isn't what I promised you, Anna," Hunt said. "But—"

"You're wrong. You promised me you'd take care of us. You haven't failed at that. Your daughter and my niece are upstairs, healthy and happy. They wouldn't even be alive if it weren't for you."

He cupped her chin in his hand. "What about you? Are you happy?"

"Are you?" she asked right back, softly.

"I was, up until Triggs showed up," Hunt said honestly.

"I knew what I was getting into when we moved here, Pierce. I'm no dummy."

"I never said—" Hunt started, but Anna put a finger on his lips.

"Let me finish, will you?"

Hunt nodded.

"You're the one thing in my life that makes total sense. You, Sophia, and Leila. You guys are my world now. You know that, don't you?"

"I think that's the nicest thing anyone has ever said to me," Hunt replied. He had to make an effort to keep his voice even.

They had moved to the Bahamas to escape the nonstop violence their lives had been filled with. For Hunt, it could be argued that the violent lifestyle had been his choice all along. Nobody had forced him to join the army or to volunteer for Ranger School. Truth be told, he had enjoyed the vast majority of his time in the military, and he could say the same about his time with the DEA. But for Anna it was different. She hadn't chosen that life. It wasn't her fault her father, then her brother, had controlled the most powerful crime syndicate in Florida. Every time she had wanted to get out, she'd been sucked right back in. And what about Leila and Sophia? In Hunt's opinion, they'd been the true victims.

That was why they had moved away from it all. To start fresh. A new beginning. The girls deserved it. Anna deserved it. And he did too. Now, he was being sucked back in. But did he have a choice?

Damn! They had made such progress. Since the death of her brother a year ago, Anna had legally adopted her niece and shut down the Garcia crime syndicate. She'd nearly been killed in the process, but her integrity and strength were only two of the many qualities Hunt loved about her.

He kissed her on the forehead. "I don't know how long I'll be gone for. You'll stay here with the girls?"

Anna nodded. "It's not the best timing, though. Have you forgotten we have houseguests coming? At least Leila will be glad to see her mother and Chris."

Hunt started to open his mouth when he felt his cell phone vibrate in his jeans pocket. He reached for it and looked at the call display.

Unknown caller.

Hunt debated whether to answer it or not. Everyone who mattered the most to him was safe and sound, either right next to him or sleeping upstairs. Then he thought about Charlie Henican, and he took the call.

CHAPTER THREE

John F. Kennedy Drive, Nassau
New Providence, Commonwealth of the Bahamas

Dorothy Triggs was so concentrated on preparing her upcoming briefing that she never saw the two dark-colored sedans until they were next to her SUV. Their high speed drew her gaze, but by the time she looked over at the first sedan, its front passenger window had already been lowered, and the muzzle of an automatic weapon was pointed directly at her.

Oh no.

"Threat left! Threat left!" Max yelled next to her. But he was too late.

The shooter opened up with his rifle, blasting rounds directly into the side of the armored SUV and sending ricochets off into the night. Some rounds must have found one of the tires, because the driver lost control and veered right toward the ditch dividing the highway.

"Hang on!" he shouted.

Triggs's heart crawled into her throat. Anticipation of crashing into the ditch at high speed stiffened every muscle in her body. At the last moment, the driver straightened the SUV and managed to stay on the road. To her right, Max had unfastened his seat belt and was reaching for the SUV's radio, presumably to call the embassy and request backup. But he never got the chance. The second sedan slammed into the right rear panel of the SUV in a perfectly executed and well-timed pit maneuver, forcing Max back into his seat. The rear wheels lost traction and started to skid. This time the driver wasn't able to recover. The bulky SUV swerved across the road, still going way too fast. It hit the ditch and flipped once, the world coming unhinged, shattered safety glass pricking her skin like a million microscopic needles. Triggs's seat belt dug into her torso. She screamed. The airbags deployed. The SUV hit a large tree and came to an abrupt halt with a metallic crunch. Dead silence reigned for a few seconds, and then the SUV's engine began to hiss, steam curling out of the hood.

Blood trickled from Triggs's forehead into her eyes. She lifted a hand to wipe it away, but an airbag prevented her from doing so.

"Mom? You okay?"

Triggs turned her head toward the sound of her son's voice. The muscles in her neck and shoulders protested the effort.

"Mom, we need to get out of the truck," Max pleaded, pushing away the airbags. "They're coming."

Images of the SUV going up in flames spurred her to fumble for her seat belt. But she was unable to stop her hands from shaking; the exercise was more challenging than it should have been. Her son had already climbed out of the SUV and was now issuing orders to the driver, who was on the radio with the embassy.

Triggs tried the door handle, but the door wouldn't budge.

Bullets fired from an automatic weapon pinged off the door, ricocheting everywhere. With a grunt, the driver kicked his door open and exited the vehicle, firing his pistol at the nearest attacker. Powerful hands grabbed Triggs's arm and pulled her from the SUV.

"Stay down," Max said, forcing her to take cover behind the right rear wheel of the vehicle. "The marines are on their way. Ten minutes."

"Who the hell ambushed us?" Triggs asked.

"Don't know, don't care," Max replied, inserting a fresh magazine into his pistol. "We just need to stay alive until the marines get here.

Stay down!" he repeated before standing up next to her. Using the rear of the SUV as a barricade, he fired his pistol into the darkness.

There was no QRF—quick reaction force—in the Bahamas, but there was a small contingent of US Marines assigned to protect the embassy. At Max's suggestion, she had traveled to the Bahamas off the books, which had meant leaving her security detail behind. They'd borrowed the ambassador's SUV and driver to get around.

A barrage of gunfire split the air above the SUV. Bullets riddled the rear of the car, and the driver cried out. He ran in front of the headlights and jumped for cover behind the front right wheel. The driver was holding his stomach with one hand, but his pistol remained in his other. The moonlight was bright enough for Triggs to see the pain on his pinched face. A moment later, his head slumped forward onto his chest. Triggs had no way to know if he was dead or simply unconscious, but what she did know was that she needed to help her son. There were an unknown number of assailants and only the two of them left. She duckwalked to the driver and grabbed his pistol. She ejected the magazine and checked how many rounds were left.

Six.

She pulled the slide back just a touch to see if there was a round already in the chamber. It was too dark to be sure, so she didn't chance it. She much preferred to lose a round than to pull the trigger on an empty chamber. She reinserted the magazine and racked the slide back, chambering a new round. She risked a look over the hood, only to feel something bite into her shoulder. The force of the impact spun her around, and she fell to the ground, dropping her pistol. She felt as if she'd been kicked by a horse. The edges of her vision were going black, excruciating pain radiating from her shoulder. She sobbed for breath, fighting off unconsciousness.

I've been shot, she thought. She hadn't even seen where the shot had come from, and for some unknown reason, she found that to be so unfair.

"Mom!" Max shouted in horror, bringing her back to reality.

"I'm okay, just a flesh wound," she called out, knowing that wasn't the case. Never in her life had she been in such pain. Her right arm was dead and useless. She felt hot blood running down the length of her arm as she staggered to her knees. Her head was spinning.

"Go this way," her son shouted at her. He seemed angry at her for some reason.

She looked at him. He was pointing toward the brightly lit Baha Mar resort two miles to the northeast of their position.

"Go, I'll cover you."

"No, I'm staying—"

"Goddamn it, Mom! Just go!" he yelled. "Go! I'm right behind you."

What else could she do? She had no weapon, her right arm was as stiff as a tree trunk, and Max had promised he'd be right behind her. She took off toward the resort, doing her best to stay in the shadows, where it would be more difficult to see her. After a minute, she looked back, surprised at how little distance she had put between herself and the SUV.

"Max!" she called out, not seeing him. "Max!" It had been at least a few seconds since she'd last heard gunshots.

Suddenly, a small white burst flared in the night, followed by a brilliant white exhaust plume. She knew instantly what it was. *RPG.* Her heart sank as she helplessly watched the rocket-propelled grenade scream toward the SUV. There was a flash of red-and-yellow light as the grenade hit its target.

Max!

A tick later, she felt the shock wave of the explosion against her chest. She was pushed back, the air knocked out of her lungs. She tripped on a root and fell backward, knocking her head on a rock. Winded, she lay there for a minute or two, numb.

Get up! Get up! Triggs urged herself. She forced herself to sit up and shook her head from side to side to try to clear her vision. Every move she made exhausted her.

"Max! Max! Where are you?" she yelled, not caring if the attackers heard her. "Max!"

Against the light of the burning SUV, she saw the shapes of at least four men. Then a muzzle flash. And another. She gasped. Though she wanted to get to her son, she knew it was hopeless. If the RPG hadn't killed him, whoever had ambushed them just had. The guilt she felt for abandoning him was crushing, and Triggs found herself choking up.

No time for this. Move! Regroup. Find out who did this. Kill them all.

Using all of her strength, she stood up but didn't waste energy on wiping away the tears that had found their way onto her cheeks. She hurried down a steep embankment, keeping one eye closed in an effort to safeguard a bit of her night vision. She hadn't been up for more than half a minute when her feet stumbled over something and she fell down, rolling and hitting rocks and branches. The pain in her shoulder was overwhelming. Blackness threatened to swallow her whole. She landed in a bed of rusted cans and bottles. Litter was all around her. Dead batteries, empty plastic bags, foil packets, rotten food. The smell was awful. The odors of decaying trash and animal filth all mixed into one.

Get up! You wanna live. Get up!

Then Triggs was upright again, climbing the bank on the other side, clawing her way out of the garbage. Voices behind her forced her to go faster. The beams of powerful flashlights crisscrossed around her. Then the first gunshot cracked. The bullet hit a glass bottle behind her, sending some type of lukewarm liquid onto her ankle. More gunfire. Fast and brief. Bullets chewed the ground a few feet to her right. She hurried faster. There were only a few more feet before she reached the top and the safety of the other side. In the distance, other lights appeared. Blue and red flashing lights. At least two police cars were fast approaching, their sirens blaring. She didn't stop to see what happened. She hoped for the best for the officers, but she wasn't confident they would survive their encounter with whoever had ambushed her.

Where are the marines? What's taking them so damn long?

She went down the steep hill, careful not to fall face-first. She couldn't afford to wait for them. How would they find her, anyway? The Baha Mar resort was still far away. In her condition, it would take way too long to reach it. She needed help. Mercifully, there was a small road perpendicular to the highway they'd been traveling on. She hadn't seen any car driving on it yet, but she figured it was because the road wasn't visible from the other side of the hill.

My phone! My goddamn phone! She reached for it in her back pocket. She looked at the screen, half expecting it wouldn't have any service. But the phone was still working and had three solid bars. She thought about calling the embassy but changed her mind. She needed Pierce Hunt. And medical attention.

She'd started to pull up Hunt's phone number when she saw a pair of headlights moving in her direction. The headlights picked out the turns in the road, and Triggs quickly estimated that if she hurried, she could intercept the car. She selected Hunt's phone number and pressed the call button. Then she half walked, half jogged down the hill toward the road.

CHAPTER FOUR

John F. Kennedy Drive, Nassau
New Providence, Commonwealth of the Bahamas

"Goddamn it, Mom! Just go!" Max Oswald yelled. "Go! I'm right behind you."

He watched his mother, one of the most powerful women in the United States, totter away in the darkness.

Once she was a safe distance away, he came out from the rear of the SUV and walked to his men, who had taken cover behind the two sedans.

"Who the fuck shot my mother?" Max hissed, furious.

These three men were the best. All were former special operators. Mistakes like this weren't supposed to happen.

Chiang Tay, a former Special Operations Force commando from Singapore, put up his hand. At five feet six inches, Tay wasn't tall, but he was built like a bull, with the thick neck, broad chest, and powerful arms of a man who had spent years in the wrestling room.

"I did, sir," Tay admitted. "I thought—"

Max raised his hand, interrupting him. At least Tay was man enough to own up to his blunder. That was something Max respected.

"We'll talk about it at debrief," Max said. "Where's the launcher?"

"Back seat." Tay pointed a finger at the second sedan.

Max walked briskly to the rear passenger door, yanked it open, and grabbed the RPG launcher.

"Take cover," Max yelled for the benefit of his men.

He mounted the weapon system on his shoulder, took a knee, and checked the back-blast area behind him. Once assured none of his men would be incinerated, he sighted on his target and pressed the trigger, sending the high explosive antitank warhead sizzling toward the SUV.

The warhead hit the armored SUV and exploded in a massive fireball, sending flaming pieces of wreckage in all directions. Max walked to Tay and handed him the launcher, exchanging it for his M4. He checked the magazine, then made sure the selector lever was flicked to single shot.

"Follow me!" he called. He led his men around the burning SUV. Twenty or so feet past the SUV, Max saw the driver. The poor man's dead body had been thrust in the air by the explosion and had landed next to a small bush. Even though the man was clearly dead, Max shot him anyway. Two seconds later he fired another shot.

"Sir?" Aidan Wood asked.

Max looked behind him. Wood had served two decades with the New Zealand Special Air Service—New Zealand's premier combat unit, closely modeled on the British SAS—and had been decorated twice for valor in Afghanistan. He was tall and thin, built for running. He had thick eyebrows and a pencil-thin mustache like the one movie stars had worn in the forties.

"I want my mother to think that whoever attacked her is finishing the job by making sure the driver and I are dead," Max replied.

He peered through the three-power night-vision scope attached to the M4 and swept the steep hill in front of him. He picked her up in no time, a distinct green heat signature. He fired one shot, missing intentionally. The round hit some sort of glass receptacle a couple of feet behind her. He then fired six or seven shots in quick succession, all of them to her right, his intention being that his mother continue on her way without looking back. A few seconds later, she started the descent on the opposite side of the hill, out of sight.

Max smiled, satisfied. For his plan to work, his mother had to live.

"Two police cars are approaching," Wood said. "What do you want us to do?"

Max hesitated. Killing police officers wasn't something he particularly relished, and his men felt the same way. Collaterals were expected, but it didn't feel right to ask his men to do his dirty work for him.

"Go back to the cars. I'll handle the police," he said.

Wood nodded, and with the fourth member of their team— Thomas DeLarue, a former member of the Second Foreign Parachute Regiment of the French Foreign Legion—they retreated to the sedans. Chiang Tay followed them but came back seconds later with Wood's M4 in his hands. Tay joined Max, who had positioned himself in the ditch about sixty feet behind the still-burning SUV in order not to cast a shadow that would be easily visible to the approaching police officers. No words were necessary between them. Tay was paying his dues for his mistake in shooting Triggs. He wouldn't let Max alone carry the burden of what they were about to do.

By the time the police cars were within range of their rifles, DeLarue and Wood had moved the two sedans down the road so they wouldn't be immediately identifiable by the officers.

"There's no going back now," Max said. "We'll do our best to stop the cars, but if the officers shoot back . . . I'll take the one on the left. You take right."

"Copy that," Tay replied as he raised his rifle.

Our cause is just. It's bigger than we are, worth more than we are, Max repeated to himself while taking aim. An image of his dead wife passed within his mind. *I'm doing this for you, Zehra.* His old life was over. He wouldn't get it back. In one horrific moment of violence, his wife and unborn child had been stolen from him. Filled with rage from the CIA's refusal to help him and in the midst of indescribable grief and anger, he'd done unspeakable things to quench his thirst for vengeance. But shortly after his return to the United States, his conscience, like an avenging spirit, had begun to torture him. Nightmares about the things he had done in Istanbul had become even more vivid than his actions had been in reality. His life had become a living hell, and if it hadn't been for his newfound mentor, who'd helped Max channel his frustrations into a worthy cause, Max had no doubt he'd be dead by now.

Probably by my own hand, Max thought, as the police vehicles continued racing toward the burning SUV.

With their flashing blue and red lights, Max didn't need to use his night-vision scope. The police cars were easy targets. Max was the first to fire. He squeezed the trigger five times, each round finding its mark. His bullets tore into the engine of the first car, causing it to sharply skid to the left. It slammed into a large tree, then burst into flames.

Fuck!

Next to him, Tay was firing short controlled bursts into the engine block of the second cop car. He wasn't having much luck. The driver, instead of turning back upon seeing what had happened to his colleague, punched the gas pedal and barreled toward them. Muzzle flashes appeared from the front passenger seat. It took Max half a second to understand what was happening. One of the officers was firing rounds through the windshield with his service pistol.

As the police car sped past the burning SUV, Max, ignoring the rounds coming at him, leveled his sights and returned fire. The windshield deflected the bullet, but a spiderwebbed hole appeared at the height of the driver's chest. Max took a millisecond to reassess and fired twice more. This time the windshield shattered, and the police car violently swerved to the left and away from them. Tay fired the next volley, and it hit the driver in the shoulder and neck. The surviving cop in the passenger seat tried to grab the wheel, but the vehicle was traveling too fast. Then came a horrid wrenching sound as the police car slammed into a lamp pole.

Max could barely believe it, but by some miracle the officer in the passenger seat was still alive. The officer slowly moved his head toward Max. Max raised his rifle, but before he could fire, the lamp pole toppled and crashed down directly on the roof of the car.

Max sighed. A bitter resignation took hold. The night had started well, but it had ended on a much different note.

"Let's go," he said to the former Singaporean commando. "We don't want to be here when the marines show up."

Max climbed into the first sedan, while Tay ran to the second. Wood was behind the wheel. Max told him to drive to the Bay Street Marina.

"The South African team you hired for security just called," Wood said. "They said everything was clear at the marina. Same goes for Norman's Cay. Plane's ready for us."

"Good," Max replied. The plan was to take the fifty-five-foot fishing boat they had chartered to Norman's Cay, a small island in the Exumas about forty nautical miles from Nassau. From there, they would take a small plane directly to a private airfield in Turks and Caicos to regroup and debrief.

They made the remainder of the ten-minute drive to the marina in near silence. At least half a dozen police cars raced past them toward the ambush site with their lights flashing and sirens wailing.

"Find out the names of the Bahamian police officers," Max said. "Add them to our list. I want their families to be taken care of."

Four officers had died tonight, doing their job. It was up to him to make sure they hadn't died in vain. *Our cause is just. It's bigger than we are, worth more than we are.*

CHAPTER FIVE

Palm Cay Marina
New Providence, Commonwealth of the Bahamas

"Pierce . . . I need help . . . now!" a female voice said, out of breath.

It took Hunt a couple of seconds to realize who the voice on the phone belonged to. *Dorothy Triggs?* Her voice was tight, barely recognizable, at least two octaves higher than usual. Hunt looked at Anna, who had taken a seat on the bed, and mouthed, "It's Triggs."

"Pierce . . . hello?"

He put the call on speaker so Anna could hear. "I'm here. What's going—"

"I was . . . ambushed. Max's dead. I think," Triggs said, sounding as if she was running. "Get the fuck out! Get out!" she yelled. "I said get out!"

"What's going on? Where are you?" Hunt asked, getting up and signaling Anna to grab his go bag. "I'll come to you."

"No! Stay put," Triggs replied, sounding like she had regained some sort of control over her situation.

"What just happened, Dorothy? Who were you yelling at?" Hunt asked.

"I hijacked a car," the deputy director of the Directorate of Operations replied. "I'm on my way to you."

"Are you hurt?" Anna asked.

"I've been shot. Shoulder."

"Where are you?" Hunt asked, trying to pinpoint her location in his mind.

"Close to the Baha Mar resort. You know where it is?"

"There are two hospitals close by," Hunt replied. "There's the Doctors Hospital and the Princess Margaret Hospital. Go to one of them."

"I can't go there," Triggs said. "The people who ambushed us know I'm still alive and that I'm injured. They'll be sending people to look for me."

"Send the marines to secure the emergency room," Hunt suggested. "Nobody will dare attack you with them on site."

"The marines are already on their way to the ambush site. There are only four of them. Before today's attack, the Bahamas wasn't considered a high-risk assignment."

"How bad is it?" Hunt asked. "Truthfully."

"What do you think?" Triggs barked back. "They killed my son."

"I understand, and I'm sorry," Hunt replied, keeping his voice neutral. "I was talking about your physical injuries."

"It hurts like a bitch, but the pain keeps me awake. Which is good. I can't move my right arm, but I don't think I've lost too much blood."

"Understood. Drive carefully. We'll be ready for you."

———

The second he hung up, Hunt ran to his neighbors, a pair of Canadian orthopedic surgeons who had purchased the unit next to Hunt and Anna's. Most of the beachfront residents in Palm Cay knew each other pretty well, so Hunt didn't feel bad waking them up—especially since he'd seen Marguerite and Keith in action the week before when another of their neighbors had been attacked by a barracuda during a diving expedition in the Exumas. The fish had managed to sever an artery in the guy's pelvis. Even in combat, Hunt had rarely seen so much blood in so little time.

The way Marguerite and Keith had taken immediate control of the situation had impressed him. During Ranger School, Hunt had been told over and over that blood loss was extremely dangerous and had to be taken seriously, on and off of the battlefield. Once a person had lost approximately one-fifth of his blood volume, they went into a condition called hypovolemic shock, which in turn often led to the failure of major organs.

"Isn't it a bit late to go fishing?" Keith joked, opening the door to Hunt's knock. In his midforties, the Canadian doctor had cool, blue, intelligent eyes. Despite his friendly tone, there was something guarded in it, as if he knew this wasn't just a late-night social visit.

"A friend of mine is on her way to my place," Hunt said. "She's been injured."

"What kind of injury?" Keith was fully awake now, all signs of sleepiness gone.

Behind him, Hunt saw Marguerite approaching, dressed in a Minnie-and-Mickey-Mouse pajama set.

"She's been shot in the shoulder," Hunt replied.

If either of them was surprised, they didn't show it. "How long until she arrives?" Marguerite asked, all business.

"Eight, maybe ten minutes," Hunt replied.

"Okay," Marguerite said, tying her long blonde hair into a ponytail. "We'll see her here, but we'll need about that much time to set things up. Can you help?"

CHAPTER SIX

Palm Cay Marina
New Providence, Commonwealth of the Bahamas

Triggs hung up from her phone call with the ambassador. The call had been disheartening to say the least. The marines were now at the ambush site and had recovered the body of the SUV driver but not Max's. How could that be? She'd seen the explosion. She'd seen the men finish him off. It didn't make sense.

Unless . . . could Max be alive? Could he have survived the explosion? The firefight? For a blind moment, hope surged through her, only to be followed by a deep sadness.

Then I truly abandoned him, she thought, her heart sinking like a stone.

Overwhelmed by emotion, she began to cry. A bone-deep exhaustion and grief overtook her. Tears ran freely down her face. For a moment, she thought about ending it all by crashing head-on into an oncoming car but pushed back the idea almost immediately. The car hit a large pothole, and a strong jabbing pain shot through her shoulder. Her jaw tightened.

Get a fucking grip on yourself!

Triggs took a long, deep breath. Then another. It cleared her mind and helped her to focus on what she had to do next. The ambassador had informed her to expect a call shortly from the United States secretary of defense. She'd start there. With the limited resources available in the Bahamas, her first consideration was to return to the safety of the United States. The SecDef would help accomplish that goal.

She was turning into the Palm Cay neighborhood when she felt her phone vibrate between her legs. She held the steering wheel with her knees while she pressed the talk button.

"This is Triggs," she said, surprised at how weak her voice sounded.

"This is James Flynn, Dorothy. This line isn't secured," he warned her. "Can you talk?"

"I can. Were you briefed on what happened?"

"I spoke with the ambassador a few minutes ago, and he filled me in," the SecDef replied. "Listen, Dorothy, I'm not sure what you're doing in the Bahamas, but I'm told you're now on your way to Pierce Hunt's place. That true?"

"I'm there now," Triggs said, parking her car in front of the beach-front townhome.

"Very well. Stay put. I'm sending a Seahawk to pick you up. It will be there shortly. Talk soon."

A gentle knock on the sedan window startled Triggs. Anna Garcia stood there, Hunt right behind her. Triggs turned off the car and opened the door with her good arm.

"Follow me," Anna said, holding the door for her. "Do you need help?"

Triggs shook her head. "I'm all right."

It took everything she had to climb out of the car. Peering back at the driver's seat, she was surprised at the amount of blood she had left behind. The seat was soaked with it. A strange sensation enveloped her, and then she felt herself spinning and falling.

CHAPTER SEVEN

Palm Cay Marina
New Providence, Commonwealth of the Bahamas

Hunt and Anna stood outside the town house, their feet in the cool sand, watching the dark ocean meet with the night sky. The air was dead calm; no breeze swayed the palm trees in passing; there was only the noise of waves crashing gently on the shore. The calm before the storm. Looking at the stars, Hunt wondered where Charlie Henican was at that moment. He doubted Henican was in a good place.

"You remember Simon and Emma are scheduled to fly in tomorrow, right?" Anna asked.

Hunt smiled at the thought of his best friend and his wife. "Cost me fifty bucks to fill the fridge with Simon's favorite Bahamian brew. I remember all right."

Simon Carter had been his second-in-command when Hunt had been in charge of one of the DEA's rapid response teams—or RRTs. Not only had they kicked down hundreds of doors together; Carter had risked his life and given up his career to accompany Hunt to Mexico to rescue Leila and Sophia when they'd been kidnapped by a cartel. More recently, Carter had accompanied Hunt to South America to retrieve vital intelligence left behind by a murdered DEA agent. That intelligence had been crucial in removing the president of Venezuela and his top lieutenant from power and stopping the spread of a dangerous drug that had killed Leila's boyfriend. The mission had been a complete success.

Well, thought Hunt. *Almost a complete success.* Carter had lost the top of his left pinkie during a firefight.

"Will you ask him to come with you?" Anna asked.

"Not this time," Hunt replied. "One of us needs to stay behind in case the DEA decides to call, you know?"

"You sure it doesn't have anything to do with what happened tonight?"

"Maybe a little," Hunt replied honestly, reaching for Anna's hand.

It's true that he would have loved Carter to come with him to look for Henican. But with what had happened to Triggs, Hunt wasn't convinced that leaving Anna alone in the Bahamas was the right call. She'd have a full house to contend with between Leila's mom, Jasmine; her husband, Chris; Simon and Emma; and the girls. He felt better having someone with Simon's skill set watching over all of them.

Anna leaned forward and kissed him on the cheek while grabbing his arm. He felt himself being pulled toward her. His lips met hers, and for a moment he forgot everything but the two of them.

Their moment was brief.

He heard the helicopter before he saw it. The roar of the engines was deafening. It took a while for the gray helicopter to appear out of the night as it descended toward the beach, its rotors slapping the night air. A Seahawk was a twin-turboshaft-engine, multimission helicopter used by the United States Navy. The chopper was similar to a Black Hawk but had been adapted with a folding main rotor and a hinged tail in order to reduce its footprint aboard warships.

The downdraft rippling across the sand forced Hunt to shield his eyes with his forearm. The rhythmic beat of the blades pulsed in his ears. Memories of his last mission and the terrible helicopter crash he'd been in flashed through his mind. It made him think of Henican again, and his muscles tensed. Years ago with the DEA, he'd traveled to a Turkish prison to interrogate a prisoner. The overpacked facility had had an insufficient number of windows to let in clean air, and hundreds of flies had swamped the sleeping area where eighty men had shared a room designed to accommodate only twenty-five. Torture and other kinds of prisoner abuse had been rampant. He needed to get to Turkey now. His friend's life depended on it.

Before the blades came to a stop, four heavily armed men jumped out of the side door. Three men took position around the helicopter while a single sailor jogged toward Hunt.

"Mr. Hunt?" He was tall and clean shaven, but his eyes betrayed his true self. The man was a warfighter.

"In the flesh," Hunt said, shaking the man's extended hand.

He introduced himself to Hunt and Anna as a senior chief with the United States Navy.

"Nice to meet you," Anna said, then added for Hunt's benefit, "I'll go check on the girls."

"Follow me, Senior," Hunt told him. "I'll take you to her."

As the men walked toward Keith and Marguerite's townhome, Hunt could see lights being turned on inside some of his neighbors' houses. Some had even ventured out onto their back decks to check out what the commotion was all about. Sophia and Leila were among the curious. It was hard to believe they'd be high school juniors this year. Every day, he admired the resilience they'd shown after their kidnapping. Hunt waved at the girls. He didn't blame them for their curiosity. He would have done exactly the same at their age. It wasn't every day that a big United States Navy helicopter landed in your backyard.

———

Keith and Marguerite had managed to stabilize Triggs, but she needed to get to a hospital. She insisted Hunt accompany her on the Seahawk rather than flying out the next day as he'd planned. It irked Hunt and reminded him why he didn't like working with Triggs. She was a bully, and there was nothing he disliked more than a bully. Then he remembered what she had been through and chastised himself for being such an asshole. It was normal for Triggs to be on edge. She had just witnessed her son getting killed.

Anna, Leila, and Sophia were waiting for him by the terrace. Anna had his go bag in her hand. Sophia was the first to give him a hug.

"Thanks for everything, Pierce," Anna's niece said, kissing him on the cheek. "How long will you be gone for?"

"Can't say for sure, I'm afraid. I'm sorry."

"Don't be," the teenager replied. "People need you. I get that."

Leila came to him next and wrapped her arms tightly around him and hung on. Hunt buried his face in his daughter's hair. Not long ago, she'd had to grieve over her boyfriend's death. She'd been through so much these last couple of years, and he was proud of her strength.

"I'll be back as soon as I can," Hunt said. "I promise."

"Don't worry, Dad. I'll be fine. We'll be fine. Just be careful, okay?"

"You know I will."

"By the way, can I Instagram this?" Leila nodded at the helicopter, a twinkle in her eyes. "It's kind of cool."

Hunt stared back at her, wondering if she was serious. Her mouth turned up just slightly at the edges.

"Good one, monkey," he said, giving Leila one last hug. "I love you."

Anna handed him his go bag, and then she kissed him passionately. No words were necessary. After a few moments, she gently pushed him away.

"Go," she mouthed.

He squeezed her hand one more time before reluctantly letting it go. It was time to get to work.

CHAPTER EIGHT

Hook-2-Long—fifty-five-foot fishing boat
Three miles south of Nassau

Max Oswald switched to generator power and asked DeLarue to disconnect the shore power cables and stow them in the aft compartment of the 2004 Viking 55 Convertible. The docks and slips were well lit, allowing his men to work without their flashlights. Max turned the ignition switch for the starboard engine, which sparked to life in a small cloud of blue smoke and began its cadenced thudding. He repeated the process with the port engine, then asked his men to start casting off the dock lines.

Max gently tapped the joystick. It was enough to push the big fishing boat forward. Once the swim platform had cleared the slip, Tay gave him a thumbs-up, and Max put the starboard drive in forward and the port drive in reverse. The boat began a ninety-degree rotation in front of the slip. When it was pointed in the right direction, Max moved the port drive into forward and steered the boat toward the marina exit. Left and right, scattered among the multimillion-dollar yachts, were ragged sailing yachts and rusty motorboats for sale. Once they were out of the no-wake zone, Max throttled the engines up to full power and felt the bow come up as the speed increased. The boat rose out of the water, and in no time they were traveling at thirty-five knots. At that speed, they'd reach Norman's Cay in less than two hours.

They had traveled less than five nautical miles and had just navigated past the southeastern tip of New Providence when Tay tapped him on the shoulder.

"What is it?" Max shouted to be heard above the deep growl of the engines.

Tay pointed toward the stern. Max glanced in that direction and saw the navigation lights of a helicopter at low altitude.

He inadvertently held his breath, half expecting the helicopter to sink them.

"Go get the launcher," Max said.

"I don't think they've seen us," Tay replied. "Or if they did, they don't care. This is their second go around that neighborhood."

Then it came to him. Max yanked the throttles back, bringing the engines back to idle. Almost immediately, the bow sank into the ocean. They glided for about one hundred feet, and then the boat came to a stop.

"I know where the helicopter is going," Max said.

———

Max let go of his NVGs and let them hang from his neck. He hadn't anticipated his mother returning to Hunt's place, but it made sense. She wasn't in any danger, but she had no way of knowing that. It was to be expected that she wouldn't want to go to one of the two large hospitals in Nassau. With only four marines stationed at the embassy, there was no way they could have attended the ambush site and secured the emergency room of a hospital.

The US had no permanent air assets in the Bahamas, so Max was confident that the Seahawk helicopter he had witnessed landing in front of Hunt's townhome came from the USS *Jason Dunham*, an Arleigh Burke–class guided missile destroyer. If Max was to believe the latest reports from the Office of Naval Intelligence, the *Dunham* was operating roughly one hundred miles north of Havana. Its mission was to closely monitor a new Russian frigate that had entered the Caribbean Sea via the Panama Canal ten days ago. The same reports indicated that the Russian warship was preparing to make several port calls across the Caribbean, a tactic to project the power of Russia in international waters. The ONI believed the Russian ship was armed with a new weapons system designed to successfully counter night-vision devices, laser range finders, and other electro-optical sight systems.

Yeah, thought Max, *the navy's right to keep an eye on these bastards.*

He became conscious of footsteps behind him. He turned and saw Aidan Wood smoking a cigarette. The former New Zealand SAS trooper joined him on the aft deck.

"Seems like your mother is getting premium treatment, isn't she?" Wood said, a taint of jealousy in his voice. Or was it contempt? Max couldn't tell.

"Looks like it," he replied.

"No expenses spared, right?" Wood pushed on.

Max understood Wood's frustration. Wood wasn't breaking international laws and his oath to his country to enrich himself. He was following Max for one reason: to provide financial assistance to the families of the New Zealand Special Operations Force operators who had died on clandestine missions but whose deaths had never been compensated or acknowledged. The same was true for Chiang Tay and Thomas DeLarue, though they were doing it for the military operators of Singapore and France. Every single one of his men was a former special forces operator who had witnessed how ludicrously their governments treated combat veterans upon their return from the battlefield. Some would call the men mercenaries, but Max didn't like the stigma attached to the term. His men were more than guns for hire. They believed in his cause.

Like Max, all of them had colleagues who had made the ultimate sacrifice fighting for what they thought was freedom, while others had lost limbs, only to be spat upon at home by the same people who had sent them to fight their wars in the first place.

And for what?

During his first combat deployment, it hadn't taken long for Max to understand what he was really fighting for. He wasn't fighting for the politicians; he was fighting for his brothers-in-arms. His loyalty was to the men and women fighting next to him, not to the political establishment back in Washington, DC. Max was done with their empty promises—especially after the tragic event that had taken his wife away from him. He had begged for assistance to go after the men responsible, but his plea had been denied by the risk-averse bureaucracy the CIA had become. But the worst thing, the thing that angered him the most, was that he'd known all along that once he returned to the US, no one would even acknowledge what he'd been through. After all, he was a NOC, a shadow warrior, right? He was supposed to deal with the pain and know how to suppress his heartache and misery. Even his mother had simply assumed he'd get over the loss of his wife and unborn child in no time.

Well, he hadn't. And as his mentor had pointed out, if someone like him couldn't do it, how could the government expect the widows and children of special warfare operators to overcome their grief with the limited resources offered to them?

Max had thought about different scenarios for getting his hands on $250 million. With that much money, he'd be able to help most if not all of the families in need. None of these families would get rich with that, but at least there would be enough money to give their children an education. Max would give them back their dignity.

He'd run a multitude of simulations, but the only option that made any sense was to extort the United States government. And recent events in Venezuela provided the perfect opportunity. When he'd gotten word that the narco-terrorist Jorge Ramirez was hiding out in Turkey and looking for a buyer for the intelligence he had on Colonel—now

President—Carlos Arteaga and his link to the CIA, Max had known he had to seize the opportunity. If it became public knowledge that the United States government had supported Arteaga with arms and funding despite knowing that he had tortured and killed American agents operating clandestinely in Venezuela, there would be years of inquiries and investigations. People would lose confidence in their government—it could even cripple the economy, or at least perturb it greatly.

This was the one piece of intelligence that could force the United States government to play ball. The intelligence was so damning, so explosive, that they would be happy to pay to keep it secret. Max was sure of it.

Unfortunately, he'd had to play catch-up since his mother had already sent Charlie Henican to Turkey to eliminate Ramirez. Thanks to the contacts he'd developed during his tenure as a NOC, Max had been able to stop Henican before he could take out Ramirez. Four years out from a failed coup that had nearly overthrown the government, the Turkish authorities were still paranoid about the possibility of another assassination attempt against the president. A few lies planted in trusting ears was all it took to set the wheels in motion for Henican's arrest.

Where Henican was at that moment, Max didn't know. But that didn't mean he didn't care. Henican was one of them. A soldier. A patriot. He'd simply been in the wrong place at the wrong time, serving the wrong person: Max's mother.

"You think she'll be okay?" Wood asked, finishing his cigarette.

Max watched him toss the glowing butt overboard with a flick of the wrist.

"Dorothy Triggs is a survivor, my friend," Max said, clapping Wood on the shoulder. "She'll be fine."

CHAPTER NINE

Somewhere in Turkey

Charlie Henican struggled slowly toward consciousness. He had something in his mouth. A cloth of some sort. A revolting stench made him queasy with every breath he took. It smelled of unwashed bodies and soiled clothing, of urine and human excrement. Henican forced himself not to panic. If he vomited, he would choke. *That* would be a wretched death. Drowning in his own puke wasn't part of his grand plan.

However hard he strained his head and neck, he could see nothing but the haziest hint of light through the cloth bag over his head. He wondered if this was because his eyes were swollen shut due to the savage beatings he had endured. His legs were numb, and his wrists were tied behind him onto a cold metal chair. A blaze had been set in each of his shoulders. Every time Henican tried to move, they flared up more, spearing flames through his joints and strained muscles.

Henican had been through SERE—Survival, Evasion, Resistance, and Escape—training, and it had sucked. But this was worse. Much worse. He had to stay calm, because the more he struggled against his restraints, the more it hurt and the harder it was for him to draw the next gulp of oxygen. Something brushed against his ankle—something long and prickly.

Like a damn rat's tail, Henican thought, disgusted.

The last beating had been the harshest. They had beaten him sense-less, two torturers taking turns so they could conserve energy. The worst was that his jailers hadn't asked him a single question. He hadn't even been given the chance to lie yet!

Then he heard something. He held his breath and tilted his head, closing his eyes so he could hear more clearly. Footsteps were approaching, the steps of not one man but three. The beatings would soon resume. His breathing sped up, forcing him to inhale more of the ran-cid stench that filled the space he was in. The footsteps stopped behind him. Henican shivered, fear taking hold.

"I see you're back with us, Mr. Henican," a man said. His English was marked by a strong Turkish accent.

Even if he'd wanted to, Henican couldn't reply. The cloth in his mouth prevented it.

"My mother used to say that a fox always smells his own hole first. Have you heard this before, Charlie?

"Well," the man continued, "I disagree with my mother on this one. Truth is that the fox is not aware of his own stink. It's part of it. It's immersed in it, just like a fish in water. You, Charlie, you have your own signature stench. It belongs to you and to nobody else. You understand what I'm saying so far?"

Behind Henican, men were chuckling. Henican didn't think any of it was funny.

The man persisted. "You walk down the street, and your nose picks up a certain smell. You say, 'Somebody's barbecuing.' You smell some-thing else, like a flower, and you say, 'That's a rose!' Well, it's the same thing with you, Charlie. Your nose picks up a special, eye-watering stench, and you say, 'It's Charlie Henican!'"

The men behind him burst into laughter.

Suddenly the cloth bag over his head was ripped away. He blinked several times. His vision seemed okay, but even the dim light made his head hurt. There was a throbbing pain behind his eyes. The gag was pulled out of his mouth.

"Who hired you to kill our president?" The voice was deep and resonant now. Its owner, while remaining out of sight, spoke in an unhurried manner.

Who hired you to kill our president? Henican sighed heavily. He was in much more trouble than he'd thought.

His eyes darted left to right in an effort to learn a little more about where he was being held. *A pool.* He was in the deep end of an abandoned swimming pool. The last time they'd beaten him, he'd been in a cell.

They must have moved me here while I was unconscious.

The swimming facility had been closed for at least a decade; its once–light blue tiles were now cracked and smeared with gunk. It had been converted into some sort of detention center. This was a world away from the pool he'd been in only a few weeks ago in Costa Rica. Henican closed his eyes. An image flashed.

Harriet Jacobs.

In his mind's eye, he could see her lying in bed, her naked body stretched languorously across the white sheets in the afterglow of their lovemaking. Despite the desperate situation he was in, his body responded to the memory.

Then, out of nowhere, a hard punch landed between Henican's shoulder blades. He winced in pain.

"Answer the question," the man hissed.

Henican didn't even remember what the question was.

"I'd . . . I'd like . . . to speak with the . . . Canadian embassy," he managed to whisper. His mouth was dry, and he could feel broken teeth with his swollen tongue. His tongue brushed over a raw nerve, and a shooting pain ignited in his skull.

"We kind of wished you would say something stupid like that, Mr. Henican," the man said. "My friends have been begging me to let them have another go at you, you know. Should I let them?"

Henican knew there were no good or bad answers to rhetorical questions like this one. He remained quiet.

"I have great respect for American warriors like you, Mr. Henican," the man said. "Delta Force, then CIA paramilitary. You had a great career."

Henican hoped the man would keep talking. He was desperate for any intelligence that would tell him who he was dealing with and what his captors knew about his operation on Turkish soil. He needed to find some way to persuade them to release him.

"You don't talk much, do you?" the man said. "Would you like some water, maybe?"

Henican nodded. "That . . . that would be great."

The man snapped his fingers. Moments later, Henican heard him twist open the cap of a bottle of water. His tormentor walked in front of him. The man was in his fifties, tall, and clearly fit. He had broad shoulders, hard eyes, and a firm-set mouth. The man put the bottle of water against Henican's lips. It hurt. His lips were dry and split by the numerous punches he'd received at the hands of the man's thugs. The man tipped the bottle up, giving Henican a few tiny sips. Henican had to work on swallowing. It was as if he had forgotten how to do it.

"I was an officer with the OKK, or the Maroon Berets, if you prefer," the man continued, taking a quick sip from the same water bottle. "I attended level-C SERE training in the United States."

Henican knew a few Turkish Maroon Berets from his time with Delta. They were a special operations unit made up of volunteers selected from all the branches of the Turkish armed forces. They were hard core. Their training regimen was as intense as any he had seen in the United States. In fact, the Maroon Berets were one of the remaining special ops teams in the world to still perform the trust shot—an exercise in which one candidate fired at a target near another candidate from fifty feet away.

"You'll talk, Mr. Henican. You know it. I know it," the man said. "Seriously, I don't know why you're being so difficult."

"Can I have a bit more?" Henican asked.

"Water? Yes, why not."

Henican took a few swallows of lukewarm water before the man pulled the bottle away.

God, the water feels good, Henican thought. But the act of drinking had made him realize that his chest and ribs were on fire, possibly with a broken rib or two. Pins and needles bit into his arms and hands. He was in no shape to make a flashy getaway. He wasn't even sure he would survive another beating.

"How come you know so much about me?" Henican asked.

"Who hired you to kill our president?"

Henican decided to go out on a limb. "Your president wasn't my target."

The man's face froze in an expressionless mask. "I gave you water, and you thank me by lying? You're dumber than you look, Mr. Henican."

The former Maroon Beret officer once again walked out of sight.

Before Henican could protest, a plastic bag came down over his head and locked around his neck. Henican gasped for air. The plastic bag formed a concave hollow around his mouth, which popped out and then in again with each pump of his lungs. He felt his temples swell with the pressure. There was no escape, no breath he could take. He tried to stay conscious, but he was losing the battle. He hung his mouth open, desperate for one more breath. Just before he choked to death, there was a small release around his neck, and some oxygen slipped in. Not much, but enough to keep him conscious.

"Like you've probably guessed, my friend, this isn't my first time at this," the man said. "I know exactly how tight to pull for suffering, and how tight to pull for a quick and merciful death."

Suddenly, there was no more air coming through. The horrible feeling of suffocation consumed Henican as his lungs demanded oxygen that he couldn't get. His head was burning, and for several panic-filled seconds, he really thought this was it. Then, as swiftly as it had come on, the bag was pulled off his head. He coughed several times. His entire body was shaking.

"Would you like me to repeat the question?" the man asked, walking back in front of Henican.

Henican was terrified to answer the question. His heart was racing. Never in his life had he been so thoroughly frightened. Never before had he felt his legs tremble so much.

Another punch landed between his shoulder blades, in exactly the same spot as the first one. This time, a stab of pain so sharp that it brought tears to his eyes stripped him of his ability to speak. Something inside him was burning up, as if he had drunk an entire bottle of peroxide.

"We can do this all day," the man spat. "How much suffering you endure before I put a bullet in your head is entirely up to you."

But Henican was only half listening. He coughed a few times, blood spattering from the back of his throat to the floor. He gasped a few more times, struggling for each breath, and then total blackness enveloped him.

CHAPTER TEN

CIA headquarters
Langley, Virginia

Dorothy Triggs ignored the burning ache in her shoulder as she strode down the hall to the seventh-floor briefing room. The trauma surgeon who had treated her had insisted that she keep her arm immobile for at least four weeks if she wanted to give her shoulder the chance to heal properly. So far, she had completely ignored the professional opinions of her physicians and had worked nonstop since her release from the Walter Reed National Military Medical Center earlier that morning.

Triggs refused to believe Max was dead. Whoever had ambushed them would have had no reason to take his corpse away from the site. Which meant they'd taken him alive.

The FBI had been charged with investigating her son's disappearance. The legal attaché from the FBI office in Barbados was already on his way to Nassau to meet with the two FBI special agents assigned to the American embassy. The three of them were to assist the Royal Bahamas Police Force with their investigation. As much as Triggs wanted to send her own officers to conduct an independent investigation, she'd been warned by the director of the CIA not to do it.

"Let the bureau handle it, Dorothy," Walter Helms had told her. "You need to understand the situation in the Bahamas."

Her boss had gone on to say that the Royal Bahamas Police Force had lost four of its officers trying to protect her. The Bahamians had made an official request of assistance to the FBI, not to the CIA.

"I don't want to hear that you've sent CIA personnel to the Bahamas," Helms had warned her. "Am I making myself perfectly clear?"

"Absolutely."

"Good. I know how hard it must be for you. The minute I hear something, I'll let you know," Helms had promised.

If it had been any other situation, she would have agreed that the CIA had no business in the Bahamas and that the FBI was more than capable of conducting a swift and thorough investigation. But this wasn't any other situation. This was her son.

As she got closer to the briefing room, an idea popped into her head. If she'd hired Pierce Hunt to find Charlie Henican, why couldn't she offer a contract to Simon Carter to sniff around in the Bahamas? She was confident Carter could get her the answer she was looking for much quicker than the FBI ever could. And hadn't Hunt mentioned that Carter was already on his way to Nassau?

She made a mental note to call him after the briefing.

———

Triggs entered the briefing room through a secure glass sliding door. The door slid shut behind her, and everyone sitting at the long conference table stopped talking. She sat at the head of the table. Pierce Hunt was directly to her right and Paramilitary Operations Officer Harriet Jacobs to her left. As one of the few female members of the CIA Special Activities Center—the division responsible for the agency's overseas paramilitary operations—Jacobs was a rare commodity. For the last two years, she had worked with Charlie Henican on many long deployments and assisted Hunt in Venezuela. She was well suited for what Triggs had in mind, and so was Hunt. Also present at the meeting were intelligence research specialists Colleen Crawford and Barry Pike, both of whom had formerly worked for the DEA and were now independent consultants.

Triggs cleared her throat. "Thank you for being here. It's greatly appreciated. I know some of you have traveled quite a bit to make it this morning."

She proceeded to pass folders around the table.

"Please take a few minutes to go through the file. It will give you a general idea of what's going on. These files were updated minutes before I walked in."

The first one to react was Hunt. He didn't say anything out loud, but Triggs could tell by his body language that his mind was racing, probably wondering why she was sending him to Switzerland instead of Turkey. Once she was certain that everybody had read the file twice, she said, "Prior to the ambush, I had Max working round the clock trying to figure out how the Turkish authorities found out about Paramilitary Operations Officer Charlie Henican's location. Fewer than ten people were aware of his whereabouts and of his mission."

"Any luck?" Hunt asked.

"Yes and no," Triggs said. "As of early this morning, Pike and Crawford have taken over the search for the leak. They're presently going through every bit of intel we have. Isn't that right, Mr. Pike?"

"Yes, ma'am," Pike said in his baritone voice. "We're making progress."

"Good to know," Triggs said. Director Helms would be pleased. The agency didn't need another Aldrich Ames. The sooner Pike and Crawford found out who had either leaked a sensitive operation or, perhaps worse, hacked into CIA communications, the better. "As far as Henican's current location—"

Before she could continue, Harriet Jacobs jumped in. "Is it possible that Charlie simply got hit by a bus and is now in a hospital?"

"We now know this isn't the case. What you'll see happened four days ago in Istanbul."

Triggs pointed a remote at a television and pressed a button. The screen swirled with colors and then cleared into a view of two dark SUVs. Six men, all of them heavily armed and dressed in black battle dress uniforms, were in the process of climbing out of the SUVs and entering the lobby of a small hotel.

Triggs fast-forwarded a few seconds and said, "This is more or less four minutes later."

The six men were seen exiting the hotel. But this time they had one more person with them.

Charlie Henican.

CHAPTER ELEVEN

CIA headquarters
Langley, Virginia

Hunt heard Harriet Jacobs gasp at the sight of Charlie Henican being led out of the Istanbul hotel. He, too, was relieved to see that his friend was still alive.

At least he was four days ago, he thought, keeping his emotions in check.

"Do we know who these people are?" he asked. "How did we get this video?"

Triggs paused the video. "These men are Maroon Berets," she said. "They're bad news."

"Why are they bad news?" Colleen Crawford asked.

Hunt answered the intelligence researcher's question. "The Maroon Berets are Turkey's best of the best. They wouldn't get deployed into Istanbul to arrest someone unless they'd received intel that this person represented a threat to their national security. Common criminals get arrested by regular police officers. Terrorists—or spies, for that matter—get the Maroon Berets."

"Pierce is right," Triggs said. "But now that I know who took him, the State Department will be able to apply some pressure. Unofficially."

"Unofficially?" Hunt asked. "What does that even mean?"

"It means exactly that, Pierce," she said. "I've collected many IOUs at the State Department over the years. They have to tread carefully; we weren't supposed to be there."

Triggs was protecting her ass, but Hunt didn't blame her. At least she was trying to get Henican back.

"Understood," he said. "But again, how did we get this video? And who took it?"

"We found it on Instagram," she said.

"I'm not following," Jacobs said. "How did Charlie end up on Instagram?"

"The videographer is a twenty-one-year-old student at Istanbul University. We don't know why she was there in the first place, but we can only assume that the arrival of two SUVs full of armed men isn't a daily occurrence in this neighborhood.

"Anyway," Triggs continued, "one of our methods of searching for Henican was to look online for specific keywords and hashtags. The student used the hashtags *HotelNiles* and *Istanbul* when she posted her video on Instagram. These keywords had been programmed into our algorithm."

Hunt wished she'd posted her video right after taking it instead of waiting days to do so. "How did you establish that the men taking him were Maroon Berets?" he asked.

"That was the easy part," Triggs said. "We cross-referenced the license plates to our database and found out that they belonged to a shell company. This shell company is explicitly used by the Maroon Berets for the purpose of conducting black or covert operations within Turkey."

"And we're sure about this?" Hunt pressed.

"We are," Triggs said dryly. "The intel is good. Understood?"

Hunt took a moment to examine Triggs. Her blonde hair was pulled back in a no-nonsense ponytail. She had wide-spaced brown eyes that were tired, but it was the shadows beneath them that he noticed more. She had been through a lot in the last twenty-four hours, and it showed.

"So what's the plan?" Jacobs asked, showing signs of desperation. "We're not going to Turkey to get Charlie, but I read in the file that you're sending us to Switzerland? What the hell?"

Hunt knew Henican and Jacobs were close. Very close, even. He suspected that the two of them shared more than just a professional interest in each other.

"As I said earlier, my friends at the State Department are taking the lead in Turkey," Triggs replied. "This is a tricky situation that will require finesse—"

"I can do finesse," Hunt said, trying to lighten the mood. He failed miserably.

Triggs shot him a dirty look. Hunt raised both hands and retreated deeper into his seat.

"The failed coup is still fresh on many people's minds," Triggs continued, her gaze still on Hunt. "It had devastating effects on the country's political sphere, and the same could be said about the rest of Turkish society. I'm not sure if you're all aware, but controversial arrests continue to happen daily. Over eighty thousand people have been arrested for links to terror organizations, and more than one hundred and thirty thousand have been purged from the public service sector. The path the Turkish government chose to follow since the failed coup has created a rift between their country and ours."

"That rings true for all of Turkey's Western allies," Hunt mentioned. "We're not the only country having issues with them. If I remember correctly, the European Commission pulled no punches when they documented the Turkish authorities' human rights infringements during the purge."

Triggs nodded. "That's correct, but when it came to military collaboration, the United States was the country hit the hardest."

"How so?" Jacobs asked.

"Because for over a decade, we had built robust relationships with many senior military officers in the Turkish armed forces. Unfortunately, many of those generals were arrested within days of the failed coup. Several of them are now serving life terms in prison."

Hunt grunted, not satisfied with the explanation. In his mind, the structured chaos in Turkey was the perfect environment for a small team of operators to be clandestinely inserted with a high degree of success. He was about to say so to Triggs, but Jacobs beat him to the punch.

"Pierce and I could easily slip into Turkey and—"

"No," Triggs snapped. "You'll do no such thing. Weren't you listening to what I just said? State is taking the lead in Turkey. I've made my decision."

Hunt came to Jacobs's rescue. "Listen, Dorothy, I'm having problems figuring out what I'm doing here. You hired me for one thing, and one thing only: to find Charlie Henican. We now have a lead, something we didn't have twenty-four hours ago, but you don't want us to go to Turkey to get him out?"

"It's not that—" Triggs started, but Hunt interrupted her. He'd had enough of Triggs's bullshit. Did she want to get Henican or not?

He grabbed the file that Triggs had given him at the start of the meeting and lifted it angrily in the air. "You don't want us to go to Turkey, but you have this incredibly detailed plan on how to get us to Switzerland. I'm confused. What am I missing?"

"I'm sorry," Triggs said, nodding her head in acquiescence. "I should have gotten to this sooner. I think we all got sidetracked for a minute. Believe me, Pierce, it was my intention to send you chasing after Henican. I think it's fair to say that all of us around the table know how close you are with Charlie and that you're the most qualified person to do it. I believe that too. I really do."

"Then the only thing you need to do is to set me loose," Hunt said, almost pleading.

"I can't do that."

Hunt heaved his bulk out of the chair, sending it thumping against the wall. "Then I think I'm done here. This was a waste of time."

"Hear me out," Triggs said. "You owe me that much."

Hunt had no idea what she was talking about. He owed her nothing. In fact, the opposite was true. But out of respect for her recent loss, he sat down.

"Thank you," she said. Then, "If you'll allow me to explain, I think you'll understand. If I don't convince you of the importance of going to Switzerland, I'll let you go back to your family. Deal?"

She looked at him expectantly. Hunt drew a long, slow breath.

"Why not?" he said. Now that Henican had been located, the only other potential operation that would justify having him here was going after Jorge Ramirez. And he was right. Triggs confirmed it when she next opened her mouth.

"We just received confirmation that Jorge Ramirez is in Switzerland. I want you to hunt him down."

Hunt smiled. *That* was something worth his time. He had unfinished business with Ramirez. It had been Ramirez's amphetamine pills that had killed his daughter Leila's boyfriend.

"Carte blanche?" Hunt asked.

"Absolutely not. You'll follow the ops plan."

Hunt looked around the briefing room. Pike and Crawford weren't CIA employees; nor was he. Jacobs was, but she was a deniable asset. *This mission is off the books,* Hunt thought.

"Who knows about this?" he asked.

"The people around this table, a couple of analysts and security officers, and the director. You get in, you take out Ramirez, then you get the hell out of Switzerland."

CHAPTER TWELVE

Grand Hotel Villa Castagnola
Lugano, Switzerland

As a former paratrooper of the 993rd Special Operations Battalion of the armed forces of Venezuela, Jorge Ramirez wasn't accustomed to making rash decisions, but he was about to. He was running out of options. And money. The last few months hadn't been kind to him. His only protectors in Venezuela—including the former president—had been arrested and were now awaiting trial for treason and murder. Colonel Carlos Arteaga had now assumed the presidency. And Arteaga wanted his head.

Ramirez was well aware that Arteaga's path to the top spot had been cleared by the Americans. Not only did he know it, but he could prove it too. That knowledge made him dangerous to the Americans, since it threatened Arteaga's already-precarious position among the Venezuelan people. Hyperinflation and a dire shortage of supplies were even more rampant than they'd been under the last president. It broke Ramirez's heart to see his country suffering, but he had done what he could.

For a while, Ramirez had aided the former president on a plan to bring cash into Venezuela by manufacturing and distributing a new type of ultra-addictive amphetamine pill. But the plan had gone awry after the drug had been rushed and several American teenagers had died. Turkey had seemed like a good place to resume his operation, but he had misjudged how much the country had changed since the attempted coup. To Ramirez's surprise, most of his trusted contacts in the Turkish underworld hadn't responded to his calls. In fact, only one had agreed to see him, and *he* had forced Ramirez to wait a full week before granting him an audience. The man, a high-ranking officer of the Turkish National Police named Doru Kazak, had encouraged Ramirez to take the few men still loyal to him and promptly leave the country. Not only wasn't Kazak interested in what Ramirez had to sell, but he'd made it abundantly clear that this was the last time he wanted to hear from him. Before leaving, the man had nevertheless given Ramirez a lifeline.

"As a departing gift and in memory of our past successful transactions, I'm offering you a special present, my friend," Kazak had said while pulling at his cigarette.

"You're too generous," Ramirez had replied.

Kazak had shaken a finger at Ramirez's sarcasm. "Don't begrudge me for being honest with you, Jorge. I can still change my mind."

There was nothing Ramirez would have loved more than to break the old man's finger and gouge out his eyes with it. Instead, he'd apologized.

"Call this number," Kazak had said, giving Ramirez a piece of paper. "I vouch for him. The man's always looking to buy intelligence. He'll pay well for what you have on the Americans. I contacted him the moment I heard you were in town. He's expecting you."

Ramirez hadn't recognized the number. "This isn't an Istanbul number, is it?"

The Turk had laughed out loud. "Business isn't as good as it used to be, I'm afraid. Istanbul has changed quite a lot since the purging of suspected disloyalists following the failed coup. To survive, I had to branch out. The number is Swiss."

Before Ramirez had been able to thank him, Kazak had continued, "There was an American in town. I don't think he was here for you, but in this business of ours, who really knows?"

Ramirez had nearly had a heart attack. He knew the Americans were after him, but he'd been so careful. Could they have found him? Kazak hadn't seemed to think so, but it would be foolish of Ramirez to assume otherwise. He had to anticipate the worst-case scenario. It was a matter of survival.

"Where is he now?" Ramirez had asked.

"I said 'was,' didn't I? The American's gone," Kazak had assured him. "I took care of him. He won't be a bother to anyone."

A quick look into the Turk's hard eyes had been enough to convince Ramirez the man had been telling the truth.

"How can I thank you?"

"Don't ever come back to Turkey."

Cornered, Ramirez hadn't had much choice but to reach out to Kazak's Swiss friend. Now that the Americans had gotten his scent, they wouldn't let go. They wanted him dead, and that complicated things immensely. Ramirez was on his own. He couldn't reasonably expect to get any help from the cartels with which he had done business in the past. With President Reilly threatening to label them foreign terrorist organizations, very few cartels, as powerful as they were, were willing to cross the Americans nowadays. Branding the cartels terror organizations opened up the possibility that Reilly could authorize the use of US military force against them without Mexico's sanction. Ramirez understood why the cartel leaders didn't want to rattle the cage too much. But it left him with very little wiggle room.

Even if he could have found a way to continue to manufacture his amphetamine pills in Turkey, it had become clear that his chances of successfully distributing them in Europe or in the United States and repatriating most of the profits back to Venezuela were almost nil. Most of his associates within Venezuela's government had been terminated or were rotting in jail. Ramirez had to give it to Arteaga. The new Venezuelan president was thorough and merciless.

The Americans, through their support of Colonel Arteaga, had made Ramirez a man without a country. Ramirez had always considered himself a businessman, never one to harbor ill will for long, but his current quandary resulted in a situation where he constantly fantasized about the deliberate, cold-blooded murders of Pierce Hunt and his traitorous bitch girlfriend, Anna Garcia. Over his years of service, he had taken no personal pleasure in killing his adversaries, but if he ever got his hands around Hunt's and Garcia's necks, he'd take great satisfaction in suffocating both of them. Until now, everything Ramirez had ever done, good or bad, he had done for Venezuela.

That was about to change.

Following his meeting with Kazak, and under an assumed name, Ramirez had traveled from Istanbul to Geneva. From there, he had rented a car and driven five hours to the Grand Hotel Villa Castagnola.

Set on the shores of Lake Lugano and nestled within a private, subtropical park, the five-star property had once been the home of a noble Russian family. He might have been there for business, but that didn't prevent Ramirez from enjoying the hotel's tranquil atmosphere and its discreet but friendly service. The scenery was spectacular, too, and while admiring the stunning views of the lake from his fourth-floor suite, Ramirez caught himself wishing he could simply disappear and start a new life here in Switzerland. To vanish for good, he needed money. Lots of it. Money he didn't have.

Yet.

Sliding the patio door open, Ramirez stepped onto the balcony and leaned against the railing. His eyes settled on the majestic lake below. Several sailboats and a couple of fishing boats were moored not far from shore, tugging gently at their tethers.

The phone number Kazak had given him belonged to a man named Aram Diljen. There wasn't much information available on Diljen. The only thing Kazak had said was that Diljen had his finger in many pies, including arms sales and drug dealing, and that he controlled most of the underworld in and around Lugano. Diljen had agreed to meet with Ramirez and was sending a car to pick him up.

Would Diljen be interested in what he had to sell? That was a tricky question. The chemical formula for the amphetamine pills could be worth something to the right buyer, but what Ramirez truly wished to sell was the intelligence he had. On a thumb drive, he had evidence of Colonel Arteaga's direct link to the Americans and of the atrocities he had committed with the complicity of the CIA in order to solidify his position within the Venezuelan government. That thumb drive could easily bring down President Reilly's administration. *That* could be worth a fortune. Ramirez doubted Diljen would himself be in a position to exploit the intelligence, but maybe he'd know someone who could.

Unfortunately, that leverage against the Americans was all Ramirez had for bargaining power. He had hidden the thumb drive containing the incriminating information in a safe place. If this first encounter with Diljen went well and the Swiss criminal was willing to pay, Ramirez would give it to him, but only once his own safety was assured.

Ramirez walked back inside his suite, closed the patio door behind him, and stood before the wall-mounted full-length mirror. He made an adjustment to his blue tie so it was evenly placed in the white space of his shirt between his dark jacket's lapels. It was an old habit. Appearances were important. His pistol, a Beretta 92FS, was secured in a shoulder holster under his left arm. Two extra magazines were safely tucked away under his right arm, and a small combat knife was sheathed on his hip.

It was time to go. The car Diljen had sent for him would arrive any moment. His hand was on the doorknob when his cell vibrated inside his jacket pocket. Since Diljen was the only one who had his number, Ramirez answered.

"The man you're about to meet isn't who he says he is."

"Who's this?" Ramirez asked, not recognizing the deep, slightly raspy voice. If he had to guess, he'd say that whoever was on the other end of the line was using a voice changer.

"I'm the man who's ready to pay you handsomely for what you have."

"I already have a buyer," Ramirez said.

Ramirez heard a dry laugh at the other end. "Aram Diljen is a CIA officer," the man said bluntly.

"That's impossible," Ramirez replied without thinking. "He's been vouched for."

"Oh, I see. *He's been vouched for*," the man said with cold disdain. "Are you serious?"

The contempt and sarcasm pouring out of the man's voice angered Ramirez, but he checked himself. He had to admit that the man had a point. Had he been played by his Turkish contact? This could also be a trap set by Diljen to test Ramirez's loyalty. The thought sent a shiver down Ramirez's spine. He would have to tread carefully.

"Can you prove it?" Ramirez asked.

"Does it matter? Can you take that chance? That's the real question."

The CIA had eyes everywhere. It was possible the man on the phone was telling the truth.

Ramirez wished he had half the resources he'd had only months ago. But he didn't. Here he was in Switzerland, certainly not defenseless, but not in a position of strength either.

"How did you get this number?" Ramirez asked, stepping away from the door.

Instead of answering his question, the man said, "I want everything you have on Queen Bee."

Ramirez froze in place.

Queen Bee. That was the CIA's code name for Colonel Arteaga. Very few people knew that, and he hadn't shared it with his Turkish contact. Whoever this was, he was well connected.

"If you'd called me earlier, maybe we could have worked together," Ramirez said, seeing no point in lying. "Now's too late, I'm afraid."

"If you hang up now, you'll be dead within the hour."

It was Ramirez's turn to laugh. "I've been in this business for quite some time. And I'm still here," he said.

"Oh, is that so?" the man said. Despite the voice changer, Ramirez could feel that his tone had turned glacial. "Maybe I should have let the American kill you in Turkey."

A lead ball had suddenly formed in his stomach. Kazak had been wrong. Ramirez had been the American assassin's target after all.

"Let me tell you what will happen in the next few minutes, Jorge Ramirez," the man said, making a point by using Ramirez's full name and not the one he'd registered his hotel room under. "In two minutes, a three-vehicle motorcade will arrive at that fancy hotel of yours. Aram Diljen will come out of his SUV to greet you personally. You'll then climb into the same SUV, and the motorcade will make its way to Ristorante AnaCapri. You're with me so far?"

The lead ball had now morphed into a major cramp. Was he being watched?

"I'm still listening," Ramirez replied, making his way to the closest window. He pushed the heavy curtain aside and peered out. He didn't see anyone standing out in the garden, but his suite was facing Lake Lugano, not the street. There was no way to know if a surveillance team was already in place. He had to assume it was.

The man continued, "Once you're in the vehicle, any attempt to speak about our conversation to Aram Diljen will be interpreted as a challenge to us."

"Who's 'us'?" asked Ramirez.

"Not something you need to concern yourself with at the moment. What you need to understand, though, is that we have men everywhere. And I truly mean that. Play along, and you'll learn soon enough who we are."

Ramirez hadn't survived this long in the underworld by being naive or stupid. He needed to consider his next step with care.

"I don't have what you seek."

"We know. But it's nearby. We know that too."

"What is this information worth to you?" Ramirez asked, pacing the length of his suite.

"You mean in addition to letting you live?"

"If I die, you'll never gain access to what I have on Queen Bee."

"Again, can you take that chance?"

"How much?" Ramirez pressed on, stopping in front of the mirror to take another look at his tie.

"Your life, plus one and a half million euros."

Ramirez frowned. One and a half million euros wasn't what he had in mind. Not even close. In order to accept an unsolicited preemptive offer for the intelligence he had on Colonel Arteaga, he'd need at least ten times that amount.

"It was nice talking to you, but I'll take my chances with Diljen," Ramirez said before ending the call.

He was in the process of putting his phone back into his jacket pocket when a high-caliber bullet broke the window where he had been standing seconds ago and embedded itself in the wall. Ramirez hit the ground and rolled to his left. He pulled out his pistol and aimed it at the doorway, knowing the real danger wasn't coming from the balcony. The shot had probably come from one of the boats he had spotted earlier, but the only entry point he was concerned about was the main door.

Unless they have a team on the roof or in one of the rooms directly above mine ready to rappel down to the balcony, he thought.

His cell phone vibrated on the thick beige carpet of his suite. Keeping his pistol pointed at the door with his left arm, Ramirez extended his right arm and grabbed it. He pressed the talk button and placed the phone against his ear.

As he expected, it was the man with the deep, slightly raspy voice. "I hope you'll reconsider my offer."

"When it comes to making a first impression, you certainly have a way," Ramirez replied, his heart racing.

"We're short on time, Mr. Ramirez. The motorcade is rolling in as we speak. You need to make a decision."

"I don't like to be pushed around."

"This wasn't my intention, but the clock is ticking."

"Ten million."

Ramirez heard the man sigh heavily. "My first offer still stands. One and a half million euros and your life. Take it or leave it."

Ramirez shook his head. He was outgunned, outmanned, and out of his comfort zone. For now, he'd have to play along.

"Very well. What do you want me to do?"

CHAPTER THIRTEEN

Lugano, Switzerland

Hunt studied the restaurant's outside terrace through the scope mounted on his Steyr SSG 08 sniper rifle. The restaurant was unusually busy for a Wednesday afternoon. A large group of German tourists had arrived by tour bus twenty minutes earlier and, despite the cooler-than-normal temperature, had taken possession of most of the sought-after tables. Hunt didn't blame them. He had himself dined at Ristorante AnaCapri a couple of years ago, and not only had he enjoyed the food, he had also marveled at the splendid views of Lake Lugano and its surrounding mountains that the terrace offered to its privileged guests. It didn't matter that Hunt was almost a quarter of a mile away from the restaurant. His stomach growled as he watched the patrons settle in for a late lunch.

The CIA had caught a lucky break when Doru Kazak had contacted Aram Diljen to tell him that Jorge Ramirez would be contacting him. Unknown to Kazak, Diljen was a CIA deep-cover asset who had been embedded with the 'Ndrangheta—one of the most powerful crime syndicates in Italy—for ten years and had become the de facto leader of the organization in Switzerland. Diljen had in turn contacted his handler at the Directorate of Operations. This was the intelligence that had initiated Henican's deployment to Turkey a little over a week ago.

Diljen was scheduled to meet Ramirez at Ristorante AnaCapri, but Hunt was starting to doubt if it was going to happen. Diljen was late, and so was Ramirez. By more than an hour.

To Hunt's right and standing four feet back from the window ledge, Harriet Jacobs mumbled something under her breath.

"What is it?" Hunt asked.

"I can't believe we're here. We should be in Turkey searching for Charlie, damn it!"

"Charlie's not the mission, Harriet," Hunt replied. "Focus, will you?"

"How am I supposed to focus when the only thing on my mind is Charlie?"

Such honesty coming from a hardened veteran took Hunt by surprise. He liked Jacobs. She was a capable CIA officer who wasn't afraid to get her hands dirty. Dark skinned, tall, and athletic, Jacobs had a great sense of humor and curiosity about life that Hunt loved. He understood why his friend had fallen for her. But he needed her to get her head back in the game. Their lives depended on it.

"Just do your job," Hunt snapped. "You're supposed to be the one in charge. Start acting like it."

For a full minute, they didn't speak, and Hunt wondered if he had pushed too hard. Then Jacobs broke the silence.

"It's that white tour bus," she muttered, her eyes glued to her spotting scope. "I can't see the south half of the terrace."

Hunt swung the scope crosshairs to the right. "Shouldn't be a problem. All the tables on that side of the restaurant are occupied. They won't sit there."

"Copy that."

He was relieved that Jacobs was back to thinking about their mission. But he couldn't fully push away his concern about his friend. He'd rather be going after Henican too.

"Where the hell are they?" Jacobs asked.

63

Simon Gervais

As formidable as she was, Hunt was starting to learn that patience wasn't one of Jacobs's numerous virtues. But she had a point.

"Whiplash, this is Sierra-Two," he said via the wireless bone microphone in his right ear.

"Go ahead for Whiplash," came Barry Pike over the radio.

"Any news for us?"

"Negative, Sierra-Two. We haven't heard from Diljen's handler or Blank Eagle since earlier this morning."

Hunt presumed that like most deep-cover intelligence officers, Diljen had only one or two handlers and would keep his contacts with them to a bare minimum. Surviving a nonofficial cover for ten years was no small feat. Having done a two-year undercover stint for the DEA, Hunt knew better than most what a juggling act it was. As for Blank Eagle, it was the code name for the communication office of Dorothy Triggs. All operational messages coming from Blank Eagle had to be personally approved by Triggs before trickling down to Hunt and Jacobs.

There were a ton of legitimate reasons why Diljen and Ramirez could be late, so he forced himself to relax. He had been in similar situations dozens of times before. Lying on his stomach behind a scoped rifle, ready to kill, wasn't something new, but he wasn't getting any younger. His shoulders and neck were starting to ache, and the years of physically pushing his body beyond normal limits were taking their toll.

And I'm only thirty-nine, he thought. At least he wasn't in Afghanistan, or Venezuela for that matter. The small one-bedroom apartment they were in, selected for its perfect view of the outside terrace of Ristorante AnaCapri, had been rented for five nights via an online booking system. The building, which was nothing more than a large house whose interior had been remodeled to provide a number of small but adequate apartments, was nonetheless much more comfortable than his regular sniper's nests. It had taken him and Jacobs less than thirty minutes to transform the dining room. They had built a prone firing position from deep inside the room that was high enough to fire through the double-wide french doors and over the balcony railing. They had first positioned six wooden dining chairs facing inward atop the apartment's dining table. They had then put the double bed mattress from the bedroom on top of the chair seats. Using chair cushions and bed pillows, they had made a stable spot for the Fortmeier bipod that supported the Steyr SSG 08. From that position, they had a clear shot 450 yards to the east—all the way to the front door and outside terrace of the restaurant.

Hunt had been on the gun for close to twenty minutes now. In another ten minutes, he'd switch position with Jacobs. Even though Hunt could stay fully alert behind the rifle for much longer than that, it was good practice to change every thirty minutes or so if the tactical situation allowed for it.

"Sierra-Two, this is Whiplash," came in Pike.

"Go ahead for Sierra-Two."

"Traffic cams indicate a convoy of three dark blue SUVs approaching your location. They're four minutes out."

This might be it.

During the initial operation briefing, Triggs had said that Diljen would be traveling in a three-vehicle convoy. Was it possible that Diljen had picked up Ramirez along the way? Hunt unconsciously pulled the rifle tighter into his shoulder.

"Sierra-One, this is Whiplash."

"This is Sierra-One," Jacobs replied.

"We just received a priority message from Blank Eagle."

"Go ahead with the priority message," Hunt heard Jacobs say, her voice composed despite the last-minute change they both suspected was coming.

"You have a new primary target. I say again, you have a new primary target," Pike said.

Hunt and Jacobs exchanged a look. She seemed as confused as he was. A new target? So late in the operation?

"Whiplash, this is Sierra-Two. Who's the target?" Hunt asked.

"Diljen," Pike replied, his voice betraying his obvious concern. "Your new target is Aram Diljen."

CHAPTER FOURTEEN

Lugano, Switzerland

Hunt shook his head in frustration.

"Diljen? They want us to take down one of ours?" he asked Jacobs in near disbelief.

Her response was a simple shrug of the shoulders.

"Whiplash, this is Sierra-One. That doesn't make any sense," Jacobs said. "Are you sure about this?"

"One hundred percent," Pike replied. "And there's more. Under no circumstances are you to engage Jorge Ramirez."

"What the hell?" Hunt exploded. "This is pure bullshit!"

Pike continued, "I just received the target profile package from Blank Eagle. I'm forwarding it to you now. Pictures of the target are on page two. Please note that it's been confirmed that Ramirez is traveling aboard Diljen's vehicle."

Hunt fought to keep his focus while he heard Jacobs rummaging through her backpack to get the secured laptop. Last-minute changes were never good. But this was beyond last minute.

"I can't believe this," Hunt said. He looked at Jacobs and added, "I say we get out of here, regroup, and figure out exactly what's going on."

"Let me check the target package first," she replied, powering up the laptop. "I'm logging in now."

Hunt didn't like any of it. Triggs had appointed Jacobs as the lead for this operation, but Hunt had spent much more time downrange than she ever would. Something told him that this entire operation was about to go belly up.

"This is a legitimate target package, Pierce," Jacobs said after a minute. "Triggs authenticated it."

"So we're supposed to kill one of ours? And what about that puke Ramirez? He lives?"

"C'mon, Pierce. You're not at your first rodeo. They don't have to tell us why."

"I don't like it."

"Neither do I, but our orders couldn't be clearer."

Could Triggs have learned something about Diljen? Was it possible that he was the one responsible for Henican's capture? Maybe the story he'd told about a Turk referring Ramirez to him was a lie. If that was the case, Hunt would happily put him down. Maybe Diljen had been too deep for too long and had somehow been turned. That was a possibility. But why this last-minute change?

Hunt swore out loud. He knew his place. He was an operator. A shooter. He wasn't a decision maker at the strategic level.

But still, something was off.

"Are you still logged in?" he asked Jacobs.

"Affirmative."

"Can you send a message directly to Blank Eagle?"

"I can, but Pike and Crawford will see it," she replied, obviously wondering where this was going.

"That's okay. Ask Triggs what Diljen has done that warrants his execution."

"There's no time, Pierce—"

"Do it or I walk," Hunt threatened. "Hurry the hell up!"

Jacobs didn't answer, but he heard her type on the laptop. Half a minute later, she was done. "Now what?" she asked him.

"We wait."

CHAPTER FIFTEEN

Lugano, Switzerland

Max Oswald read the message he had just intercepted. It had come from Harriet Jacobs, but he was certain it was Hunt who had insisted on it. Max shook his head in disbelief. Hunt was proving himself to be a major pain in the butt. Max was familiar with how Jacobs operated. She was a good soldier who carried out orders without questioning them. Hunt, on the other hand . . .

"What's the problem?" Wood asked, stroking his mustache.

"Nothing I can't fix," Max said, rattling away on his Toughbook as fast as his two-finger typing would permit.

"You should really learn how to—"

"Not now!" he growled.

Max, Wood, Tay, and DeLarue were parked in a rented BMW X5 less than two minutes away from Hunt and Jacobs's location. Before his abrupt departure from the CIA, Max had cloned all of his mother's mobile devices and work computers. Her phones, laptops, and even security tokens were now his. He had unlimited access to intercept or allow through any messages she received or sent. He could issue or rescind orders, modify operational plans, and even create new ones if need be. And that was exactly what he was doing. By diverting Jacobs's message to his shadow account, he was making sure that his mother would never see it and that she had no idea what was actually going on in Lugano.

"Sir," Tay called from the back seat, holding an earbud to his ear. "The TOC just called it. The motorcade is one minute out. Our men are in position."

"Copy that," Max replied. He read his answer one more time, then pressed send.

And another one bites the dust, Max thought sadly.

CHAPTER SIXTEEN

Lugano, Switzerland

"Sierra-One, this is Whiplash. Motorcade is one minute out."

"Good copy, Whiplash. Motorcade is one minute out," Jacobs replied.

Hunt glanced once again toward Jacobs. She had returned behind her spotting scope but had left the laptop open. "Anything?" he asked.

A soft ding emanating from the laptop answered for her.

"It's confirmed. Diljen is the leak," Jacobs said. "The bastard sold out Charlie."

Unreal, Hunt thought, surprised. *I was sure it was the Turk.*

Hunt took a long look at her. Were they really about to kill a CIA officer? Despite the concern he had seen on her face only minutes ago, Jacobs now exuded confidence and determination.

"We're doing this, Pierce," she said, acknowledging his nonverbal question. "You with me?"

"Yeah, I'm with you," he said after a rare moment of hesitation. He had voiced his concerns, but now that the decision to go through with the mission had been made, he'd give it his best.

"Good," she said.

"Updates?" he asked briskly, getting back to the business at hand.

"Wind is coming from your left at about five knots. You'll see the first SUV moving from your left to your right in just a few seconds. Windows are tinted."

Hunt adjusted the rifle to account for the estimated wind. He could feel his stomach starting to tighten with tension. He took a deep breath, filling his lungs with the cool Swiss air coming in from the opened french doors, and then breathed out slowly. He repeated the exercise three more times. When the first of the three SUVs pulled up alongside Ristorante AnaCapri, Hunt was ready, steady as a rock. He was in his zone. Composed but prepared. Watchful but relaxed.

Two men who had been inside the restaurant came out to greet the new arrivals. They must have been there for a while since Hunt hadn't seen them before and Jacobs hadn't called them out. They were dressed in slacks and sports jackets over open-collar shirts, and both had on dark sunglasses. Even from a distance, the men looked as though they meant business.

"These two must be Diljen's advance team," Jacobs said before adding, "Or Ramirez's men."

It didn't matter either way. Hunt wasn't planning on firing more than one shot. Diljen might have been the top 'Ndrangheta guy in Switzerland, but Hunt was nevertheless surprised he traveled with such an entourage. In Hunt's experience, hardened criminals kept a low profile.

Three men poured out of the front SUV and took up defensive positions around the convoy. Hunt noticed that the driver remained inside the vehicle.

"I didn't see anyone getting out of the rear SUV," Jacobs said. "You think they have a CAT?"

"Hard to say."

A CAT—or counterassault team—was a group of heavily armed men well trained in counterambush tactics who would usually remain low profile inside their vehicles unless things turned ugly. Hunt had served on CATs before, and although the dignitaries he and his team were tasked to protect oftentimes had their own security details, CATs were regularly needed to provide heavier firepower in war zones. Hunt couldn't fathom why Diljen would need to travel with a counterassault team. It was odd. This was Switzerland, not South Sudan. The TOC—tactical operations center—needed to be advised of that possible development. Hunt was glad that it was Pike and Crawford who were manning the TOC. They were used to working in high-pressure environments. Their timely input and ability to remain cool under stress had saved his life more than once.

"Whiplash, this is Sierra-Two," Hunt said over the radio.

There was no response.

"Whiplash, this is Sierra-Two. How copy?" Hunt repeated, but there was only silence coming from the other end.

Damn it!

This wasn't a good time for communications problems. The communication system he and Jacobs were using to talk with the TOC was encrypted, and only another radio operating the unique encoding algorithm could hear them. Anyone else trying to listen in would hear static. They could have tried to reach Pike or Crawford with their satellite phone, but with the motorcade already parked in front of the restaurant, that time had come and gone.

"Movement at the second SUV," Jacobs said. "One of the bodyguards is about to open the rear passenger door."

Hunt watched as the rear passenger door opened and a medium-height, well-built Hispanic man in his thirties climbed out. Hunt got a good profile look.

"It's him. That's Jorge Ramirez," Hunt said, allowing his finger to caress the smooth, curved face of the trigger.

"I confirm," Jacobs replied without any hint of hesitation.

Another man, who had also been riding in the back of the SUV, got out on the opposite side. He wore a pair of designer jeans and a neatly ironed pink shirt and sported a well-trimmed beard. Diljen, Hunt assumed. The man exuded confidence even from afar.

"I confirm this is our target. This is Aram Diljen," Jacobs said. "Whenever you're ready."

For a moment, Diljen stood on the sidewalk and seemed to wait for Ramirez, who was flanked by one bodyguard, to walk around the front of the SUV.

Hunt took a deep breath, exhaled, and stabilized the crosshairs a couple of inches under Diljen's neck. He began to squeeze the trigger, which was adjusted for a forty-ounce pull, and then he stopped.

"I'm about to lose visual, Pierce," Jacobs warned him. "What are you waiting for?"

"It doesn't feel right," Hunt said, his finger resting on the trigger guard.

Jacobs's reply was uncompromising. "For God's sake. Henican might be dead because of him, and if Triggs sanctioned this, that means the man's a traitor or a threat to our national security. How many more of us does he need to sell out for you to take him down?"

"Diljen's loyalty was never questioned during our briefing," Hunt argued. "On the contrary—"

"Sierra-Two, the message has been authenticated. Take the god-damn shot," Jacobs ordered.

Hunt groaned but got back in his firing position. Jacobs was right. Diljen was a menace. Through his scope, Hunt surveyed the scene. Walking side by side, Diljen and Ramirez were about to enter the res-taurant. Hunt estimated that he had less than two seconds to take the shot before his window of opportunity evaporated. His finger curled around the trigger. So steady was his trigger pull that the recoil took him by surprise. Hunt's hand automatically worked the bolt, ejecting the empty casing and chambering another round. The bullet took a hair under half a second to travel the distance. It struck Aram Diljen at the base of the neck. On hitting the spinal cord, the bullet fragmented, creating secondary missile-like projectiles. Two of these bullet fragments found their way to Diljen's heart, killing him instantly.

Even though the rifle was outfitted with a suppressor, it still sounded as if a weapon had been fired, but at least the shot hadn't been as deafening. By the way the bodyguards were reacting, they had no clue what had just happened. With the exception of Jacobs, Hunt thought it was likely that no one else in the building or on the nearby street had heard the gunshot.

"Good hit," Jacobs said. "Time to go."

Hunt felt a sick twist in his stomach. It wasn't a "good hit." He had killed a CIA officer. A fellow American. There was nothing remotely good about it.

Shit! What have I done?

A glance through his scope showed that Diljen was sprawled on the sidewalk with blood running from beneath him. Hunt rested the crosshairs on Ramirez, itching to pull the trigger and be done with it. Why would Triggs want to keep this piece of shit alive? One minute he was enemy number one, and the next he wasn't to be touched?

Hunt swore under his breath. As much as he wanted to, he wouldn't defy his orders. He wouldn't kill Jorge Ramirez.

Ramirez turned, and for an instant, Hunt was positive that his eyes were peering directly at him. Hunt's heart fluttered, bile rising at the back of his throat. Ramirez didn't look surprised to see his newfound friend with a bullet hole in the back. It was as if he'd known all along what would happen to Diljen at the restaurant. Less than ten seconds after Hunt had fired the shot that had killed Aram Diljen, Ramirez climbed aboard the third SUV and departed the scene.

The third SUV isn't a CAT—it's a goddamn getaway vehicle! Hunt thought. Who was behind the wheel of that SUV? Diljen's men or Ramirez's? Or a third and yet unknown party?

"Let's go, Pierce! Get a grip." Jacobs's voice snapped him back to reality. She was right. It was time to go. Now wasn't the time to become bogged down in self-doubt. He'd get his answers later. Hopefully from Triggs herself.

Hunt rolled away from the Steyr SSG 08 and off the table. He picked up the rifle and took it to the bedroom, where he placed it on the bed. He closed the bipod, unloaded the rifle, then swiftly dismantled it. He stuffed the rifle in his carry-on luggage. By the time he was done and back in the living room, Jacobs had packed up the spotting scope and undone the sniper's nest. In the distance, Hunt heard sirens and wondered if the first on scene would be the police or the paramedics.

"All set?" Hunt asked, closing the french doors.

Jacobs shook her head. "Still can't reach Whiplash. I'll call Pike on the sat phone to give them a quick sitrep."

"Understood," Hunt replied, heading toward the door. "I'll bring the car around."

Their exfil plan was simple. They would drive to a safe house in Agno—a small historic town west of Lugano—and lie low for seventy-two hours or until notified otherwise by Whiplash.

Shouting over his earpiece caused Hunt to stop midstride. It was the emergency channel. Barry Pike was yelling something unintelligible, almost deafening Hunt in the process. Hunt couldn't be sure, but he thought he had heard a burst of machine-gun fire in the background.

Shit! Now what?

He cupped his hand over his earpiece so he could hear better and distinguish the sounds from one another.

"Whiplash, this is Sierra-Two. Say—" Hunt started, but he was interrupted by an out-of-breath Pike.

"They knew our codes, Pierce. He's sold us out . . . and Henican! It's the goddamn—"

In the background, Hunt discerned urgent shouts and more gunfire. A few shots were so sharp Hunt reckoned that it was Pike who had fired them. Hunt looked at Jacobs. Her face had drained of color, and her eyes seemed to grow to twice their normal size.

Pike continued, his voice a hysterical pitch, "Colleen! Nooo! Fuuuck!"

Hunt heard one more gunshot, then the thud of a body hitting the floor followed by a loud gasp. And then nothing.

"Whiplash? Whiplash, this is Sierra-Two, come in," Hunt said.

Damn it!

"We need to get to the TOC," Jacobs said, rushing past him. "Everything's going to shit."

Hunt couldn't agree more. Protocol in case the TOC was attacked or overrun was for him and Jacobs to get out of Switzerland in the most expedited way. If the two CIA security officers assigned to protect the TOC had been unable to repel the attack, Langley's solution was to cut its losses, not risk the lives of two more officers by asking them to intervene. Hunt understood the theory behind it, but he didn't agree with it. Not one bit. He had never left friends behind. Today wasn't the day he was about to start.

CHAPTER SEVENTEEN

Lugano, Switzerland

Ramirez didn't hear the shot, but he felt the zip of the bullet and the wet thudding sound it made entering Diljen's back. Propelled forward by the impact, Diljen fell onto his face. By the way Diljen had been driven forward, Ramirez quickly assessed the likely position of the shooter. The bodyguards, caught by surprise, took longer than they should have to check on Diljen. Not that it mattered. Their employer was dead. The man with the raspy voice had kept his end of the bargain.

Ramirez, unlike the bodyguards, didn't waste any time. His instructions were clear. He was on a tight schedule. He hurried to the third SUV. On his way, he glanced at the probable location of the shooter and almost waved. It didn't take a genius to understand that if the shooter had wanted Ramirez dead, he'd be so by now. Ramirez opened the door of the SUV and climbed in the front passenger seat. The man with the raspy voice had told him that the third SUV, the one that would be riding at the back of the motorcade, would be manned by men loyal to him and that Ramirez would receive his next set of instructions from the driver. Partnering with turncoats wasn't what Ramirez had had in mind when he'd landed in Geneva, but he was going with the flow.

Two men were seated in the back, both wearing semimilitary clothing and armed with MP5 submachine guns equipped with sound suppressors. The driver, who was wearing a white T-shirt and a pair of light-colored blue jeans, had a pistol holstered on his right hip. His arms were as big as Ramirez's thighs. His right forearm was decorated with a series of tattoos Ramirez had seen before on Russian convicts.

The SUV sped down the road, away from the scene.

"In the glove compartment," the driver said by way of introduction, his thick Russian accent confirming Ramirez's guess about his origins.

Ramirez reached out and opened the glove compartment. From it he took a small Smith & Wesson .38 five-shots revolver. He checked the cylinder, and satisfied that it contained five rounds, he snapped it back in place.

"What do you expect me to do with this?" Ramirez asked the driver. The small-caliber revolver's stopping power was far less than the Beretta he'd been asked to dispose of by the man with the raspy voice.

"Not much. Stay in the car. Stay alive," the driver replied.

"Where are we going?"

"Geneva. Soon. But now, we do small detour first."

Ramirez left it at that. It wasn't like he had much control over the situation. He hadn't yet handed the intelligence he had to the man with the raspy voice. And his promised €1.5 million hadn't been deposited in his Andorran bank either.

But you're alive, he thought. *That's more than Aram Diljen can say.*

The driver drove fast, whirling down the narrow streets of Lugano. He made several right turns and revved the engine going up a short, steep road. It didn't take Ramirez long to figure out where they were going.

"We're on our way to pick up your sniper, aren't we?" he asked.

Despite the high rate of speed they were traveling at, the driver took his eyes off the road and looked at Ramirez. "Not really," he replied, a thin smile on his lips.

Less than two minutes after they'd left the restaurant, the SUV came to a sudden stop next to a four-story apartment building. Without a word being spoken, the two men seated in the back of the SUV climbed out, their suppressed MP5s up. The way they moved and held their weapons left no doubt in Ramirez's mind. These men were more than Russian convicts. They were trained soldiers.

They're not here to pick up the sniper, Ramirez thought. *They're here to kill him.*

CHAPTER EIGHTEEN

Lugano, Switzerland

Max Oswald clenched his fists, his neck muscles involuntarily tightening.

"Goddamn it!" he said, slamming his fist into the dash. "Who the fuck just attacked the TOC?"

"What do you want to do?" DeLarue asked, his voice heavily tinged with a French accent.

Max had a decision to make. He could either rush to the TOC and try to stop the bloodshed, or he and his men could stay at their current position for the next phase of the operation, which was to collect Jorge Ramirez from the Russian mercenaries. Max wondered how long it would take Hunt and Jacobs to figure out that they had been tricked into killing the wrong man. Not that Aram Diljen didn't deserve to die. He did. Diljen hadn't climbed to the top of the 'Ndrangheta in Switzerland by being a good boy. The man had murdered and tortured countless adversaries in his quest to control Lugano's underworld. Aram Diljen was a piece of shit, although Max conceded that most of his victims had been fellow criminals.

So I guess that evens things out, Max thought.

He made his decision. "Drive to the TOC," he ordered Wood. "Fast."

Wood didn't need to be told twice. He peeled out of their parking spot and headed north. He took advantage of the light traffic to pick up speed, weaving in and out between the slow-moving vehicles, pushing the BMW X5 to its limits. In the back seat, Tay and DeLarue fastened their seat belts. In front of the BMW, a small group of cars was stopped at a red light. Max held his breath. They were going way too fast.

Shit! We're gonna plow into them! He braced for impact.

At the last moment, Wood drove the car onto the sidewalk and steered around the cars without killing anyone. Moreover, they got through the intersection without being hit by another vehicle. As Wood maneuvered the car back into the street, Max looked at him.

"Nice driving," he said, finally breathing.

"We're less than three minutes out," Wood said.

Way too long, Max thought. *Damn it!*

"Okay, guys," Max said. "I want you to spring from this vehicle at a moment's notice. You've all seen pictures of Barry Pike and Colleen Crawford, as well as of the two CIA security officers. Everybody else is to be considered hostile. You got me?"

Everybody did.

Max double-checked his MP5, making sure the magazine was well inserted and that he had a round in the chamber. Then he settled in his seat with a deadly coolness born of years of combat. He was ready.

———

Max was relieved to see no first responders at the scene. That would make their job much easier. The TOC was located on the ground floor of a medium-size, two-story office building just outside the city limits of Lugano.

"Slow down," Max told Wood once they were two hundred meters away. He wanted to survey the area to make sure they weren't walking into an ambush. There were only a few cars in the parking lot since most people had already gone home at the end of their workday.

They were still fifty meters from the building entrance when Max saw four armed men running out of the building, heading toward an idling white Toyota Sequoia SUV.

His heart stopped.

What the fuck is this? What are they doing here?

These men were the backup team of Russians he had hired in case additional security was needed or something happened to the team that was supposed to pick up Ramirez. They were supposed to be five miles away from here, in the rooms he had booked for them at a local hotel. He'd never even given them the TOC location.

Why had they attacked the TOC? Max wanted answers.

"Wood, you stay in the car."

"Understood."

For the benefit of the others, Max added, "I want one alive."

One of the Russians scanned the area as he was about to climb into the passenger seat of the white SUV. His gaze came to rest on the BMW X5. Then he found Max's eyes.

"On me!" Max shouted, leaping out of the BMW while it was still rolling. He fired his suppressed MP5 six times before the Russian managed to warn the others. His first five rounds missed, hitting the SUV and shattering the passenger-side rear window. His sixth round struck the man square in the chest, knocking him off balance and pushing him against the car.

Max sprinted toward a parked Honda to his right and skidded to a stop, taking cover behind the front wheel and the engine block. The white SUV was thirty meters in front of him, and Max had a clear view of the driver. To his left, Tay and DeLarue advanced toward the SUV, covering each other. Max took aim at the driver, but just as he was about to pull the trigger, the first man he had shot popped back up.

Max shot him in the head. The Russian's head snapped back, coating the windshield with a red mist. The driver panicked and put the transmission in reverse. He floored the gas pedal and hit one of the remaining Russians. Despite the firefight, Max heard a guttural scream as the rear passenger-side tire rolled over the Russian, crushing both his hips.

By backing up, the driver of the SUV had unwittingly exposed another Russian shooter who had been hiding behind the driver's side front wheel. Instead of sending lead downrange to cover his retreat, the man shouted at the driver to come back. Max dropped him with a double tap, both rounds hitting the man in the upper chest. To Max's left, the white SUV crashed into a parked car after Tay pumped rounds into its interior, killing the driver.

Max scanned the area for other threats. One Russian sat in the middle of the parking lot, holding his leg. A small pool of blood had formed beneath it. The man's rifle was out of reach. Tay and DeLarue were already on him, holding him at gunpoint. Max asked Tay to follow him inside the building while he ordered DeLarue to secure the Russian mercenary and make room for him inside the BMW.

Tay opened the door, and Max entered, his MP5 pressed against his shoulder. A short hallway led to two doors and two separate office spaces. It was standard operating procedure to rent out the entire space to limit staff movements during an operation. The office to the left was where the team ate and slept, while the one on the right was where the TOC was located.

Max signaled Tay to cover the door leading to the TOC while he cleared the sleeping quarters. The door was unlocked. Max pushed it open and rushed in. He encountered the first body almost immediately. A Russian mercenary was sprawled on the floor with at least four bullet wounds in his chest. His weapon, a semiautomatic pistol, lay on the floor beside him. Max stepped over the body and scanned the office. It consisted of a small bathroom and a larger open-space area, with four folding camp cots with sleeping bags, two portable refrigerators, and two Coleman compact two-burner gas camp stoves. It took Max less than twenty seconds to clear the space. One CIA security officer was lying against the far wall, a single gunshot wound to the head. His lifeless eyes stared past Max into the ceiling. His pistol, a nine-millimeter Beretta, was still in his right hand.

Max left the office and tapped Tay's shoulder, letting him know he was ready. It was obvious that a shotgun had been used to breach the door leading to the TOC. The entire doorknob and locking mechanism had been blown off. Going in, Tay turned left, clearing the left corner, while Max hugged the right wall and cleared the far corner. They both rotated toward the center of the room. The TOC was much smaller than the one on the seventh floor of the CIA building. The focal point was four flat-screen monitors placed on a series of tables arranged in a U shape. Two work desks were positioned at the opening of the U, on which were computers and communication equipment.

Barry Pike had turned over his desk and used it as cover from the assailants. The desk was riddled with bullets. Pike was on his back, a satellite phone in his left hand and a pistol clutched in his right. For a moment, not seeing any visible gunshot wounds, Max thought Pike was still alive. The thought was short lived. Stepping closer, he saw that Pike had been shot in the right eye, probably with a subsonic round.

"His lady friend is gone, too, and so is another security officer," Tay said. "I'm sorry, boss, but we need to get out of here."

Tay was right. Max didn't need to see Crawford or the second CIA security officer. He felt guilty enough as it was. His only solace was to see two more dead Russian mercenaries sprawled on the carpeted floor. Pike, Crawford, and the others had died fighting.

Wood had parked the BMW in reverse right next to the exit door. Instead of climbing into the SUV, Max walked past it and toward the Russian mercenary who had been crushed under the Toyota.

Max kicked him in the back. The man grunted. He was still alive. Max pressed his knees against the man's left leg and his right hand over his mouth, keeping him quiet. The pain on the man's face was obvious. His face was red, and his neck muscles were working as he tried to scream. He tried to bite Max's hand, but Max had seen it coming and punched him straight on the nose, breaking it. Before the man could scream, Max placed his hand back over his mouth, his glove becoming red from the blood gushing from the man's flattened nose.

"Do you know who I am?" Max asked in English.

The man shook his head.

"Do you speak English?"

The man shook his head again. Max punched him twice on his broken nose, his fist landing in exactly the same place. This time, even with Max's hand on his mouth, the man managed to scream.

Once the man's lungs were empty, Max asked, "What are you doing here? Who paid you to attack this place?"

He could see that the Russian wanted to lie but was too weak to do so.

"Water—" the Russian pleaded in English. Max increased his pressure on his injured leg.

"Who paid you to attack this place?" Max repeated.

The man moaned. Max removed his hand and made it a fist, ready to strike if need be.

"We were . . . told to attack two different . . . two different sites—"

That answer confirmed Max's suspicion that someone had bypassed him and had gained direct access to his Russian mercenaries.

"Which sites? Are we presently at one of the sites?" Max asked.

The man nodded weakly.

Damn it! I'm losing him, Max thought. He had to hurry.

"Where's the other site?"

"I . . . don't . . . know. Two teams. We're . . . two teams."

"Who asked you to attack this site?" Max asked, releasing some of the pressure on the man's leg.

The man's eyes were glassy and unfocused. Max had almost given up when the man mumbled something. "Max . . . Oswald. The . . . name of the man who . . . who asked us to kill the Americans is . . . Max Oswald."

CHAPTER NINETEEN

Lugano, Switzerland

Max Oswald looked down and deep into the Russian's brown eyes and searched for some hint of a lie. He didn't find any.

Shit! That can't be.

"Have you ever met him?" Max asked, but the man wasn't even listening anymore. His eyes had rolled back in his head.

Max released the pressure he'd been applying to the man's leg and stood up. He took two steps toward the BMW, then stopped. He turned around and unceremoniously shot the Russian mercenary in the head with his MP5, putting him out of his misery.

Max climbed into the passenger seat of the BMW without a word. He signaled Wood to start driving. Behind him, DeLarue had applied a tourniquet to the injured Russian's leg and had slapped a four-inch-wide strip of gray duct tape on his mouth to keep him quiet. This was a good thing since Max needed to think.

The name of the man who asked us to kill the Americans is Max Oswald, the dying Russian had told him. It was as if someone was doing to him exactly what he was doing to his mother. Had someone gained access or taken control of his virtual network? If so, it could also mean that his numerous passports and credit cards and his bank account information had been breached. Was his safe house compromised too?

Who stood to benefit the most from Pike's and Crawford's deaths? Who else outside his team knew the TOC location? Who had the technical expertise to pull this off? He'd have to brainstorm about this and come up with a list of names. Unless an organization was behind this? Could it be a foreign intelligence service?

And then, like a well-aimed punch to the gut, another thought struck him. If the Russian mercenaries had raided the TOC, it was possible that the other team had already assaulted the apartment where Hunt and Jacobs had taken the shot.

Max twisted in his seat, pulled his pistol from his hip holster, and attached a silencer. He looked behind him at DeLarue. "Remove the duct tape," Max ordered, pressing the tip of the silencer against the Russian's knee.

The Russian mercenary looked at Max. The man was scared but was trying to look tough, which was difficult, considering the wet spot between his legs.

"Think carefully about your answer," Max warned the mercenary. "Your left leg is still good, and with proper medical care your right leg will eventually heal." The man was breathing fast, almost panting like a dog. "If you lie, the first thing to go will be your left knee," Max continued, tapping the man's knee with the silencer.

"What do you want?" the mercenary spat.

"I was about to ask you if you spoke English," Max said. "Now I know."

"So?"

"Who hired you?" Max asked, his eyes locking onto the Russian's.

"Max Oswald."

Tay and DeLarue glared at Max, surprised by the man's answer. Even Wood looked at him.

Max continued, "Have you ever met him? Do you know what this Max Oswald looks like?"

The Russian shook his head. "I swear," he said, clearly terrified that Max wouldn't believe him.

"It's okay, calm down," Max said, his voice comforting. "What's your name?"

"Vasily."

"Okay, Vasily. You're doing great. If you continue like this, in a few months, this whole thing will simply be a bad memory. Would you like that?"

Vasily nodded with enthusiasm.

"Just a few questions. If you don't mind, of course?" Max said cordially. He wanted the Russian to believe that he had a chance to get out of this ordeal alive. If Max wasn't convincing, the Russian would clam up, and Max wouldn't get the answers he sought.

"I . . . I don't mind," Vasily replied.

"Good. That's good. First question: Is there another team in play?"

Vasily's facial expression told Max the Russian hadn't understood the question, so he rephrased it. "Are you working in collaboration with another team?"

Vasily's expression relaxed perceptibly. "Yes. In downtown Lugano."

"Why are they there?" Max asked.

"Max Oswald initially hired them to provide extra security for someone named Aram Diljen," Vasily explained. "They were the A-team."

Max *had* hired the Russians—and, using the security tokens he'd stolen from his mother, had informed Diljen that the CIA would be providing additional muscle for his meeting with Ramirez. That was why the extra SUV at the restaurant hadn't raised any alarms. But when Max had retained the services of the Russians through an arms dealer the CIA had used in the past, their only instructions had been to pick up Ramirez and drive him to the location Max had specified.

"What was your role in this mess?"

"At first, we were told to stay in reserve."

"Earlier, you said 'initially,' and now you've just said 'at first.' What changed?"

"A couple of hours ago we received a new set of instructions, and a big bonus too," Vasily said. "Max Oswald gave us the address of an office building and pictures of the two people he wanted us to kill."

Barry Pike and Colleen Crawford.

"What about the other team? What were they asked to do?" Max asked, not sure he really wanted to hear the answer.

"They were told to raid an apartment. There were two targets there too," Vasily said. "I don't know the specifics."

Damn! Pierce Hunt and Harriet Jacobs. Max felt sick to his stomach as the news sliced through him. He turned to Wood and said, "Go to the apartment. Hurry!"

Max's mind was spinning. So many questions, so many half-formed answers were running through his head all at the same time.

"How did you communicate with Max Oswald?" Max asked.

"Through my phone," Vasily replied, then caught himself and added, "And Igor's laptop. I'm sorry . . . I—"

"Relax, Vasily. It's fine. Who's Igor?"

"Our team leader."

"Where's Igor now?"

"He's dead. He was our driver."

Max could barely believe it. Igor, the driver, was the leader? The poor excuse of a man who'd tried to escape at the first sign of trouble and in doing so had run over one of his men? *Coward.* Max was glad Igor was dead, but he wished they had taken the time to search the SUV. It was too late to go back.

"Where's your phone?" Max asked.

"It's in my right pocket."

Tay rifled through the man's pocket and found the phone. He handed it to Max. It looked like a regular iPhone. "How do you contact him?"

"We use WhatsApp. We all do," Vasily said.

Max sighed. The rapid development in communication technologies had made it possible for gangsters and terrorists alike to communicate via encrypted platforms like WhatsApp for free. Up against mushrooming networks and altered tactics, Western intelligence services faced daunting capacity challenges. It was impossible to closely monitor everyone.

"Face recognition or password?" Max asked.

"Both," Vasily replied without hesitation. "Nine-nine-nine-one-five-six is the code."

Max narrowed his eyes and stared at Vasily. The Russian refused to look at him, much less meet his eyes. He was lying. Hadn't Max made it exceptionally clear what would happen to the Russian if he was caught lying?

Some people just can't help themselves, Max thought.

"That's really the answer you want to go with?" Max asked.

The man swallowed hard.

"I guess you didn't care about your knee that much after all," Max said, aiming his pistol at Vasily's left knee.

He was about to pull the trigger when the Russian shouted for him to stop.

"Please . . . no! I'm sorry . . . I'm sorry . . . ," he said.

"What does the number you gave me do?"

"It . . . it would have unlocked the phone, but it's a distress signal too," Vasily confessed. "The real number is six-five-one-nine-nine-nine."

Max entered the number. The phone unlocked. He smiled at Vasily, who, despite being in obvious pain, smiled back.

Max fired a single round through Vasily's front teeth.

CHAPTER TWENTY

Nassau
New Providence, Commonwealth of the Bahamas

The airport was bustling as Simon Carter walked down the concourse to the customs area. Thankfully, the line at customs was short, and in a matter of minutes Carter was standing outside the arrivals terminal. He took a taxi to the Atlantis resort on Paradise Island. Formerly known as Hog Island, Paradise was located just offshore from the city of Nassau and connected by two fixed bridges crossing the Nassau Harbor. Why the FBI had decided to lodge the three special agents they had assigned to investigate the disappearance of Max Oswald at an expensive resort like the Atlantis, Carter had no idea. But he wasn't about to complain. From the top of the Sir Sidney Poitier Bridge, he had an incredible view of the entire resort. Carter had read online that the Atlantis had a 141-acre water park, which included high-speed waterslides, eleven pools, a mile-long river ride, and a five-mile stretch of beach.

The day before, when he and his wife, Emma, had first arrived in Nassau to spend time with Pierce, Anna, and the girls, she'd been the one with the look of total awe on her face. She'd squeezed his hand, excited about the few days they were about to spend relaxing with their friends.

Then Dorothy Triggs had called, and their carefully planned beach getaway had gone up in smoke. If Emma had been disappointed about the unforeseen changes, she hadn't shown it. Carter had always known he had married up, but Emma continued to amaze him in so many ways. Carter was aware he wasn't an easy man to live with. The constant deployments, the shift work, the missed birthdays and anniversaries. And the danger. Always the danger. Despite all of this, she'd stuck by him. Sometimes he wondered why.

Ten hours later, he'd been on a flight to Washington, DC.

Upon arrival, a car had been waiting to take him to Langley, where he'd been personally briefed by Triggs. At the end of it, she'd handed him a new set of identities, which included a Canadian passport and an Ontario driver's license.

"Nobody knows about this, Simon," Triggs had told him. "You're on your own with no agency backup."

"What about Tom Hauer?" he'd asked. "What if he—"

"I took care of Tom," Triggs had said. "He doesn't know why you're not available, but he knows not to call you."

The DEA had Carter and Hunt on a monthly retainer. Hauer hadn't contacted them since they had returned from their last mission in Venezuela, but he had always treated them with respect and honesty. And the direct deposits into their bank accounts were always on time. The last thing Carter wanted to do was alienate Hauer.

"Which tower?" the cab driver asked.

Carter had to look at his reservation. "The Royal Towers," he replied.

"First time in the Bahamas?"

"First time at Atlantis," Carter said, examining the iconic pink structure.

As they made their way along the palm-lined driveway, the Royal Towers appeared—larger than life. They were impressive and absolutely stunning. Carter paid the driver and thanked him for the smooth ride.

A concierge in a white uniform welcomed him. "Checking in, sir?"

"Yes I am," Carter replied, looking around at his surroundings. In a structural sense, the Royal Towers definitely lived up to the hype. The sheer size of the hotel was mesmerizing.

"Your name?"

"Mitch Steck," he said without hesitation. He handed his Canadian passport to the concierge.

The concierge typed a few keystrokes on his computer, then picked up the phone. "Is Mr. Steck's room ready?" the concierge asked.

He smiled at Carter and hung up the phone. "Follow me."

The concierge led Carter through a massive covered walkway from which he enjoyed terrific views of the Atlantis Marina, where a small fleet of multimillion-dollar yachts lined the docks. The lobby was grandiose and didn't disappoint with its soaring ceilings and murals.

The concierge gave Carter his room key and wished him a pleasant stay. His room was on the seventh floor, two doors down from Special Agent Bill C. McGhee, the lead FBI agent for the case. Carter entered his room and placed his carry-on luggage on the bed. The first order of business was to perform a complete sweep of the room. He visually inspected every lamp, light fixture, vase, and flowerpot as well as the smoke detector and the air vent for any camera or transmitter. He didn't find any. Next, he unzipped his suitcase and removed a signal-detection device he used to sweep the space one more time.

Same result. Satisfied that, to the best of his knowledge, he wasn't being watched, he returned to his carry-on and picked up a sticky wireless mini–spy camera and two miniature listening devices. He exited his room and walked toward the bank of elevators, where he remembered seeing a narrow table against one of the mirrored walls. On the table were a house telephone and two vases of fresh flowers. It took Carter less than ten seconds to stick the minicamera to one of the vases.

He took the elevator down to the main floor and found a seat at Plato's, a sports lounge just off the lobby. After ordering a large coffee and a Western omelet sandwich with fries, Carter sent a message to

Triggs to let her know that he had checked in without issue. He opened the application linked to the mini–surveillance camera he had installed on the seventh floor and waited for it to load. Using the application, he panned the camera left and right to make sure he'd placed it properly, then spent the next five minutes looking at the pictures of the three FBI agents assigned to Max Oswald's case. He read each bio twice and committed their faces to memory. On paper, the agents looked competent enough. That said, Carter understood why Triggs was reluctant to trust the FBI. As a former DEA special agent, Carter had worked many cases in close collaboration with the FBI. They were great at investigating and building cases against criminals and terrorists alike, but they weren't very fast, and everything was always done in accordance with the law—which was the right thing to do when you wanted to convict someone, but maybe not the best option when the ultimate objective was to kill whoever had perpetrated the deed. That was why Triggs had sent him to the Bahamas; he didn't have to follow the rules.

When his omelet sandwich finally arrived, he ate with appetite. Carter briefly considered ordering another one but changed his mind when a notification popped up on his phone that the camera had captured someone waiting at the bank of elevators. Carter didn't hold his breath, since the last twelve notifications had been false alerts.

Not this time. It was game time.

So when Special Agent Bill C. McGhee exited the elevator two minutes later, Carter was ready.

CHAPTER TWENTY-ONE

Lugano, Switzerland

Hunt cast a final look around the apartment. Satisfied they hadn't left anything behind that could be easily traced back to them, he joined Jacobs in the small vestibule of the apartment.

"We good?" she asked, her hand already on the doorknob.

"Yeah. Let's go," he replied, anxious to leave. As much as he wanted to help Pike and Crawford, Hunt feared they'd be too late.

Hunt knew something was wrong the moment Jacobs cracked the door open. The pounding of heavy, hurried footsteps coming along the hallway told him everything he needed to know.

They'd been compromised.

Was it the local authorities? Aram Diljen's bodyguards? Or whoever had attacked the TOC? It didn't matter. They were in trouble. The only other exit was through the double french doors.

He grabbed Jacobs by the shoulders and yanked her away from the door just as he heard the first muffled shot. A strangled cry escaped Jacobs's lips as she was thrust against Hunt. A nanosecond later, something whispered by his right ear.

Shit! Whoever was shooting at them was using silenced weapons. In his arms, Jacobs had become limp. Hunt dragged her four feet back and around the corner leading to the living room and the kitchen. He sat her up against the wall, her legs splayed, and drew his pistol from his holster. He peered around the corner and fired three shots, but the attackers had already sought cover. Next to him, Jacobs's head had fallen to one side. The front of her shirt was steeped in blood where two bullet holes were easily visible. Jacobs's eyes were partly closed, and her lips were parted. A watery red-pink bubble had formed in the corner of her mouth.

Oh fuck. Harriet.

Hunt knew it was pointless, but with his right hand he checked her pulse anyway while keeping his left arm extended with his pistol pointed toward the threat. There was no pulse. She was gone. Hunt fought hard to maintain emotional control. He had to survive this. He had to find out who was coming after them.

That was when a grenade rolled next to him. Hunt jumped to his feet and took two quick steps before leaping over the kitchen counter. He landed on the other side of the counter, hard on his right shoulder. He just had time to bury his head in his hands and close his eyes before the grenade exploded. Even through his squeezed-tight eyelids, Hunt saw a pure white light that momentarily blinded him. The noise from the explosion was so loud that he thought he had accidentally discharged the pistol he was still holding next to his ear.

Knowing the two attackers were about to make their entry to dispatch any potential survivors, Hunt got to his knees but fell to his side, disoriented. He crawled around the kitchen corner just in time to see one of the men enter the living room. Hunt, still befuddled, fired five times in quick succession, hitting the man in the arm and neck. The second attacker, seeing his friend collapse, cut the corner too fast and tripped over one of Jacobs's legs. Hunt shot him in the head at point-blank range as he was falling. Struggling to get his bearings, Hunt slowly got to his feet. The first man he had shot was still moving, writhing in pain on the living room floor, his silenced MP5 still slung around his chest. Hunt moved toward him with caution while making sure there were no other immediate threats coming from the two entry points. He couldn't help but take a quick look at Jacobs. From her arms and legs to her neck and face, the shrapnel had shredded her skin. He'd make sure the CIA recovered her body; she deserved that much. And so did Henican.

By the time his eyes returned to the injured man, he had stopped moving. Hunt checked his pulse. The gunman was dead.

Damn it!

The whole situation had become a nightmare, but he had no time to think. He needed to take action now. He had to get out of the apartment and head to the TOC. Hunt changed his magazine and pocketed the half-empty one for future use. This whole mission was a clusterfuck of humongous proportions.

Hunt was just about to start searching the dead gunmen's clothes when he paused. Breathing through his mouth to facilitate his hearing, Hunt was convinced he'd heard additional footsteps coming from the hallway. These new ones weren't hurried like the previous ones. They were controlled, measured. Pistol pointed toward the door, Hunt began a slow, soundless passage toward the junction with the living room. He held his position for thirty seconds—which seemed like an eternity—hearing no sound. Then there came the low, almost imperceptible squeak of hinges as the front door slowly opened. Aiming his pistol at the front door at shoulder height, Hunt waited.

CHAPTER TWENTY-TWO

Lugano, Switzerland

Jorge Ramirez heard three gunshots. The driver had heard them, but he didn't seem concerned.

"These aren't coming from the MP5s your guys are carrying," Ramirez warned him. "These were pistol shots."

"It's okay," the driver said, but nonetheless he pulled his pistol from his hip holster. "Nothing to worry about."

The sound of a grenade exploding reached Ramirez and then, a few seconds later, came more pistol shots. Ramirez unconsciously counted them.

Five quick pistol shots.

Then a single shot.

The driver had lost his cool and had become agitated. "No good," he said. "Now we go."

"So *now* it's time to worry?" Ramirez asked the driver, following him outside the SUV. "Where are we going?"

When the driver rose to his full height, Ramirez noticed how tall the man was. His skin was dark, tanned, and his shaved hair was so blond it looked almost as white as his T-shirt. He locked eyes with Ramirez and, to Ramirez's surprise, came up with a tactical plan.

"There are two enemy shooters inside the apartment," the driver said. "There are only two entry points. Front door and balcony. I take balcony. You take front door. Capito?"

Capito? Ramirez understood, but it was the first time in his life he had heard a Russian speak an Italian word. It didn't sound good. In Ramirez's opinion, Italian was an exceptionally beautiful language, but not so much when spoken by a Russian brute.

"You want me to go up there with this?" Ramirez asked, holding the five-shot revolver.

The driver didn't bother to answer. He glanced at his watch. "You go now. In ninety seconds I come balcony. Draw their fire. I kill."

And with that, the driver left in a light jog around the apartment building. Ramirez was at a crossroads. With the tall Russian gone and the two first assaulters probably dead, he could chance a quick getaway. But that would mean abandoning the promised €1.5 million. Furthermore, the man with the raspy voice had proved himself to be a man with considerable resources. Ramirez couldn't say the same about his current status.

He sighed, then hurriedly set the timer on his watch for eighty seconds.

The edifice was a low-rise, three-story building that looked more like a house than an actual apartment complex.

Holding his Smith & Wesson revolver in a high-ready position, Ramirez began his slow ascent of the stairway. He hugged the left-hand wall, making sure to check behind him every few seconds. Once he had reached the landing, he saw a hallway that led to a single half-open door twenty steps away. A quick look at his watch told him he had forty-five seconds left. Ramirez's heart was racing. The excitement of the unknown and the adrenaline rush of living on the edge made him feel powerful and in control. He crept toward the door, stepping carefully to avoid any noises that would give him away.

Thirty seconds.

He stopped, listening for any kind of noise from inside the apartment. Nothing. Whatever battle had raged inside the apartment was now over.

Ten seconds. Time to go in.

Ramirez eased the door open, careful not to make a sound. The hinges squeaked ever so slightly. He stiffened. Ramirez held still, his heart pounding in his ears.

One second.

Ramirez rushed inside just as he heard a loud thump coming from the back of the apartment. He was three steps in when the first two shots were fired.

CHAPTER TWENTY-THREE

Lugano, Switzerland

With agonizing slowness, the door opened. Hunt had already pulled the slack out of the trigger when the double-wide french balcony doors swung open behind him. Hunt cursed himself. He'd had tunnel vision, focusing all his attention on a single threat, and had forgotten about the second entry point—definitely something the second wave of attackers had counted on.

He ducked on instinct and rolled to his right just as two bullets punched the wall where his upper back had been a quarter of a second ago. Hunt got a quick sight of his target—a tall, heavyset man wearing a white T-shirt—and fired before the man could get off another shot. Hunt double-tapped him in the chest and put an additional round in his mouth, splattering brain, bone, and blood everywhere.

Before the man had even hit the ground, Hunt had already leaped back to his feet, knowing someone was about to rush in. Conscious he was a beat late doing so, Hunt was in the process of pivoting back toward the relative safety of the corner separating the living room and the vestibule when he saw a man enter in a combat crouch, his knees slightly bent, his head tucked in, and a small revolver pointed in Hunt's direction.

Jorge Ramirez.

———

Ramirez, revolver extended in front of him, was totally caught off guard.

Pierce Hunt!

Could it really be him? A thousand questions popped into his mind, which cost him a millisecond of hesitation before he pulled the trigger. In his defense, he only had a small target, as three quarters of Hunt's body was behind the corner. Hunt seized on Ramirez's hesitation to duck completely out of sight. Ramirez had to push in, or he was dead. He sidestepped right, over the dead body of one of the Russians, opening his angle on the living room.

He didn't expect what happened next. Hunt, legs coiled, lunged at him low and hard, his hands successfully grabbing Ramirez's wrists before he could shield his pistol by bringing it closer to him. Ramirez fired, more to distract Hunt than in a realistic attempt to hit him. Ramirez used Hunt's momentum against him by allowing himself to be pushed back two steps before pivoting 180 degrees on his left foot.

Ramirez fired again.

———

Hunt winced as Ramirez's revolver discharged less than six inches from his left ear. Hunt felt himself gaining forward momentum, which wasn't good. Ramirez was planning on throwing him over his left hip. Hunt couldn't let that happen. He would lose control of Ramirez's wrists. A deadly sin.

Instead of fighting against his own momentum, Hunt dropped to his knees while continuing to move forward. His right knee crashed into Ramirez's quadricep, squeezing it against his thigh bone. Ramirez yelled in pain, and Hunt used the moment to move his hands from Ramirez's wrists to the revolver barrel, which he clamped down on. Hunt stood and drove the revolver straight up above his head, pivoted to his right, and, with all his strength, pulled Ramirez's hands back down on the other side, successfully putting Ramirez in an agonizing arm bar.

———

Jorge Ramirez cried out. He had lost the advantage—if he'd ever had it in the first place. The sudden agony in his arm was so great that it took his breath away. The revolver dropped from his nerveless fingers. Ramirez's feet flew out from under him, and he was thrown to the floor in a heavy heap.

———

Hunt pinned Ramirez to the floor, vaguely aware of numerous police sirens approaching. He grabbed Ramirez's collar and started choking him. Ramirez's eyes widened in terror, but he managed to strike Hunt on the side of the head with a hammer fist. The strength of the blow didn't amount to much, but it was its precision that hurt. Hunt leaned forward and ducked his head, not wanting to be hit on the temple again. Letting go of his now-ineffective hold, he slammed his elbow toward Ramirez's windpipe but missed, instead hitting his chin. Ramirez riposted by wrapping his legs over his and torquing right, effectively flipping Hunt to his side. Hunt rolled away, wanting to create some distance.

Both men jumped to their feet, out of breath, the police sirens getting closer by the second. Hunt caught Ramirez searching for his revolver with his eyes, but it had slid under the dining table.

How the hell did Ramirez end up here? How did he know? How could he?

Hunt had a feeling that Ramirez was as surprised as he was. Was his order not to kill Ramirez still valid? Hunt decided it wasn't.

He reached for his gun.

———

Anger boiled deep inside Ramirez's guts. Seeing Pierce Hunt in the flesh was almost surreal. The man standing in front of him wasn't only responsible for Ramirez's current vulnerable status; he was also partly to blame for his failure to restore his beloved Venezuela to greatness.

What was the American doing in Switzerland? Had he been the one to shoot Aram Diljen, a supposedly deep-cover CIA officer? Nothing made sense. Hunt was a true patriot, brainwashed by years of service with the Rangers and the American DEA. Never would a man like Hunt willingly kill one of his own.

But Hunt would certainly not hesitate to kill *him*. As Hunt's hand moved to the small of his back—where Ramirez assumed Hunt had holstered his pistol—two Swiss police officers entered the apartment, weapons drawn.

"Polizia! Non muovetevi!"

Knowing the Swiss police weren't likely to shoot an unarmed suspect in the back, Ramirez bolted. He reached the dead Russian driver in two strides and took half a second more to pick up the pistol.

"Polizia! Polizia! Non muovetevi!"

Ramirez didn't turn around. He didn't even slow down once he was on the balcony. He threw the pistol in front of him and launched himself at the railing, seeing too late the ladder leaning against the balcony that the Russian driver must have used to climb up.

Shit!

Ramirez flipped over the side of the railing and barely managed to grab the metal bars. He slid down them way too fast and burned his hands so severely that he involuntarily let go.

Pierce Hunt's face was the last thing on his mind as he felt himself falling backward.

CHAPTER TWENTY-FOUR

Lugano, Switzerland

Hunt heard the police announce their presence and flattened his back against the wall, knowing that they couldn't see him from the vestibule. But they saw Ramirez. The officers yelled at Ramirez to stop, but in only a few strides, Ramirez had jumped over the railing of the balcony.

Holy shit! Hunt had to give it to the man. Ramirez was fearless. Or crazy.

Hunt, still flattened against the wall, waited for the first officer to run past him. As Hunt had done a few minutes ago, the officer focused only on the threat he'd seen and completely missed Hunt hiding less than two feet to his left. When the second officer went past him, Hunt sprang into action. A swift chop to the officer's forearm was all it took to disarm him. The officer turned toward him and yelled something in Italian that Hunt didn't understand. To the officer's credit, he didn't give up and lunged for Hunt's neck. Hunt grabbed the officer's right hand and bent it back while twisting it over his forearm, forcing the officer to fall in order not to break his wrist. The officer landed square on his back, hitting his head solidly against the hardwood floor.

The first officer, warned by his partner's shout, turned toward Hunt, who had already drawn his pistol. His eyes opened wide, like a deer caught in the headlights, when he realized that Hunt had him in his sights.

Hunt's Italian was almost nonexistent, but he nevertheless tried to warn the officer. "Non farlo! Non farlo!"

It was a big bluff. Hunt wouldn't dare shoot a police officer. The Swiss cop took in his surroundings, and Hunt could only guess what was going through his mind. From where he stood, the officer could see that there were at least four dead bodies in the small apartment and that the man responsible for the carnage was holding him at gunpoint, having disarmed his partner in a matter of seconds.

The officer gently placed his gun on the ground. "I speak English," he said with a soft British accent. "Lived in London for a few years."

"My Italian is crappy," Hunt replied.

"My partner, is he okay?" the officer asked, his concern evident.

"He knocked his head. He'll live."

"Did you do this?" the officer asked, looking around.

"What do you think?" Hunt said, approaching the police officer. "Get on your knees and interlock your fingers. I'm sure you know the drill."

The officer obeyed. "Up until now, I wasn't sure. Now I know you didn't. Why keep me alive if you had?"

Hunt grabbed the officer's handcuffs from his duty belt and holstered his pistol, half expecting the officer to make a move. He cuffed the officer without a problem. Hunt walked in front of him so he could look him in the eyes.

"I don't know who the three guys are," Hunt said. "But if I had to guess, I'd say they're Russian mercenaries."

The officer nodded toward Jacobs. "What about her?"

"No idea," Hunt lied. "I've never seen her before."

Hunt frisked the pockets of the last man he had shot. He found a set of keys, an extra magazine for the pistol Ramirez had picked up, and a cellular phone.

Hunt looked at the officer, thought about saying something, but didn't. He grabbed his suitcase and left the apartment, closing the door behind him.

CHAPTER TWENTY-FIVE

Lugano, Switzerland

As a former paratrooper, Ramirez knew a thing or two about hard landings. As his hands involuntarily let go of the metal bars of the balcony, he instinctively bent his knees, tucked in his chin, and allowed his feet to strike the ground first. He hit the ground jarringly hard but remained uninjured by distributing the landing shock from the balls of his feet to his calves, thighs, hips, and finally back. He rolled twice to his right, picked up the pistol he had thrown over the balcony, and ran.

He sprinted for one minute, putting as much distance as he could between himself and the apartment building. Turning into an adjacent street, Ramirez switched to walking. He had only traveled a few steps when a dark sedan with tinted windows stopped at the next street corner. Ramirez didn't even react. He kept going as if he couldn't care less about the car. Inside his chest, though, his heart was pounding. He wished the car would move along, but for some reason it remained immobilized at the intersection.

Had someone called in with his physical description? Was he about to be summoned by plainclothes police officers? Even though he couldn't see the occupants, he could feel their eyes on him, sharp as knives. Ramirez glanced behind him and, seeing no oncoming traffic, decided to cross the street to create some distance between him and the dark sedan. Once Ramirez reached the middle of the street, the sedan's bar lights lit up like a Christmas tree, and with its tires screaming on the pavement, it accelerated toward him.

¡Mierda! ¡La policía!

Ramirez reached for the pistol he had tucked at the small of his back, but he wouldn't have time to make good use of it before the unmarked police car hit him. Instead, he jumped out of the way of the oncoming vehicle, then fell to the ground and rolled against the curb. The sedan came to a screeching halt, and a man bolted out of the front passenger seat. He wore a navy business suit, but Ramirez saw a police badge clipped to his belt. Ramirez had time neither to draw his pistol nor to get out of the way. The policeman plowed into him like a runaway freight train, whacking him to the ground and knocking the wind out of his lungs.

Ramirez swung at the policeman's head but was a second too slow. The policeman raised his right arm and blocked the blow. Then he drove his fist into Ramirez's sternum, sending a wave of pain radiating throughout his body. Before Ramirez could catch his breath, he was hit on the chin by a right hook. His jaw throbbed; his ears were pounding. Ramirez threw a wild punch, got lucky, and hit the policeman on the right side of his head. But the policeman barely flinched. The blow only seemed to make him angry, and he threw a violent left hook into Ramirez's face. Ramirez actually felt his brain bump into his skull.

Fighting for breath, Ramirez was aware that the policeman's partner had joined the fight. Two strong hands grabbed his legs, pinning them to the street. Ramirez tasted blood; his eyelids sagged. He was vaguely aware of being rolled onto his stomach. One of the policemen disarmed him and forced his hands behind his back. Ramirez felt the cold steel handcuffs around his wrists, the final click telling him that his struggle was over. He was hauled upright and rammed against the police sedan's hood.

It was then that he saw the fast-approaching BMW X5.

CHAPTER TWENTY-SIX

Lugano, Switzerland

Hunt, his head on a swivel, left the apartment building. He spotted the parked SUV and hurried in its direction, conscious that more police were on their way. He unlocked the SUV with the keys he'd taken from the dead Russian, placed his luggage on the back seat, and sat behind the wheel. He started the engine, looked at the fuel gauge, breathed a sigh of relief, and put the transmission into drive. He drove down the road and headed toward the TOC.

His mind whirled and twirled. The whole operation was FUBAR—fucked up beyond all recognition. Part of him wanted to call Triggs, but a little voice in his head told him to hold out a bit longer. He needed to think before making the call. He had to put some order into his thoughts.

Someone with detailed knowledge of the operation had betrayed them.

Could it be Triggs? What did she have to gain?

Not much, Hunt thought. *But she did have a lot to lose.*

He might not have trusted Triggs entirely, but she had the greater good of the United States at heart. She'd never willingly sink an operation. By Hunt's count, there were about a dozen people who knew the details of the operation. To simultaneously attack his sniper hide and the TOC required a lot of logistics, financial means, and manpower. Who could provide such things among these people?

Taking for granted that Triggs wasn't involved, the answer was obvious.

No one.

No single person had the financial resources and the access needed to pull off that kind of operation. It was just too complex. That meant that a foreign intelligence agency had gained access to their operation in some way.

Or a foreign agent deep within the Directorate of Operations. The thought sent a cold shiver down his spine.

The TOC had been in contact with Triggs's team, so Hunt was confident that by now Triggs had heard about the fiasco. He wondered if she would take his call. There was a reason she had sent him and Harriet Jacobs to Lugano. Jacobs was a deniable asset, and so was he. In case of their deaths, the only differences between them were that Jacobs would get an anonymous star on the wall at Langley, and a death benefit check would go to whoever's name she had written down. He, on the other hand, wouldn't get a thing.

Hunt never reached the TOC. The police had set up a roadblock across the main route leading to the industrial square where the TOC was located. The small amount of traffic was being stopped in both directions. As Hunt drove by, he saw teams of officers thoroughly searching every vehicle with the help of a pair of Labrador sniffer dogs. In the distance, at least five police vehicles were parked in front of the office building that housed the TOC. Also at the scene were numerous ambulances and a fire truck.

I'm too late, Hunt thought. He had known all along. Realistically, Crawford had died during Pike's frantic phone call, and Pike had followed her a few seconds later. Hunt's stomach sank, and a veil of sadness overcame him.

I can't believe they're gone. His throat tightened. They had been through so much together during the last year. It felt surreal. His mind went back to Pike's last call. What had his friend tried to say?

They knew our codes, Pierce. He's sold us out . . . and Henican.

What had Pike meant? Then it came to him. Pike had said *he*. Not *she's sold us out*. Not *they sold us out*. He had said *he's sold us out*.

Pike had found the mole.

And it cost him his life, Hunt thought.

Chances were that Triggs wasn't involved, but the CIA had been compromised. Hunt was now sure of it. He'd been right not to call Triggs. For now, there was no point risking exposure by attempting to go through the police roadblock. Hunt had no idea to whom the SUV he was driving belonged. It could have been stolen for all he knew. He needed a new means of transportation. He'd been so caught up with all the questions in his head that he had forgotten basic tradecraft. Hunt drove silently, lost in his thoughts, trying to make sense of everything.

He failed.

He couldn't stay in Lugano. He needed to put distance between himself and the city. Hunt had memorized the location of the two nearest CIA safe houses. The closest one, where he was supposed to go with Jacobs, was in Agno, a small town to the west. The other one, which was more than one hour away, was in Como. Located on the Italian side of the Italian-Swiss border, the city of Como overlooked the southwest end of Lake Como and was surrounded by ridges of green hills. Unlike Agno—which had barely any visitors—Como was the third-most-visited city in Lombardy. Hunt would have no difficulty swapping his SUV for another car there.

The border crossing was easy and painless, but the police on the Italian side were slowing down the traffic to make a quick visual inspection. Since both countries were in the Schengen Area, there was no passport control, and Hunt drove through the border without coming to a full stop. He directed a wave at the Italian officer but didn't get one back.

On any other day, the drive to Como would have been made charming by the pleasing scenery and the sunny skies of Italy—which were in sharp contrast with Hunt's mood. Lake Como was impressive. The heights and edges of the mountains surrounding it were sprinkled and lined with astonishing villas. Higher up, the facades of the mountain flanks were one lush mass of foliage.

Once in the city, Hunt followed the directions to the underground parking on Via Antonio Sant'Elia. It was more than time to get rid of the SUV. He pulled up to the parking ticket machine and reached out to take the voucher. The security arm went up, and Hunt drove through. He parked the SUV and went to work wiping it down to get rid of his fingerprints.

He grabbed his suitcase, snapped out the handle, and pulled it behind him toward the exit.

———

Even though the CIA safe house was only two blocks from the parking lot exit, Hunt thought it would be smarter to check into a hotel first. If his sniper hide and the TOC locations had been compromised, what guarantee did he have that the Lake Como safe house was still secured?

None. If he was right that the mole was someone at the CIA, Hunt had to assume that the safe house was being monitored.

Prior to accessing the safe house, Hunt would need to conduct surveillance to make sure he wasn't walking into a trap. That triggered another issue. A simple walk-by wouldn't be enough. To determine if there was surveillance around the safe house, Hunt would need a few days. Days he didn't have. If he'd had a few more guys with him, they could do it in less, but by himself Hunt needed to be extra careful.

Conducting surveillance alone was never a good idea, especially with this much at stake. It was frustrating to know that the weapons and communication devices he desperately needed were only two blocks away, but out of reach.

Maybe gaining access to the safe house wasn't the only option. Maybe he didn't need to risk it all by going there. Then he thought about someone, and he smiled. The person he was about to call wouldn't be happy. In fact, Hunt was convinced it would drive the man mad with righteous anger. But in the end, he would help Hunt. He would do the right thing.

Tom Hauer always did.

CHAPTER TWENTY-SEVEN

Lugano, Switzerland

Max was the first to see the police cars. There were three parked in front of the apartment building from which Jacobs and Hunt had taken the shot. A couple of ambulances waited for the four medics who were carrying a pair of stretchers down the stairs. On each of the stretchers lay a covered body. Max signaled Wood to continue driving.

"What do you want to do?" Wood asked.

"We need to find Ramirez," Max said, powering up his laptop. "He's the mission now."

"We'll need to get rid of this guy too," Tay said from the back seat, pinching his nose against the fecal stink.

Shooting Vasily in the head hadn't been Max's brightest idea, but it had felt good at the time. And now they were all paying the price for his impulsiveness. Like many other victims of sudden death, Vasily's bowels and bladder had relaxed. Tay had a point. They couldn't operate with Vasily continuing to stink out the SUV—and they had to at least remove the blood and brain matter splattered on the ceiling and rear window.

"Move him in the back for now," Max said. "We'll switch vehicles when we can."

Tay and DeLarue grunted as they shoved Vasily into the cargo area of the BMW.

Max hoped Ramirez hadn't dumped his phone. Triangulating his location using the cell towers was the easiest way to pinpoint his location, but it would be useless if he had discarded his phone or, worse, if he had given it to someone else or thrown it in the back of a pickup truck. If this was the case, Max could lose hours chasing after the wrong person.

The app Max opened on his laptop came with a built-in hack into most of the wireless carriers in Europe and the United States. All Max had to do was enter Ramirez's number. The app would automatically find the wireless carrier assigned to the phone and ping the number. Max had no idea how many cell towers were in the vicinity, but he hoped for at least three. Pinging a cell from a single tower would indicate the distance but not the direction of the phone in relation to the cell tower. To triangulate Ramirez, the application would need to ping a minimum of three cell towers. A ping would be sent from each tower to Ramirez's phone. Using the time it took the ping to travel to Ramirez's phone and back to the cell towers, a distance would be calculated and a radius drawn from each cell tower. Ramirez's location would be at the intersection of the three circles.

"Hmm, boss," Wood said, one hand on the steering wheel, the other stroking his mustache. "You might not need your fancy app to find Ramirez."

Max raised his eyes from the laptop. Half a block away was an unmarked police car—with its emergency lights turned on—blocking the street. Two plainclothes officers were holding a man against the hood of the vehicle.

"You must be kidding me," Max muttered. "Keep going, keep going. Slowly."

When they were within fifty feet of the police car, Max confirmed that the man the police had in custody was indeed Jorge Ramirez. If the Swiss police brought Ramirez in for questioning, they wouldn't let him go. Ramirez might have good fake passports and other credentials, but his fingerprints would do him in.

Max made an executive decision. They were going to rescue Ramirez. Now.

"We're going in, guys," Max said. "Wood, you stay behind the wheel. Tay and I are going nonlethal on the officers. DeLarue, you cover us. Understood?"

They all did.

A second later, Wood stopped the SUV, and Max, DeLarue, and Tay climbed out. Tay and Max had their Tasers ready, with DeLarue covering their advance with his M4.

Then all hell broke loose.

CHAPTER TWENTY-EIGHT

Lugano, Switzerland

Ramirez knew something was up when the BMW slowed down fifty or so feet away from his position. The two plainclothes police officers—one was patting his legs down for a secondary weapon while the other one was using his body weight to keep him pinned down on the hood of the police car—didn't seem to notice until three armed men climbed out of the BMW. Upon seeing them, the immediate reaction of the officer pinning him was to bring down Ramirez with a powerful punch to the kidney. It was a stinging blow that sent streamers of pain through Ramirez's back. As he crumpled onto the pavement, Ramirez heard the officer yell something to his partner. The next moment, the officer fell flat on his back next to Ramirez, his whole body quaking in spasms. Curly wires had attached themselves to the officer's clothing. The officer had been shot with a Taser, and the strong electric current flowing through his muscles had rendered him completely helpless.

The second officer, though, had ducked behind the police car and was in the process of pulling his pistol out. From his position on the pavement, Ramirez saw the feet of the approaching men. They were less than fifteen feet away.

Then the second officer decided to make his move.

Max, in a combat crouch, his Taser extended in front of him, aimed at the officer who'd knocked Ramirez to the ground. Tay, on his left, would engage the other officer, who was standing slightly left of the first officer. Max fired, breaking open the compressed-gas cartridge inside the Taser, which in turn launched the electrodes toward his target.

The outcome was instantaneous. The officer fell backward, straight like a piece of plywood. The other officer had disappeared, and Max assumed that Tay had successfully tased him. The disadvantage of the Taser was that you only had one shot. In order to fire again, the operator needed to wind up and repack the electrode wires and load a new gas cartridge. So when the second officer popped up from behind the police car less than two seconds after Max's target had dropped, Max was still in the process of transitioning to his pistol.

To Max's horror, the officer had his pistol already up and fired two rounds at Tay before DeLarue took the officer down with a head shot. Max's peripheral vision caught Tay collapsing to the pavement, but he had to push through. He had to secure the first officer. With his pistol now out of his holster, Max quickened his pace and reached the other side of the police car just as the first officer—who was now in a seated position—was reaching for his own pistol.

The men locked eyes, neither blinking, neither moving for a second or two. Then the officer drew a quick breath and pulled his pistol out of his holster.

"Don't—" was the only thing Max had time to say before the officer's index finger reached the trigger of his service pistol.

Max fired once. His bullet caught the man just above the right eye. The officer was dead before his back touched the pavement, even though the twitching nerves in his arms didn't know it yet.

DeLarue, who had already kicked the pistol of the first officer away, looked at Max. "What now?"

"Grab him!" Max pointed to Ramirez. Then he ran to Tay, who lay in the street, his Taser a few feet away. Max felt a knife of pain. Tay

121

had caught two rounds in his upper chest, only a few inches below his throat. A large red stain covered his shirt. Tay's breathing was slow and shallow, but he opened his eyes when Max took a knee next to him.

Tay tried to say something, but Max told him to be quiet. To examine his wounds, Max tore Tay's shirt open and tried to wipe away some of the blood from around the entry wounds with his sleeve, but Tay gently pushed his hands away and pulled him close.

"You're . . . a good man . . . Max. A good man," Tay whispered. "Take . . . care of my . . . guys. Yes?"

Max grabbed Tay's hand with both of his. "I will. I'll take care of your brothers-in-arms. I promise."

"I . . . sorry for . . . for your mom," Tay said in a fluid-filled murmur. "Didn't mean to . . ." Then his eyes closed.

Max's throat tightened as he tried and failed to find a pulse. *Shit!*

The whole intervention had lasted less than one minute, but Max knew they were pushing it. They needed to get out of there before more police showed up.

The BMW rolled to a stop next to him. Max gave Tay one last look before climbing into the front passenger seat. DeLarue and Ramirez were already in the back.

"What about Chiang?" Wood asked, frowning.

"Chiang's gone."

"We can't leave him here," DeLarue said, his French accent heavier than usual.

It tore Max apart inside to leave Tay behind, but his loyal Singaporean friend would play one last role.

"He might slow the cops down," Max said. "There's nothing on Chiang that can connect him to us."

"That's bullshit!" Wood spat, punching the steering wheel with his fist. "We can't just—"

"Just fucking drive!" Max shouted. "Go!"

Wood slammed his foot on the accelerator, and the BMW shot forward.

Max's original plan had called for them to cross the border to Italy and head toward Lake Como, where one of the CIA safe houses was located. Max was confident he would have been able to access it without triggering any alarms at Langley. But with the shooting of two police officers so close to the Swiss-Italian border, Max was afraid that by the time they reached the border, the Swiss and Italian authorities would have set up roadblocks in and out of both countries. The only place he could think of where they could regroup and reassess the situation was at the rental house they had used as a base. It was only ten minutes north of Lugano, and with any luck, they could get there before the police got their act together.

CHAPTER TWENTY-NINE

Somewhere in Turkey

Charlie Henican sipped from his bowl of soup, wincing at the rancid taste. He hadn't eaten anything since the stomach-turning stew he'd been given the day before. The soup was far worse. He took another sip, then drank his watered-down tea in silence. His entire body, stricken and weak, needed the calories. But with only two green peas and a yellowish piece of carrot floating in lukewarm water, Henican wasn't convinced his calorie requirements were met.

He looked around his small cell. There was a certain finality about it—no windows, a tiny lice-infested mattress to nap on, and an old wool blanket slightly larger than a bath towel that never covered Henican's freezing body regardless of how he balled himself up. And the bucket. The damn bucket he used to do whatever he needed to do. There was no need for a sink since he was given—in addition to his copious meals—a small cup of water twice a day. At least he wasn't tied to a chair at the bottom of an empty swimming pool.

Henican coughed. His cough seemed to come from the depths of his lungs. Not only did it hurt his throat, but every coughing fit radiated pain from the top of his stomach up through his chest. The two goons working with the former Maroon Beret had really messed him up.

I'm gonna need to find a way out of here, Henican thought, *because if I don't, I'll catch a goddamn disease and die a much more painful death than with a round to the head.*

At least they had left him alone since his last beating.

Henican heard footsteps coming down the hallway. He wasn't sure how many people were coming to say hello, but it was definitely more than one. Three men appeared outside the bars. These weren't the same men as before. Two of them wore black battle dress uniforms. The third, a bit smaller than the other two, wore civilian clothes and a balaclava to mask his identity. Henican wasn't sure if this was something he should celebrate or be terrified about.

One of the uniformed men unlocked the door and pushed it open. The one dressed in civilian clothes came in and eyed Henican.

"My friend told me you aren't in Turkey to kill our president," the man said, crossing his arms over his chest. His English was excellent. "Is that true?"

This was an interesting development. Henican didn't recognize the man's voice. He'd never seen or spoken to him before. Had the former Maroon Beret believed him? If so, that meant he had probably ordered the beatings to stop until he could convene with his superiors and make a decision on what to do next.

"Killing your president is the last thing on my mind," Henican replied.

The man remained silent for a moment, as if he was contemplating what to say next. "What is an American assassin doing in Turkey?"

Henican shook his head, and his forehead furrowed. "I wish people would stop calling me that. I'm no assassin," he said.

"I beg to differ," the man said. "I've read your file, Mr. Henican."

"I don't know why you—"

The man raised his hands, but it was his eyes that convinced Henican to stop talking.

"You can play games all day long, Mr. Henican, but it won't be with me. I don't have the time. Do you understand? Am I making myself clear? Because if I'm not, and you try more of your bullshit, I'm done. You'll never see me again, and you'll rot in this hellhole for a long, long time."

Henican sighed. "Ask your question."

"Why are you in Turkey?"

Henican's eyes drifted up to the man's covered face. Where he expected to find the eyes of a bored investigator, he found himself staring into eyes as focused, committed, and angry as he'd ever seen. Their eyes met and locked for several still, quiet moments. It was as if nothing else existed around Henican.

Sometimes you need to take a leap of faith, Henican thought.

"Jorge Ramirez," Henican said.

The man nodded. "Now we're getting somewhere," he said.

CHAPTER THIRTY

Atlantis
Paradise Island, Commonwealth of the Bahamas

Simon Carter watched FBI Special Agent Bill C. McGhee exit the hotel elevator. McGhee, a tall, serious black man in charge of the FBI Barbados office, oriented himself for a moment before walking toward the lounge area. Forty-nine years old, McGhee had been with the bureau for twenty-two years, and before that he'd been a police officer with the NYPD. His file said he was a thorough investigator well liked by his superiors and respected by his subordinates.

McGhee was the first of his group to arrive, and he sat at the bar in front of a large flat-screen TV. From where he was seated, Carter had no problem hearing McGhee order a Diet Coke. His two colleagues joined him shortly after his drink arrived and ordered the same. The three men were dressed similarly: dress pants, short-sleeved collared shirts, no ties or jackets, but well-polished shoes. They looked relatively fit, but these men weren't operators; they were investigators. With their drinks in hand, they moved to a table close to Carter's.

Carter gave them the chance to get comfortable before making his move. He stood up from his table, picked up his empty beer bottle and his plate, and walked to the bar to place the items on the counter. He paid his bill and headed past the table where the three men sat. He paused for a moment, staring directly at McGhee.

McGhee raised his eyes. "Yes?" he said. "Can I help you?"

"Bill McGhee?" Carter said. "What are you doing here?"

McGhee looked thoroughly confused. Before he could reply, Carter shook his hand.

"Mitch Steck, Royal Canadian Mounted Police," he said in a slightly offended tone that suggested McGhee should have known who he was. "We were on the Critical Incident Management course together back in 2014."

McGhee nodded. "Yeah," he said. "In Ottawa, right?"

"Exactly. At the police college." Carter smiled. "You were in Jack Sutton's group, but I was with Nathan Richmond's, so we didn't have the chance to interact much."

"Yeah, right," McGhee said. "I . . . I'm sorry I don't remember you, and . . . and that's on me. I really should. I just—"

"No worries at all. I'll let you guys be. Just wanted to say hello," Carter said.

"Bullshit!" one of the two other FBI agents said. "Please excuse McGhee's poor manners. You said your name was Mitch, right?"

"Mitch Steck." The men shook hands. The files had informed him the man's name was Douglas Blair—a thirty-five-year-old former marine sergeant who'd seen action in Iraq.

"Grab a seat, for God's sake," Blair said. "You want something to drink?"

"I'm good. Just had lunch."

"Saw you a few tables away," the third FBI agent said, extending his hand. "Your breakfast sandwich looked great, brother."

"It tasted even better," Carter replied.

"So you and McGhee were on a course together?" Blair asked. "You're still with the RCMP, Mitch?"

"I am. I'm eighteen years in, so another seven will give me a good pension," Carter said.

"Right," McGhee said. "I have five kids who all want to go to college. I'll never retire."

"What are you guys doing in the Bahamas?" Carter asked, his left hand slipping into his pants pocket.

McGhee looked a bit uncomfortable, but Blair didn't seem to mind sharing a bit of information with a fellow policeman. "You heard about the shooting on John F. Kennedy Drive a couple days ago?"

Carter nodded, leaning close to the table, while his left hand peeled away a covering on the back of the listening device he had fished out of his pocket.

"Victims were Americans," Blair said, taking a sip of his Diet Coke.

Carter turned to McGhee. "I thought you were working out of the Chicago field office," he said. That was where McGhee had been posted while he'd been attending the Critical Incident Management course at the Canadian Police College.

"I moved out of the big city with the family a couple years ago," McGhee said. "I'm now the legal attaché for the Caribbean. I work from Bridgetown in Barbados."

"Awesome," Carter said. "I'm sure the family's loving it."

"Beats Chicago, that's for sure."

"What about you guys?" Carter asked, reaching under the table as far as he could without being obvious. He pressed the sticky side of the listening device to the bottom of the table.

"We're at the Nassau suboffice," Blair explained. "Our mandate is to support the Royal Bahamas Police Force investigating the shooting, but between you and me—"

McGhee interrupted Blair. "And what are you doing in paradise?" he asked Carter. "Family vacation?"

"Yep. We've been coming here for a few years now. Our kids love doing the slides."

"That's nice," McGhee said. "Anyhow, it was nice seeing you again. Enjoy your vacation."

Carter knew he was being dismissed, so he shook hands with the three agents, wished them luck in their investigation, and hustled out. He took the elevator and entered his room. He locked the door behind him and sat at the writing desk next to the window. He retrieved an earphone from his back pocket and jammed it in his left ear. He then plugged the earphone into a receiver that was tuned to the frequency of the listening device he had stuck under the table.

There was a fair amount of background noise, but he could hear the conversation McGhee was having with his two colleagues. For a while, nothing of importance was discussed. The men decided to order some food before heading out to the police station. Blair kept poking McGhee about Mitch Steck, finding it alarming that, at his age, he couldn't remember ever meeting the guy.

"The thing is," McGhee said, "I remember the class well, and the name Mitch Steck does ring a bell. I just had a different mental picture of the guy. And did you notice he was missing the top of his left pinkie? I would have remembered *that*."

Their food arrived, and the men started discussing the case. Carter took notes of what the FBI had found out so far, which wasn't much. Blair complained that the Bahamian police weren't forthright in providing them access to the ambush site or the evidence they had seized on the scene. McGhee agreed with Blair and promised to talk directly to the deputy commissioner to resolve the situation.

"I don't feel any urgency on their part," Blair complained. "This isn't acceptable. Why can't we analyze the evidence ourselves?"

"It's their case, remember?" McGhee said. "I don't like it, either, but we're guests here."

"I don't give a crap if we're guests or not," Blair hissed. "Someone ambushed the deputy director of the CIA, murdered or abducted her son, killed an embassy driver, and the Bahamians are dragging their goddamn feet."

"Keep your voice down," McGhee warned. "This isn't the place."

"But he has a point," the third man chipped in. "Why can't we at least see the evidence they seized?"

"I've told you before," McGhee said. "They want to process the evidence themselves. Four Bahamian police officers died trying to intervene. You better remember that."

"We're wasting time," Blair said. "They haven't even begun analyzing the evidence, and do you really think they know what they're doing?"

McGhee moaned. "You're a real pain in the ass, you know that?"

"We need to put a little more pressure on them, Bill," the third agent said. "I'm with Douglas on this one."

"At the very least, I'd like to get immediate access to the video footage," Blair said.

That struck a chord with Carter. *Video footage?* Had someone videotaped the ambush? Carter paid close attention to what was said next.

"It's beyond me why they haven't watched it yet," the third agent said, clearly frustrated.

"I'll see what I can do about the dashcam footage," McGhee replied. "When I inquired about it yesterday, I was told the video technician had been called to another island."

Blair exploded. "You have to be shitting me! Who gives a rat's ass if the video technician is there or not? This ain't rocket science. Unbelievable!"

"Are they keeping the footage with the other evidence?" the third agent asked.

"I think so," McGhee replied. "They're keeping everything at the Lyford Cay station."

Carter wrote the information down. He'd love to get a look at the dashcam footage.

"Why don't we go there and see what we can do?" Blair suggested. "What do we have to lose?"

Carter heard the sound of a chair being pulled across the floor. *Blair's getting ready to leave.*

"Wait a minute, Douglas," McGhee protested. "Sit down, will you? Listen, guys, I'm not against the idea, but nobody knows us at the Lyford Cay station. You think they'll simply give us the footage if we flash them our FBI credentials? You're not being serious."

"So what do you propose, Bill?" Blair asked. "Because right now I'm about done listening to you telling me what I can't do."

"Fair enough," McGhee said, his tone conciliatory. "You've made your point. It's just that I don't want us to be pushed aside even more than we already are. We all know how defensive the Bahamians get when they feel we're stepping over them. Let me clear this with the deputy commissioner first, okay?"

For the next five minutes, Carter heard only Blair and the third agent talk to each other, mostly bitching about how McGhee was dragging his feet. Carter supposed that McGhee had stepped away from the table to call the deputy commissioner. When McGhee returned, something about his tone had changed. It was much more upbeat than when he had left the table only minutes ago.

"The deputy commissioner actually surprised me," McGhee said.

"What did he say?" Blair asked.

"Seems like they're ready to release the footage to us," McGhee explained. "They've already made a copy."

"That means they watched it. Did they find anything?" asked the third agent.

"The deputy commissioner hasn't watched it himself, but he's been informed that nothing of significance was on the video."

"That's hard to believe," Blair said.

"Finish your meal, then go see for yourself," McGhee said. "Ask for Sergeant Ferguson. He's waiting for you."

Carter took the elevator down to the lobby and stopped by the in-house rental-car office. He showed his Canadian driver's license to the clerk and prepaid the rental fee for a Jeep Wrangler with the credit card attached to his Mitch Steck persona.

"Would you like the car to be brought to the front for you?" the clerk asked.

"That'd be great," Carter said, slipping the clerk a five-dollar bill.

The clerk called for a valet and told Carter his rental vehicle would be at the front in less than five minutes. Carter thanked him and walked outside into a wall of heat. The sun had reached its zenith, and Carter elected to stay under the covered walkway to wait for the vehicle. He doubted the Jeep would have a navigation system, so he took the opportunity to confirm the location of the Lyford Cay station with his phone. His traffic app showed that it would take approximately thirty-five minutes to drive the seventeen miles.

About the same time it would take by boat, he thought. That gave him an idea. He dialed Anna Garcia's number. He let the phone ring twice, then hung up. He called again.

"Who is this?" Anna said.

"Hey, Anna, it's Simon."

"Where are you? Do you need anything? Emma's here if you want to speak with her."

"I'm on the island, and I'd love to talk to Emma, but I'm actually calling for Chris. He and Jasmine are still there, aren't they?"

"They're on the beach with the girls," Anna replied. "Give me a minute."

Carter had to give it to Anna. She was one tough woman. She must have had a thousand questions, not only about what he was doing back on the island so soon after leaving but also about Hunt's whereabouts. Undoubtedly, she had felt the tension in his voice and decided to keep her questions to herself.

"Simon?" came in Chris Moon.

"Hey, brother," Carter said, "thanks for taking the call." Moon was the star quarterback of the Miami Dolphins. Despite some initial tension between Hunt and his ex-wife's wealthy new husband, Moon had proved to be a stand-up guy.

"What do you need?"

"Do you have access to Pierce's boat?" Carter asked.

"I do. I actually took everyone out for a ride this morning. Emma loved it, by the way."

Carter was glad his wife was enjoying herself even if he wasn't there. She'd been looking forward to spending time with Anna, Pierce, and the girls.

"Awesome. You have no idea how happy this makes me," Carter said.

"Anna told me you're on the island. You need me to pick you up somewhere?"

"I'm not sure yet, to be honest," Carter replied.

"Just tell me when and where, and I'll be there."

"Why don't you head out toward Lyford Cay? If I don't call you back on your cell within the next two or three hours, that will mean I don't need you."

"Understood," Moon said. "Anything *special* I should bring aboard?"

From the way he had pronounced the word *special,* Carter understood what Moon meant. *Should I bring a weapon?*

"No need for that, my friend," Carter said. "Just a couple of cold beers will do."

"Oh well," Moon said, sounding a bit disappointed. "I kind of hope you'll call anyway."

Carter hung up and laughed out loud. *Anything* special *I should bring?* Moon cracked him up every time. Moon's hundreds of thousands of fans had no idea how badass their favorite NFL quarterback really was.

Carter glanced at the long crescent driveway to see if the Jeep had arrived and wished the valet would hurry up. The last thing he needed was for Special Agent Blair to see him climb into his Jeep and actually follow him to the police station. Carter fished his earphone from his pocket and placed it in his ear. Seconds later, he was able to confirm that Blair was still seated at the table. It appeared that the omelet sandwich had been a hit with him too.

CHAPTER THIRTY-ONE

DEA headquarters
Arlington, Virginia

Tom Hauer rubbed his face with his palms. Not for the first time, he wondered if Pierce Hunt was more trouble than he was worth. He had made it a point not to contact Hunt since his return from Venezuela. In his opinion, Hunt needed time to recuperate after the op, to recharge his batteries, and especially to spend time with Anna, Sophia, and Leila. It was the same for Simon Carter. The man had nearly lost his life in Venezuela. Carter needed to heal his wounds before going back to work.

Hauer now realized he'd been naive to think that Hunt would take it easy. He should have known better. Since Hunt hadn't been able to confirm that his phone was secure, he had remained vague about why he had ended up in Italy and why he needed Hauer's help. But the fact that Hunt had trusted Hauer enough to ask him for help meant a lot.

Hunt's initial demands weren't outrageous. He had requested access to a DEA safe house, a secure satellite phone, and some firepower. In exchange, he'd promised Hauer he'd brief him on the entire situation. As the administrator of the DEA, Hauer had a lot of autonomy on how he could use the resources of his agency. But he needed to be careful. His boss, the US attorney general, often liked to poke around the DEA operations, especially those that Hauer would prefer to keep under the rug.

There was a knock on his office door, and before he could answer, Linda Ramer walked in, armed with the largest coffee mug Hauer had ever seen.

"Are you running an op I'm not aware of?" Ramer asked him, always the straight shooter.

Ramer was the director of the Intelligence Division of the DEA. She was utterly reliable and was one of Hauer's favorite people.

"Sit down, Linda," Hauer said. "Please."

Ramer took a long sip of her coffee and sat on the very edge of one of the two chairs facing Hauer's desk. She looked at him expectantly. "So? Are you running an op or not?"

"I'm not, Linda. But—"

"If you're not running an op, why do you need to know where our Italian safe houses are located?" Ramer cut in.

"I'm the administrator of the DEA, Linda. I can—"

Ramer interrupted him again. "We don't have anything going on in Italy at the moment. I just checked."

"For God's sake, Linda, ease up on the coffee and let me finish, will you?"

Ramer didn't respond immediately; instead, she studied his face for a moment, as if deciding whether she could trust him.

"I'm sorry," she said after a moment. She took another long sip of coffee. "It's been one of those mornings."

"Anything I should be concerned about?" he asked.

"I'm handling it. What do you need?"

"As I said on the phone, I need to know the exact location of our closest safe house to Lake Como."

"Can I at least ask why?" Ramer asked.

"Minutes ago, I received a distress phone call from Pierce Hunt," Hauer started, raising his hand to stop Ramer from asking another question. "He needs access to a safe house, one that preferably has a small armory."

Ramer's reply was immediate. "Milan. We have a safe house in Milan."

"Are you aware of any reason why Hunt couldn't use it?" Hauer asked.

"About a thousand," she replied instantly. "Hunt is a trouble magnet. That's not too bad when he operates in third world or failed countries like Venezuela and Afghanistan, but Italy? Did you forget what he did in San Miguel de Allende?"

"You can't argue about his efficiency, though," Hauer countered. "He gets the job done every single time."

"True, but at what cost?"

"We're still here, aren't we?" Hauer said.

That didn't seem to satisfy Ramer. "What's he doing in Italy? Why does he need the DEA's help?"

"I don't know, Linda," Hauer replied truthfully. "The minute I know, I'll share that information with you. But in the meantime, I made the decision that we were going to help him. Fair enough?"

Hauer noticed a shift in Ramer's expression from argumentative to supportive. Her massive coffee mug was in one hand, but she ground the thumb and forefinger on her other hand together fiercely—a clear sign that she was reassessing her position. Hauer knew better than to interrupt whatever thought she was mulling over.

"The safe house in Milan is one of our newest ones," Ramer said. "It's stocked with everything Hunt will need to start a small war."

Hauer smiled. "Don't be overly dramatic."

"I'm not," Ramer replied, standing up. "I'll send you the necessary info in a minute. Was there anything else?"

Hauer shook his head. As Ramer exited his office, he wondered if giving Hunt access to the safe house wouldn't end up being the greatest misstep of his career.

CHAPTER THIRTY-TWO

Lyford Cay
New Providence, Commonwealth of the Bahamas

Carter arrived at the Lyford Cay police station fifty minutes after the valet had handed him the keys to the Jeep Wrangler. The flow of traffic had been a bit messier and more congested than the traffic app had suggested. Carter had had to remind himself a couple of times to drive on the left side of the road—friendly local motorists had also done so by liberally using their horns. Carter had known about the left-side driving, but it had proved more challenging than he had expected. Not that driving on the left was difficult. It was simply that being seated on the right side of the vehicle had led Carter to unfailingly mix the blinkers with the wipers, which in turn had caused some problems for the cars following him too closely.

He had lost the connection with his listening device the moment he had driven over the bridge linking Paradise Island to the main island of New Providence. The last he had heard from Special Agent Blair was that he was going to his room to pick up his car keys and that McGhee had opted to join him. Knowing the parking garage was a good five-minute walk from the Royal Towers and that he already had a five-minute head start on them, Carter was confident he'd have enough time to grab the footage from Sergeant Ferguson and be long gone by the time McGhee and Blair showed up.

The Lyford Cay police station was the tiniest police station Carter had ever seen. It was positioned at the corner of a one-story pinkish commercial building in the gated community of Lyford Cay. Considered one of the world's wealthiest and most exclusive neighborhoods, Lyford Cay was located in a charming thousand-acre enclave on the northwestern side of New Providence and only a short distance from the Lynden Pindling International Airport. A security guard at the entrance gate had stopped Carter and called Sergeant Ferguson to confirm that Special Agent Douglas Blair from the FBI did indeed have an appointment. To Carter's relief, he simply had to show his RCMP badge to drive through—the security guard didn't bother to read the name on the credentials.

Carter entered the police station through a single white door. The station consisted of one medium-size room fitted with a counter on which a computer was installed, as well as what seemed like a waiting area with two old armchairs and a low, square coffee table. As Carter crossed the doorway, a tiny bell rang above his head, and a uniformed police officer behind the counter looked up from his cell phone.

"Good afternoon," Carter said, a big friendly smile on his face. He flipped open his RCMP credentials just long enough for the man to see the big shiny badge. "You're Sergeant Ferguson?" he asked, pocketing his credentials.

"In the flesh," the sergeant replied.

"Douglas Blair. FBI. Nice to meet you."

The men shook hands. "I was about to leave for an early lunch when the deputy commissioner called and asked me to wait for you," Ferguson said. "That doesn't happen every day. The deputy commissioner calling, I mean."

"I'm sure it doesn't," Carter replied. "I really appreciate you staying a bit longer to help me out."

"No worries. I'm by myself today, so I kind of work my own hours, if you know what I mean?"

Carter didn't but nodded anyway. His glance discreetly swept the area, looking for a surveillance camera. He didn't see one. A couple of motion detectors were mounted on the wall behind the counter, but they were part of a security system that was likely only armed when the station was closed.

"As I said," Carter continued, "I can't thank you enough for waiting for me. I'll get out of your hair. I just need to pick up what my boss asked me to."

"You mean the SD cards?"

"Yeah, the SD cards."

"Crazy what happened, I'll tell you," Sergeant Ferguson said. "Never seen anything like it. Very upsetting."

"Oh, you watched the footage?"

"Of course! We all did."

Carter didn't feel like asking who "we" meant. He just wanted to grab the SD cards and leave. The real Douglas Blair was only minutes away.

"Can I get the SD cards?"

"For sure," the sergeant replied, dropping behind the counter. "I know they're around here." He shuffled through some papers. "Here they are."

Sergeant Ferguson placed a plastic bag containing two black SD cards on the counter. He pushed the bag toward Carter. "Take it."

Carter picked up the plastic bag and stared at the SD cards.

"The clarity of the video is remarkably good. Damn impressive what you can record these days," Ferguson said.

"Couldn't agree more," Carter said, getting ready to leave. "Enjoy your lunch."

Ferguson raised his hand. "Just a minute. I need you to sign the evidence log sheet."

"No worries," Carter said, accepting a blue pen from Ferguson. "I thought these were copies."

"No, man," Ferguson replied, shaking his head. "These are the originals. I think they uploaded the footage to the cloud, but I'm not sure. What I do know is that these two disks were in the cruisers belonging to the four guys we lost. That's why we need them back."

"Of course," Carter said. "Give us a couple days, and I'll drop them back right here myself."

"No need to drive all the way back to Lyford Cay," Ferguson said. "These SD cards need to go to headquarters. You know where it is?"

Carter nodded. "East Street, right?"

"You got it."

Carter wasn't sure what kind of leverage Special Agent McGhee had used to obtain the originals from the deputy commissioner, but whatever it was, it had worked. Carter wondered how the courts—if it ever got there—would see this breach in the chain of custody. He was sure the rules in the Bahamas were the same as in the United States. Evidence had to be accounted for at all times and supported by the proper chain-of-custody documentation. So if the SD cards ended up being the evidence that would identify the people behind the ambush of Triggs and her son and the deaths of the four Bahamian police officers, the chain of custody would be broken. The prosecutors would be pissed. Carter hoped that the footage had indeed been uploaded to the cloud, since he had no intention of returning the SD cards. But he was confident that whatever Triggs had in mind for the people responsible for the disappearance of her son was probably much worse than whatever the Bahamian government could ever throw at them. The officers' families would never know it, but the punishment would give them the justice they deserved.

Carter slid the evidence log sheet back to Ferguson, who dated and timed the entry. He then signed his name next to Douglas Blair's signature.

The phone next to the computer rang. Ferguson looked at it and made a funny face, as if he wasn't used to hearing the phone ring. "Busy day, I guess," he said, picking up the receiver.

Carter couldn't hear what the person at the other end of the line said, but the reaction on Sergeant Ferguson's face prompted Carter to act. He leaped over the counter and landed on the other side just as Ferguson let go of the receiver to take a step back—a weak attempt to create some distance. Ferguson's right hand had moved to the top of his holster, leaving Carter no choice. He dropped Ferguson onto the linoleum floor with a left-handed stab to the throat, followed by a right-handed chop to the side of the neck.

Carter once again jumped over the counter and headed for the exit as the door swung open and FBI Special Agents McGhee and Blair barged in.

McGhee's jaw tightened as his eyes locked with Carter's. McGhee's mouth formed a grim line, and his eyes burned with the conviction of the righteous.

"You're not with the RCMP, are you?" McGhee asked, raising his fists.

Carter didn't like his odds. McGhee might have been past his prime, but he had an impressive stature. He was tall and wide, and Carter was sure McGhee knew how to throw a good punch and, even worse, how to take one. And if this wasn't enough, Blair seemed to know what he was doing too. He had already moved to Carter's right. Blair didn't look stressed, either, telling Carter that the younger FBI agent had seen his fair share of hand-to-hand combat in the marines. But what worried Carter most was Sergeant Ferguson.

Ferguson was the only man in the room with a gun, and with what Carter had done to him, he feared the Bahamian police officer wouldn't think twice about shooting him in the back. At best, Carter estimated that Ferguson would come around in thirty to forty seconds, which left him very little time to neutralize the two FBI agents.

"Did you kill him?" McGhee asked, gesturing to Ferguson, his anger evident.

Carter almost took offense, but from McGhee's point of view it was a legitimate question.

"I'm one of the good guys," Carter said.

"Then why don't you get your ass on the ground with your hands behind your back, and we'll clear—" started McGhee, but Carter had stopped listening. His peripheral vision had caught Blair's movements.

Blair was quick, agile, and maybe a little too confident. He used his right hand to throw the first punch, aiming at Carter's chin. Carter moved his head to the left, Blair's fist sailing past his right ear. With his right leg, Carter kicked at the outside of Blair's right knee. The FBI agent's eyes grew wide as he realized his mistake. Having thrown his punch and missed, he had most of his body weight on his right leg, so when Carter's foot crashed down on his knee, Blair fell toward Carter, who welcomed him with a direct left hook to the jaw, knocking him out.

McGhee hadn't wasted any time and was on Carter before Blair hit the floor. And as Carter had feared, McGhee knew how to use his fists. Carter tucked his chin into his chest and brought his shoulders up. McGhee's fist glanced off Carter's left ear. Carter ignored the pain and countered with a quick jab to McGhee's nose. The blow wasn't hard enough to break the nose, but it was enough to make it bleed. McGhee withdrew a few steps and brought his hand to his nose.

"Who the fuck are you?" McGhee asked. "And what do you want?"

Carter didn't feel like making conversation. There was a distinct possibility that the security guard at the gate had called for backup.

"Step away, Bill," Carter said.

"No way, you lying piece of shit," McGhee growled, taking two steps toward Carter.

Catching Carter completely by surprise, McGhee lashed out with a sweeping kick that took Carter's legs right out from under him. Carter fell flat on his back but immediately rolled to his left, expecting McGhee to jump on him. But instead of going to the ground with him, McGhee had remained on his feet and was now challenging Carter to get up. McGhee wasn't a pretty sight; his nose was bleeding freely, and the front of his white short-sleeved shirt was now painted crimson. Bringing Carter down seemed to have given him confidence. McGhee's fists struck wildly, one of them hitting Carter's mouth, splitting his lip. Carter tasted blood. Next came two quick jabs that Carter easily blocked. He then ducked under the big right-handed hook McGhee had telegraphed. The hook left McGhee open, and Carter took full advantage. He stepped forward and rammed his knee between McGhee's legs with such force that the FBI agent's feet lifted in the air. McGhee howled in pain and dropped to his knees, holding his groin.

"You fuck!" he said through clenched teeth.

Carter pushed him out of the way and exited the police station. He climbed into the Jeep Wrangler and sped toward the marina. On his way he called Chris Moon.

"Are you where you're supposed to be?" Carter asked.

"What do you think?" Moon replied, his tone joyful.

In Carter's opinion, the NFL quarterback was enjoying this way too much, but damn if Carter wasn't happy to have him around.

"You're my exit strategy, Chris. Pick me up at the fuel dock."

"Sure thing," Moon said. "I guess plan A didn't work out?"

"Who said you weren't my plan A all along?"

CHAPTER THIRTY-THREE

Just north of Lugano, Switzerland

Max carried his third cup of coffee to the large bay window and stared out at the Swiss mountains. They seemed wise and powerful, but peaceful too. He contemplated the mountain chain with fascination, trapped by a sense of beauty he couldn't express. There was nothing in the world he would have loved more than to spend his remaining years in a picturesque setting like this with his late wife, Zehra. It was hard for Max to conceive that his son would have been three years old by now if Zehra hadn't been out celebrating with her friends at the nightclub that dreadful night the terrorists had attacked it.

He chastised himself for having such thoughts. It hadn't been Zehra's fault that she had died that night, along with their unborn child. Zehra didn't deserve his anger, only his eternal love and sorrow. He wished he could have found the ISIS puke who had shot her dead. He had tried to quench his thirst for vengeance by going after the terrorist's affiliates, but despite all the men he'd killed in retribution for Zehra's death, he still missed her every damn day. Sometimes he wished that he had died, too, rather than having to survive and feel the pain he'd been condemned to endure for the rest of his life.

And the guilt. Always that guilt. How many times had he replayed the scenario in his mind? If he'd been there, maybe he could have done something. Even unarmed he would have done something. He would have shielded her. He would have wrapped his arms around her and her precious cargo, and he would have offered *his* back to the shooter. *His* back.

His coffee cup dropped from his hand. Max saw it fall in slow motion. It shattered on the hardwood floor, darkening the thick white rug behind him and splashing his leg with the hot liquid.

DeLarue and Wood gave him a look from the kitchen table, where they had unfolded a cleaning mat and set about to clean and oil all of the team's weapons. "Ça va, Max?" DeLarue asked in French. "T'as besoin d'aide?"

Max's French was poor, so he waved at DeLarue. "Too much caffeine, not enough sleep."

Max picked up one of the towels set aside for the hot tub and cleaned up his mess. He wondered what the owners of this spectacular property would say if they knew that a Russian mercenary named Vasily was stuffed in their freezer.

They'd never refund my security deposit, Max thought, smiling despite the morbidity of the situation.

"I'll go check on our guest," he said to DeLarue and Wood, taking the steps down to the lower level.

Max was glad he had rented the house for four weeks. He had booked the modern-style mountain residence under an assumed name via an online travel agency and had used a prepaid credit card to pay for it. Located in a sunny and peaceful area north of Lugano, the property faced the southeast and offered unrestricted panoramic views of the surrounding mountains. The living space was divided into three floors connected by an internal lift. What had really sold the place to Max, though, was the five-car garage on the lower level that gave him and his men the privacy they needed. The fact that the property was outfitted with imposing security arrangements that included powerful floodlights and a closed-circuit security system had cemented his decision to make this his home base for the operation.

His South African support team had flown in from the Bahamas the day before. They were the guys who had cleaned up after him when he had left Nassau by boat with Wood, Tay, and DeLarue. As much as the Russian mercenaries had disappointed him, he had nothing negative to say about these guys—all of them in their forties and early fifties and very much onboard and sympathetic to his cause. They were as solid as they came. Former South African paratroopers. Max would have bet a month's pay that at some point in their lives, they had worked for Executive Outcomes—a South African private military company that had closed its doors in 1998.

One of the first things Max had done upon the arrival of his support team in Switzerland was to establish a rotation schedule for the different security duties around the house. One of the positions was to monitor at all times the closed-circuit security system. It was a boring job, but it had to be done. One more man was required to patrol the exterior of the property. The four other South Africans could relax, eat, or sleep. Each shift lasted four hours.

How long it would take him to convince Jorge Ramirez to cooperate would dictate the amount of time he'd have to remain in Switzerland. Since he was personally financing the entire operation, time was of the essence. Even though he had siphoned a considerable amount of money out of the Directorate of Operations black budget account, he didn't have unlimited financial resources. Far from it. He had calculated that he had a burn rate of approximately $20,000 per day. With a total budget of just $3 million, he had a runway time of no more than two months considering that Ramirez's share would be roughly $1.65 million in exchange for the information he possessed.

That meant that Ramirez better start cooperating soon. Max was a patient man and a big fan of the carrot-and-stick approach. So far, he had fed Ramirez the carrot, but he wouldn't hesitate to give him the stick.

———

Ramirez was sitting in a metal chair, his ankles shackled to the legs of the chair and his hands cuffed behind his back. He had tried to make conversation with the man guarding him but had failed miserably.

They hadn't beaten him up . . . yet. Which was good. They had given him a couple of pretty good sandwiches to eat and had helped him drink a bottle of water. When Ramirez had asked for a bathroom break, the guard had nodded at him before calling one of his colleagues. By the way they'd positioned themselves and covered each other even for the simplest task, Ramirez knew he'd have a hard time escaping. These men were serious business.

A tall, athletic man entered the room. He was one of the four who had come to his rescue in Lugano. Mid- to late thirties, maybe early forties. He had sandy-brown hair and clear gray eyes. Sad eyes, though, Ramirez noticed. Full of sorrow, but not broken. Confident. He had seen that man before but couldn't place where.

"Jorge Ramirez, I'm Max Oswald."

Then Ramirez remembered, and what little hope he had of escaping vanished.

CHAPTER THIRTY-FOUR

Milan, Italy

Hunt had commandeered a late-model Audi A4 for his drive from Lake Como to Milan. Stealing a car in Como hadn't been much of a challenge. He had found what he was looking for in less than an hour, at a swanky restaurant he had spotted on the way into Como. When a car drove up to the restaurant, the valet would take the car to an underground garage two streets down. He'd then put the keys in a small box outside the restaurant but never bothered to lock it. Hunt had simply waited until the valet had left to park a car. Then he'd crossed the street, opened the little box, and taken the keys for a car that the valet had already parked.

Hunt hoped that the owners wouldn't report the car stolen before he reached Milan, which was almost two hours away since he preferred not to take the highways. As he had expected, Tom Hauer had come through with the location of a safe house. For now, the only thing Hauer had asked in return was that Hunt give him a complete situation report once he was there. Hunt had every intention of keeping that promise.

———

The two-hour drive to Milan was uneventful, and Hunt parked the Audi in an underground parking garage located at the opposite end of the city from the safe house. He wiped his fingerprints off the door handles and steering wheel and left the key in the Audi's exhaust pipe. In the morning, he'd call the restaurant to let them know where the car was.

Hunt removed his carry-on from the trunk and hailed a taxi. He gave the driver an address four blocks away from where Hauer had told him the safe house was situated. Hunt walked the rest of the way, luggage in tow. The safe house, an odd-looking red town house, was located in San Siro. San Siro, Hunt realized, was a highly residential neighborhood filled with kids' playgrounds and, if he had to judge by the prices written on the menus set on the sidewalks, somewhat affordable restaurants.

Hunt unlocked the door using the code Hauer had forwarded him. The townhome was more spacious than Hunt would have thought. It was decorated with modern furniture that was expensive enough to be considered tasteful and would have fitted perfectly in Chris and Jasmine's mansion in Florida. The first floor housed an open kitchen with a dining area, a living room, and a powder room. The upper floor featured a master bedroom with an en suite and a smaller guest bedroom that had its own bathroom too. Hunt entered the master bedroom. There was a king-size bed in the center with a thin mesh canopy hanging from the bedposts. He shook his head; he'd never seen a safe house so posh. What was the point in spending so much money on a place that might never see a single visitor?

Hunt headed toward the walk-in closet and slid the door open from left to right. Hauer had placed a lot of importance on opening it this way. Clothes, female and male, hung on three sides. Hunt pushed aside the clothes on the far wall. Behind the clothes was a keypad, just as Hauer had said there would be. Hunt's next step was to call the man.

"Are you at the safe house?" Hauer asked.

"Stop your bullshit, Tom," Hunt replied. "I haven't looked for them yet, but I know this place is filled with hidden surveillance cameras. What's the code?"

"Is the keypad illuminated?" Hauer asked.

"It is."

"So you do know how to follow instructions."

"What are you talking about?" Hunt asked. Was Hauer getting senile?

"In order to get the keypad illuminated, you need to open the walk-in closet door from left to right."

"Is that spy shit really necessary, Tom?"

"I'm glad you feel the way I do, Pierce. Because until a couple of hours ago, I didn't even know we had something in Milan."

Hunt couldn't care less about what Hauer knew or didn't know. He needed the code.

"The code, please?"

"Stand by. I'll have to ask Ramer."

Hauer had briefly explained to him that the weapons vault was protected by a token system. The access code changed every sixty seconds, and only someone with access to one of the three tokens could unlock the door. Linda Ramer had one. The two other tokens were inside the vault.

"You there, Pierce?" It was Ramer.

"I'm here, Linda."

"Okay, you have fifty seconds to enter these numbers: four-nine-two-three-four-four-three-two-nine-four."

Hunt entered the numbers, and the keypad turned green. "I'm in."

"Good," Ramer said. "The boss wants to talk to you."

"Take a few minutes to familiarize yourself, then call me back with one of the secure satellite phones," Hauer said.

"Will do."

The weapons vault wasn't as large as some he'd shared with Simon Carter and the rest of his team, but it was nonetheless impressive. Racks held a selection of rifles, pistols, and even four Tasers. In addition, Hunt counted half a dozen suppressors, as many weapons optics, at least a dozen plate carriers and tactical vests, ten gray Blackhawk Urban load-out bags, and four satellite phones. On a small wooden table were neatly piled bundles of banknotes. Hunt estimated there was €250,000 inside the vault.

Stacked in one corner were thousands of rounds of ammunition. In the other corner were enough MRE cases to feed an entire infantry platoon for a week. To Hunt's right was a black key holder attached to the wall. Inside that key holder Hunt found the two security tokens. He put one in his pocket. He then took one of the load-out bags and began filling it up. Into the bag went an HK416 with an Aimpoint CompM5 optic and a 3X magnifier, an HK45 tactical pistol, a plate carrier, spare magazines for the rifle and pistol, and enough rounds of ammunition for both weapons. Before closing the vault, he chose two MREs and added a SureFire flashlight to his arsenal.

And a satellite phone. He had a promise to keep.

CHAPTER THIRTY-FIVE

Milan, Italy

Hunt paced the living room, holding the secure satellite phone to his ear and eating a chocolate bar he had found in one of the MREs. He thought his conversation with Hauer and Ramer was going pretty well, all things considered. He hadn't held anything back and had shared everything with them, including Dorothy Triggs's visit to the Bahamas. Hunt had expected Hauer to hit back a little or at least let him know he wasn't pleased with his decision to go to Switzerland on behalf of the CIA, but on the contrary, Hauer had told Hunt he would have done the exact same thing in his shoes. Hauer had even offered to contact Triggs directly to give her a complete situation report, but Hunt had insisted he'd do it himself.

"So what's your plan?" Hauer asked.

"As far as I'm concerned, the mission hasn't changed," Hunt replied. "I need to find Ramirez."

"Why?" Hauer asked. "What makes you think you need to find him?"

Hunt was confused. Where had Hauer been during the last fifteen minutes? Had he not been listening?

"Ramirez has intelligence that could cripple the current administration and the CIA," Hunt said. There was an odd silence at the end of the other line. "Hello?"

It was Ramer who came back. "We're here, Pierce. We were just mulling over what you said earlier."

"And?"

"Tom and I aren't convinced that it's such a bad thing if the intelligence Ramirez has in his possession becomes public."

That was a shocker. It wasn't like Ramer and Hauer to float ideas without first thinking them through, but this one came so far out of left field that Hunt wondered if he'd heard Ramer correctly. He took a seat in one of the overstuffed armchairs.

"What are you saying?" Hunt trusted Tom Hauer more than any other bureaucrat, but he didn't like the direction this conversation was taking.

Hauer cleared his throat. "What I think we're saying, Pierce, is that we don't think the information Ramirez has in his possession is worth your life—"

"What about Barry's and Colleen's and Jacobs's lives?" Hunt roared back, images of the three of them appearing in his mind. He realized he was about to lose control. He took a long, deep breath. The last thing he wanted was to get into a shouting match with Hauer and Ramer, so he checked his temper and, in as composed a voice as he could muster, said, "Are you insinuating that Colleen and Barry died over nothing? Because from where I stand, that's exactly what you're saying."

"Barry and Colleen will be greatly missed," Hauer replied. He sounded sincere, and that was one of the things Hunt appreciated most about him; the man truly and deeply cared about his people. Could Hunt say the same about Dorothy Triggs? He didn't know her well enough to pass a definitive judgment, but so far, working with her, it wasn't reassuring.

"That said, and based on what you've shared with us, we're of the opinion that the mission in Switzerland was ill advised," Hauer continued. "There are pieces that we aren't seeing, Pierce. I'm sure you realize that too."

Hunt did. But that was to be expected. Unlike a soldier who openly faced his adversary on the battlefield, covert operations were a shadowy trade. Field operatives had to be able to adapt and live through the ambiguities of the job. However, there was a limit to how many uncertainties Hunt was willing to tolerate. Clearly Hunt's team hadn't been the only one in play in Lugano. Somehow, a rival element had joined the game. Could it be someone like the Venezuelan special forces? Colonel Carlos Arteaga, the current president of Venezuela, had the most to lose if it became public that he was an American puppet. Despite what Triggs had told him, the Venezuelans did care about who their president was. They were proud people, and if they learned that their president had betrayed them, there would be a revolution.

"What are you suggesting?" Hunt asked.

"I think that going forward, this should be a DEA operation. What do you say?"

Hunt pinched his nose between his thumb and forefinger and closed his eyes. There was a reason why he'd yet to give a full situation report to Dorothy Triggs. Deep down in his gut, something was bothering him. He hadn't taken the time to really think about it until now, but way too many things hadn't gone as smoothly as they should have. First among many was the capture of Charlie Henican in Istanbul. That could have been bad luck. Turkey was in a state of controlled chaos, and it was difficult to differentiate friend from foe. Then there was the ambush in which Triggs had been shot and her son had disappeared. If Triggs had learned who'd orchestrated the attack, she hadn't shared the info with Hunt. Then there was the whole situation in Switzerland that was so over the top that it had Hunt's head spinning. How had Jorge Ramirez found out where he and Jacobs were? And what about the Russians?

Then it came to him. There could be only one reason why the bad guys were always a step ahead. It was because they knew in advance when and where elements of the operation were happening.

"Pierce, are you there?" Hauer asked.

"Dorothy Triggs has a leak in her office," Hunt heard himself say. Before either Hauer or Ramer could reply, Hunt went on to explain the thought process that had led him to this determination.

"There could be another explanation," Ramer said without conviction.

"I'd like to hear it," Hunt replied.

After a few moments of silence, Hauer said, "Even if there is another explanation, something none of us can see at the moment, I believe it would be much safer if the DEA spearheaded the effort to find Ramirez."

Hunt agreed. "Makes total sense to me. And since Ramirez played a pivotal role in distributing pills that killed American teenagers, I think it's totally legitimate for the DEA to go after him."

"I won't let you go after Ramirez alone, Pierce," Hauer said. "Abigail and Dante Castillo are on standby."

"Are they now?" Hunt asked, a tiny, hopeful smile creeping onto his face. "Last time I spoke with Dante, he told me he and Abigail were retired."

"Well, they were—until I called them and said you might need assistance."

Hunt had the utmost respect for Dante and Abigail Castillo, two former DEA agents previously stationed at the Guadalajara office whom Hunt had called upon for help when searching for his kidnapped daughter.

Despite its more-than-awful start, Hunt's day had just gotten a little brighter.

CHAPTER THIRTY-SIX

CIA headquarters
Langley, Virginia

Dorothy Triggs was standing with her back against her office window, staring straight ahead and thinking about the mess she had on her hands. Reports from Pike and Crawford had been few and far between, which had surprised her since she had clearly requested to be kept in the loop. It was one of the two analysts assigned to oversee the TOC's communications who had informed her of a problem. By the time the attacks on the TOC and the apartment in Lugano had been confirmed, it had been too late for her to do anything of consequence. The Swiss police had already cordoned off the two areas.

Now, for the third time in the last hour, she had double-checked all the agency's safe houses in Switzerland, Italy, and France. Pierce Hunt and Harriet Jacobs hadn't checked into any of them, and despite her best efforts, she'd been unable to reach either of them. She hoped they'd been able to make their way out safely, but she wasn't holding her breath. In fact, she had a superstitious fear that there might be something still worse to come.

The sudden ring of her office phone startled her.

"Triggs," she said.

"There's a Doru Kazak from the Turkish General Directorate of Security for you on line two, ma'am," her receptionist said.

"Forward the call to my personal secure line, please." Triggs hung up.

This should be interesting, Triggs thought. She'd have to tread carefully with Kazak. Since the attempted coup d'état, he'd become a man of great influence in Turkey. He had his president's ear, so anything she said to him would certainly make it to the very top. She hadn't interacted with him directly much, but on a few occasions over the last four years, they had exchanged information. Kazak was a tricky man to deal with. His personal enrichment was always his first priority. The Turkish president was certainly aware of Kazak's side dealings, but since the man had proved to be loyal and trustworthy, Triggs figured the president turned a blind eye to Kazak's illegal activities as long as they didn't embarrass him.

The only reason Kazak would be calling today of all days was because of Charlie Henican. Either he knew where Henican was and wanted to be financially compensated for the information, or Henican was actually in the Maroon Berets' custody at Kazak's direction. Kazak would want to be compensated for that too.

Triggs picked up the phone and punched the blinking red light.

"Mr. Kazak, how lovely to hear from you," Triggs said.

"Thank you for taking my call," Kazak replied. "It's important to be able to communicate directly without the interference of politicians or bureaucrats. Don't you agree?"

"Of course, Doru. How could I not?" She suspected Kazak was referring to the State Department officials who were in Turkey to negotiate Henican's release.

"Let me first offer my sympathies, my friend. I'm so very sorry about what happened to you and to Max. I heard you nearly lost your life too?"

Triggs remained silent for a moment. She shouldn't be surprised that the word was out about the attempt on her life. There was no point denying it. "Thank you for your kind words. They mean a lot."

"Max was a man of many talents, wasn't he?" Kazak said. "He was a good friend of Turkey."

"How can I help you, Doru?" Triggs asked. She had no intention of discussing her son with Kazak.

"Ha! But it's the other way around, my dear Dorothy. It is I who can assist you."

"Is that so?" She was now more sure than ever that the call was about Henican—and money. Kazak was probably afraid that the State Department would negotiate Henican's release directly with the Ministry of Foreign Affairs, effectively cutting Kazak out of the loop.

"I know you're short on time, Dorothy, but so am I. So I won't beat around the bush, and I hope you'll do the same."

"I'm listening," Triggs replied. If a bit of money could buy Henican's freedom, she'd be happy to deal directly with Kazak. The State Department would cry and complain, but she was used to their lamentations. State Department officials liked to bark, but everybody knew they had no bite.

"I'd like to talk about the matter of Charlie Henican," Kazak said.

Voilà! Here we go.

"I'm still listening," Triggs said.

"I'm happy to hear that," Kazak said. The man sounded genuinely relieved. "Despite our best of intentions, sometimes it's difficult to admit our wrongdoings and transgressions—"

"Let me interrupt you, Doru," Triggs said, leaving him no choice but to listen to her. "Let me be perfectly clear about Charlie Henican. It's true that he has done some contracting work for us in the past, but we haven't heard from him in months. We only learned that he was in Turkey a few days ago when an Instagram video of him popped up in a routine check."

"Ah yes, the video," replied Kazak with just the right amount of impatience in his tone. The man clearly didn't like to be interrupted.

Especially by a woman, Triggs thought.

Kazak continued, "I had a long chat with the young woman who shot it. Did you know she used to be a student at Istanbul University?"

Triggs suddenly didn't like where this was going. "Used to be, Doru? What have you done to this poor girl?"

"We think she's a CIA asset," Kazak replied.

"That's absurd, and you know it!"

"Time will tell, I guess," Kazak said. "So far, she hasn't cooperated much. I'm afraid we might need to use different methods of persuasion. Definitely less pleasant techniques than those I've so far authorized."

Triggs was fuming. "Careful, Doru," she warned. She was about to remind him about the recent precision strike that had terminated the commander of Iran's Quds Force, but she checked herself. She had to be careful about placing Doru Kazak—one of the most powerful officials in Turkey, albeit a corrupt one—in the same camp as the leader of an organization that had been officially deemed a terrorist organization by several governments.

"How we handle our internal security shouldn't be your concern, Dorothy," Kazak said. "I think you should focus your time and energy on Charlie Henican. And wouldn't you know it, the man has made some interesting revelations."

Triggs swallowed hard. Over the years, Henican had been involved in many of the CIA's most secret operations. What Henican had in his head could cause real harm.

"As I said," Triggs said, "Henican has worked for us in the past but hasn't been employed by the agency in a while."

"So if I understand correctly, you're telling me the CIA had no idea Charlie Henican was in Turkey?"

"We're not in the business of keeping track of all our former employees," Triggs said sharply. "The United States, contrary to some of our supposed allies, isn't a police state."

"Not sure which countries you're referring to, but I'm sure it isn't Turkey. I thank God every single day for the freedoms we as Turkish citizens enjoy," Kazak said, seemingly oblivious to his own bullshit.

He continued by asking, "Would you like to know what your *former* employee told us?"

Triggs cringed at the emphasis Kazak had placed on the word *former*.

"Why don't you tell me?"

"At first, Charlie wasn't cooperating. A bit like the young videographer, if you know what I mean. Then we changed tactics, and he became much more talkative."

"Charlie Henican is an American citizen. He should—"

"He's an assassin!" shouted Kazak, losing his temper and all sense of decorum. "And stop with your veiled insults! You're starting to piss me off!"

Triggs was taken aback by the tone and fervor with which Kazak had spoken. Had she misread the situation and Kazak's true intentions? What angle was he playing? Sometimes in discussions like these a tactical withdrawal was necessary.

"I didn't mean to upset you, Doru," Triggs said, her tone appeasing. "Our countries are allies, and so are we, you and I. Why don't you tell me what you want? Maybe we can come to some sort of arrangement?"

Kazak grunted in acknowledgment. "Maybe we can."

Triggs stayed silent for a full minute, giving Kazak time to regain his composure.

"His story matches yours," Kazak said. "He claimed the CIA had no idea he was in Turkey."

"Did he tell you why he *was* in Turkey?" Triggs asked. "I'd like to know myself, because I can assure you that if he committed—"

"He said he was in Turkey for Jorge Ramirez."

"Name rings a bell," Triggs said.

"Oh, I'm sure it does," Kazak replied. "I've dealt with that cockroach before. This Ramirez guy, he isn't a pleasant man or someone to take lightly."

"I'm aware," Triggs said, privately thinking that Ramirez was exactly the kind of cockroach Kazak loved to deal with.

"Then again, Charlie Henican is a formidable operator. Exactly the kind of soldier I'd send after a man like Jorge Ramirez."

"I've told you many times already that Henican—"

"I know, I know. He doesn't work for you," Kazak said. "I doubt that very much, but I'll play with you and assume Henican is indeed a rogue former asset. That means you have a serious problem on your hands, my friend. A very serious problem indeed."

"And why's that?" Triggs asked.

A dry chuckle escaped Kazak. Triggs had a feeling that Kazak wanted to say something, but even over the phone she could feel his hesitation. She pressed on. "What's my big problem, Doru?"

"Do you know how we caught Henican?" Kazak finally asked, not answering her question. But he didn't wait for her to answer, either, before continuing, "We received precise details of Henican's whereabouts in Istanbul. We knew at which hotel he was staying. We even knew his room. And his mission."

"His mission?"

"We were told that Henican had gone rogue and that he had been paid by a foreign intelligence service to kill the president of Turkey."

Triggs felt as if she'd been kicked by a horse. She didn't know what to say.

"That's ridiculous. You must know that!"

"My men said his tradecraft was good, even excellent," Kazak said. "But we both know that doesn't really matter when you're already compromised, yes?"

Triggs had stopped listening, her mind stuck on the fact that Henican's presence and exact location in Turkey had been leaked. Once again, highly sensitive information about a black CIA operation had found its way into hostile hands.

How?

Had the same person who was responsible for Henican's betrayal also leaked the intelligence on the Swiss operation? Her mind was racing, trying to sort through the small number of people who'd known about both ops.

"You there, Dorothy? Because there are two more things I'd like to discuss."

She had a sick, twisting feeling in her stomach that told her she wasn't going to like whatever Kazak had to say. She did her best to remain stoic.

"You have my full attention," she said.

"Half a million American dollars will buy back Charlie Henican. He's a bit shaken by his formidable adventure in Turkey, and I don't think he'll ever come back to visit our wonderful country, but he's still in one piece."

Triggs took a deep breath. Half a million was less than she had been ready to pay. She had a black budget she could access to pay Henican's ransom.

"Don't play hard to get, Dorothy," Kazak said. "Just say yes, and I'll take your word for it."

"Yes," Triggs said. "And what's the second thing?"

"Thank you in advance. Glad we got that first deal done. As for the second one, it will be a bit more expensive."

"I don't even know what you have to sell," Triggs replied.

"I can tell you exactly who sent the compromising information."

"What compromising information?"

"The leak, Dorothy. I can tell you who gave me the information that led us to Henican."

"You know who it is?" Triggs asked incredulously.

"Of course. I wouldn't be a good businessman if I didn't."

"How much?"

"I'm not greedy. It's really just to cover my expenses."

"How much, Doru?"

"Two million dollars."

Two million! The man was nuts. "I'll give you half a million if the information leads somewhere."

Kazak's reply was instantaneous. "No deal."

"You have to be reasonable," Triggs said. "We don't even give—"

"You're the one who needs to be reasonable, Dorothy," Kazak cut in. "I'm offering you salvation. Be rational about this. Think it through. I'm giving you a chance to stop the hemorrhage before it's too late."

Triggs massaged her temples. She could feel the beginning of a massive headache. Kazak had her cornered. Even though he came up short of saying it out loud, she knew Kazak wouldn't hesitate to sell the information to someone else if she failed to buy it from him.

"I'll give you two million with the understanding that you'll get nothing if the information is garbage," she said.

"Then I'll say this," Kazak said. "I'll accept your kind offer with the understanding that if payment isn't made, Charlie Henican's stay in Turkey will be extended indefinitely."

"Don't insult me, Doru. I'm a woman of my word."

"That might be so, but I don't think you'll like what I'm about to tell you."

"Just tell me what two million dollars bought me. Who leaked the information, Doru? Who gave up Henican's location?"

"It took us quite a bit of time to trace back the IP address the intelligence came from. In fact, by the time we found out who contacted us, Henican was already in custody. We might not have the resources of your all-powerful NSA, but we've been around. The United States isn't the only kid on the block anymore."

"I'm not giving you two million dollars so you can run your mouth, Doru," Triggs said, her temper rising another notch. "Who the hell sent you this information? Who's the goddamn leak?"

"You are, my dear friend. You're the one who sent me everything I needed to arrest Charlie Henican."

CHAPTER THIRTY-SEVEN

CIA headquarters
Langley, Virginia

Triggs still felt as if she were in a trance.

Can this be really happening? she asked herself, the frown lines on her forehead deepening. Her conversation with Doru Kazak had shaken her to her core. The only good thing that had come out of it was the release of Charlie Henican.

That was a win, a real one. But she doubted it would be enough to salvage her career if what Kazak had told her was true. Never had she felt so isolated. Someone with detailed knowledge of her operations—no, more than that, access to her computer—had betrayed her.

How was this even possible?

Triggs brought her hands together under her chin, her fingers steepled as if she were praying. Her mind ran through a dozen possibilities, but none of them made sense. Was it possible that Doru Kazak was playing her? That he was actually selling her misinformation? It would be daring on the Turk's part, completely out of character for him. He would know that if Triggs ever found out about such a treachery, he'd never be able to sleep more than one night at the same location. She just didn't see it; self-preservation was too important for Kazak. No, the man had been telling the truth.

Could someone have been so bold as to bug her office? She doubted it; nobody would dare unless the order came from the director himself, and she knew that Walter Helms would never agree to it. Still, she'd ask support to sweep her office again—just to make sure.

Her phone rang. She tensed. She considered not answering it. But she did.

It was Simon Carter.

And just as she'd thought it would, her day got considerably worse.

CHAPTER THIRTY-EIGHT

Carter helped Moon dock the boat in its slip.

"You've done that once or twice before, haven't you?" Carter said.

"Once or twice," Moon replied, laughing. "I've had boats all my life. Almost learned how to drive them before I could walk."

As they walked back toward Hunt and Anna's townhome, Moon asked, "So what's on those SD cards?"

"I haven't watched their content yet, but it's supposedly the footage taken by the dashcams inside the two police cars that came to Dorothy Triggs's rescue."

"You think you'll be able to use the footage?"

"I don't see why not," Carter replied. "The police sergeant I borrowed the SD cards from told me he'd watched the footage and the picture quality was great."

"He didn't say anything else?"

"He didn't seem to think the footage identified anyone. We'll see about that."

Carter's wife exited the town house with a garbage bag in her hands.

"Emma!" he called.

She let go of the garbage bag and ran down the sidewalk to meet him. She jumped into his arms, and he caught her midflight. He hugged her as he spun around, and then he put her down and kissed his wife of sixteen years passionately.

As the three of them resumed their walk toward Hunt's place, Emma slipped her hand into his and groaned in pleasure when he raised her hand and brushed his lips across her knuckles.

"What's your secret?" Moon asked, looking at them in awe. "You've been together forever, right?"

Carter smiled. "It's gonna be seventeen years of happily ever after this August," he said.

"There's no secret, right, baby? I think *that* is the secret," Emma said, looking at Carter. "Simon and I are honest with each other. We don't keep stuff from each other."

"You and Jasmine, everything okay between you two?" Carter asked, suddenly concerned.

Moon stopped walking and looked around, as if he wanted to make sure nobody else was within earshot.

"I'm madly in love with her," Moon said, his eyes bright and twinkling.

"And I know she feels the same," Emma said. "She's crazy for you."

And then Carter understood. A small "oh!" escaped his lips. "You serious?" he asked.

Emma looked at him, dumbfounded. "What are you talking about?"

But Carter was smiling, and he clapped Moon on the arm. "When are you gonna do it?"

"I don't know. I guess I'm just waiting for the right moment."

"For what, you guys?" Emma asked, gently punching her husband on the chest. "What's going on?"

With his hands on her shoulders, Carter looked down at his wife's face. "He wants to renew his vows to Jasmine."

It took a moment for her to process this. Then her eyes lit up, as Carter had known they would. "Oh my God!" she said. "Oh. My. God."

"You can't say a word about this to Jasmine, okay?" Moon said.

She shook her head. "Not a word." Then, having a second thought, she asked, "Did you buy a new ring? Can I see it? Oh my God, I wanna see it."

"I'll show it to you guys later," Moon said. "It's in my suitcase."

"Thanks for sharing that with us," Carter said. "Means a lot."

"I honestly don't know why I did. It just came out—"

"Actually, I'm the one who said it. You just confirmed it by not denying it," Carter said, grinning. "But don't worry, brother, your secret's safe with us."

———

Carter knocked on the door, and Anna opened it for them.

"Hey, guys," she said, letting the three of them in. As she turned to make space for them, Carter spotted the Glock she had slipped between her belt and the small of her back.

Jasmine was seated on a barstool in the kitchen, sipping a bottle of Sands Light and laughing at Leila and Sophia's pathetic attempt at making crab cakes. Moon rolled up his sleeves and joined them in the kitchen. Emma, who in Carter's opinion was one of the greatest cooks in the universe, started barking orders.

Anna grabbed two cold beers from the fridge, twisted the caps off, and gave one to Carter. They toasted each other in silence. The first taste felt like heaven, the cold liquid easing down Carter's throat like nectar. He took a moment to savor the bitter taste.

"So?" Anna asked, guiding him toward the terrace.

He gave her the key to his room at the Atlantis. "I can't go back to the hotel, but I need my suitcase. I have stuff that I need in it."

"All right, but why can't you go back?"

"Let's just say that I ran into three FBI agents. Two of them will never forget my face." Carter took a sip of his beer.

"Ha," Anna said simply. "Anything else?"

"I need a laptop that accepts SD cards. A police sergeant from the Royal Bahamas Police Force gave me two SD cards—"

"He gave them to you?"

Carter shifted his weight from one foot to the other.

"Well?" Anna insisted.

"Let's just say he won't forget my face either."

"What's so important on these SD cards that you had to fight your way out?"

"How about you go get that laptop of yours, and we'll watch what's on them together?"

———

They set up on the terrace. Carter grabbed two more Sands Lights from the fridge and cut two lime wedges while Anna powered up the laptop. While waiting, Carter gazed at the ocean, which stretched as far as he could see, its undulating swell infinitely relaxing. He pulled the lime wedge out of his bottle neck, squeezed the juice in, and then thrust the lime down into the bottle until it dropped into the beer with a splash and a fizz.

"Want me to do the same for yours?" he asked Anna.

"No thanks. I actually prefer it without lime," she said. "SD cards, please."

Carter gave them to her and then removed the lime wedge from Anna's bottle. He added the wedge to his beer.

"You live dangerously, Simon," Anna said, watching him.

She inserted the first card into the slot. Once all the files were downloaded, she ejected the SD card and inserted the second one to repeat the process.

"We're good," Anna said a minute later.

"I think we should start with the last video on each SD card," Carter suggested.

Anna nodded. "You want me to open two windows so we can watch both at the same time?"

"I think we'll be better off by focusing on one at a time. And let's note the time stamp for each video."

Anna clicked on the last file and started the video. The time stamp was clearly indicated at the bottom of the video, and she made note of the date and time on her phone. As Sergeant Ferguson had said, the quality of the image was surprisingly good. The video was just over seven minutes long.

"Seems like the dashcam was activated when they received the call for service," Anna said.

Unfortunately, the footage had no sound. Carter wished he could have listened to what the officers were saying. It would have helped to know what the call was about and what kind of information had been forwarded to them. The first seven minutes showed the car traveling eastbound on John F. Kennedy Drive. The vehicle was traveling—if the GPS on the dashcam was accurate—at just under one hundred miles an hour. Traffic was almost nonexistent, which made sense since it was so late at night. When the video was just short of the seven-minute mark, Carter asked to pause it. His eyes had been drawn to something on the screen.

"You see this?" he asked, his finger pointing at an orange ball.

"That's probably Dorothy Triggs's SUV," Anna replied.

"Can we continue the video frame by frame?" Carter asked.

Anna punched a few keys on the keyboard. "Here you go."

The footage continued but at a slower speed. Despite the image being a little blurry at that speed, the quality was good enough for Carter to see muzzle flashes and sparks flying off the hood of the police car. He asked Anna to pause it again.

"Okay, now rewind ten seconds," he said. "Now play it at normal speed . . . pause it!" he said, three seconds later. "See there? Two shooters. There are two different shooters firing at the vehicle."

"I see two muzzle flashes, all right," Anna said. "But I think each shooter's firing at a different police car."

Carter agreed. They would have to watch the footage of the other police car to make sure.

"Let's continue at slow speed," he said.

He again counted the muzzle flashes of the shooter who was standing on the left side of the screen.

Five. Five muzzle flashes. And two sparks.

Right after the fifth muzzle flash, the police vehicle suddenly veered and started to skid. Two seconds later it smashed into a tree, still going at over sixty miles an hour. Then the camera stopped.

"Oh my God," Anna said, almost out of breath.

When Carter turned from the screen, his eyes were narrowed, his expression deadly. "I want to know who those bastards are," he hissed, clenching his fists. "I'll put them in the ground."

Even though Carter didn't know the Bahamian police officers personally, the footage was still hard to watch. These two officers were part of a big brotherhood, a brotherhood that was willing to sacrifice everything for a higher purpose: justice. Police work was a calling. Carter didn't know one officer who had chosen this profession for the money. He himself had joined the DEA because he believed he could make a difference in people's lives. The satisfaction he got out of helping a victim or putting a smile on a kid's face was priceless.

Witnessing two officers murdered like this angered him no end. He knew the heartache it would cause to the families shattered by the tragedy. He pledged that even if the killers weren't prosecuted in the Bahamas, he'd find a way to let the families know that justice had been served.

Without a word, Carter got up from his chair and took the two steps down to the beach. He needed to clear his head. He kicked off his shoes and walked slowly along the edge of the calm sea, thinking about the dead officers and their families. He wasn't sure he wanted to watch the other video. What was the point? He already knew the outcome.

The salt water was warm on his feet, and he gulped the fresh sea air into his lungs. He closed his eyes and lifted his chin a little, letting the ocean air surround him.

What are you doing? Carter asked himself. He had work to do. Now wasn't the time to go soft. Dorothy Triggs was counting on him. He took three deep breaths, jumped up and down in the sand, then shook his arms and legs. Feeling energized, he jogged back to the terrace to watch the second video.

"You're okay?" Anna asked him with a smile.

"I'm good now. Sorry."

Carter picked up the beer that he had left on the table and took a long swig.

"Let's do this," he said, once there were only the two lime wedges left in the bottle.

The duration of the second video was almost identical to that of the first. The first several minutes were once again about the police car speeding toward the ambush site. Anna slowed down the video when they reached the point where they could see Triggs's burning SUV on the left side of the screen. As they had seen in the first video, sparks flew off the hood of the second vehicle too. Then three holes appeared almost simultaneously right in front of the dashcam.

"The bullets probably passed between the two officers," Anna said.

Then Carter saw the first police car veering to the left.

"Look, Simon, they're accelerating," Anna said, her finger pointing at the screen where the speed was indicated. "It says seventy-two miles per hour."

Then more bullet holes appeared in the windshield, but this time they showed up on the right side of the screen.

"Pause it right there!" Carter said. He pointed at a reddish ball on the screen. "You know what this is, right?"

"This is the officer returning fire through the windshield," Anna replied.

"You got it," Carter said. "I hope he hit one of the bastards."

The chances of hitting a target from a car traveling north of seventy miles per hour were almost nil. *Especially with a pistol,* Carter thought. He was nevertheless glad to see that the officers had fought back.

When the police car drove past Triggs's burning SUV, it was still traveling at around seventy miles per hour. For the first time, Carter was able to see not only the muzzle flashes of the attackers but also two distinct silhouettes.

"Holy shit! We can see the shooters," Anna said, slowing down the footage even more.

C'mon, c'mon, just a bit closer, Carter willed. *I want to see their ugly faces.*

Another bullet pierced the windshield, this one directly in front of the driver's seat, and then the windshield exploded into a thousand pieces. The police car swerved violently to the right, and for the briefest moment, Carter thought the car might straighten itself out. But it didn't. Instead, it slammed into a lamp pole.

Damn it!

Carter wanted to slam his fist down on the table, break it in half, and heave the pieces onto the beach. He wanted to scream. He wanted to grab those two murderers and pound them into the ground.

He forced himself to calm down and push his rage away. He was among friends and family here; his anger wouldn't serve any purpose. At least not in the short term. Next to him, Anna was typing furiously on the keyboard, completely absorbed. Carter didn't want to interrupt whatever she was doing, so he stood up.

Anna raised her face, her fingers pausing over the keyboard. "Sit down, Simon. And wait."

Carter sat back down. He laced his fingers together and stretched out his hands, cracking his knuckles. Anna's fingers were moving so fast that Carter couldn't see them clearly. He had never seen anyone type so fast; it was hypnotic to watch. He shouldn't have been surprised, though. Anna had graduated with a master's degree in computer science from the Florida Institute of Technology. She and Hunt had first met while he'd been undercover investigating her family, who'd run a prominent drug cartel for which Anna had handled the books.

Carter couldn't make sense of all the letters and numbers scrolling up and down the screen. As if she had read his thoughts, Anna stopped typing and turned the computer toward him.

But he was even more confused by the blank screen. "What am I supposed to be looking at?" he asked.

Anna shook her head and sighed. "It hasn't started playing yet, Simon. I was just about to explain what I did."

"Of course. I knew that," he said.

For a second or two, Anna looked at him funny, then said, "Okay, so I isolated part of the footage and slowed it waaay down while at the same time enhancing the image by a factor of six."

"Okay?"

"You were supposed to ask me which part I isolated," Anna said.

"Which part did you isolate, Anna?"

"Great question, Simon. Glad you asked." Anna clapped her hands together in mock encouragement. Despite the seriousness of what they were working on, he caught a flash of amusement in her eyes. But then she grew serious again, and her eyes hardened.

"I was able to isolate the part when the second car started to lose control, when, for a fraction of a second, we thought the driver would be able to straighten out the car just before they wrapped themselves around a lamp post. You know which part I'm talking about?"

Carter nodded. "I do."

Anna pressed a key, and the clip started playing. When the police car straightened, Anna hit a button, and the video froze. She zoomed in on the shooter at the right side of the screen. The image was grainy, but there was no mistaking what they saw.

"Do you know him?" Anna asked.

Carter was almost overcome by the urge to walk behind the screen and look directly into the man's face. He was Asian; that much Carter could see. He was short, and he knew how to hold his rifle.

"Can you take a screenshot?" Carter asked. "I'd like to send his mug shot to Triggs. I'm sure the CIA will be able to identify him."

"Already done," Anna replied. "I'm creating a new file just for the shooters."

"Can we do the same thing for the shooter on the left?"

Anna ran her fingers over the track pad and started clicking away like a madwoman.

"Ready?" she asked, then hit play on the video. She went through the same procedure with the shooter on the left. As she zoomed in on the image, the picture quality became poorer. The shooter's face became a blur of colored pixels.

"Can you do better?" Carter asked.

"I'm not done," Anna replied, fiddling with the track pad.

Anna zoomed the image back out slightly to give it more clarity. She took a screenshot and dragged the newly created file into a special photo-enhancer application.

"How long is that—"

"It's almost done. Look!" Anna said.

As the image became sharper, Carter could make out more details.

The man was Caucasian and quite tall, with an athletic build. Anna then zoomed in. Her photo enhancer had made the shooter's face almost crystal clear. Carter stared at the screen, unable to believe his eyes. His stomach tightened, and the anger and rage he had been able to push aside came back with a roar. He gritted his teeth.

Fuck. Me.

Anna must have seen Carter's face drop, because she said, "You know him, don't you?"

It took Carter a few moments to put his thoughts in order. This screenshot changed everything. It also meant that Hunt might be in more danger than he had bargained for. Now the questions were: Was Dorothy Triggs in on it? Did she know her son was still alive? Did she know he'd shot and killed four Bahamian police officers?

"Simon!" Anna called out. "Do you know this guy?"

"Yeah, I know him. He's Dorothy Triggs's son. His name is Max Oswald."

Anna let out a breath as if she'd been punched in the stomach. Obviously she'd been caught off guard too. "Are you absolutely sure?"

"One hundred percent. She showed me numerous pictures of her son when I was at Langley."

"This isn't good," she said, a worried look on her face. "We need to warn Pierce."

"I have no way of contacting him, Anna. He's on a black op. He's operating inside an allied country. Everything is closed circuit. He probably left his personal phone in Virginia. Unless you and Pierce have another way of communicating?"

Anna angled the laptop closer and sat back down. Carter had seen how she usually typed, but something had changed. Her hands were shaking so badly that she was typing the wrong letters and had to delete them and type the right ones.

"Damn it!" she shouted.

"Let me help you," he offered.

She threw him a look, and he backed off. "I'm fine," she said, her anger slipping through. "This bullshit, this goddamn bullshit, is exactly why Pierce didn't work for Triggs. He fucking hates the CIA. He always did. Did you know he initially turned her down? Did you know that, Simon?"

"We haven't talked much in the last few days, Anna. The operation came together very quickly for him, I think."

"Well, I'm telling you now. He didn't want to have anything to do with her. Pierce likes working for Tom Hauer, and he told the bitch so."

"But she used Charlie Henican to draw him in, didn't she?"

She nodded, and tears welled in her eyes. Pain, and anger too. Lots of anger. Anna had been through so much in the last few years. She had finally found peace here in the Bahamas with Hunt and the girls.

"You know Pierce as well as I do, Anna. Maybe better. He's the kind of guy who—"

Anna raised her palm. "I know, but I don't have to like it."

Carter wanted to tell her that everything was going to be okay, but he knew better. Anna Garcia was as tough as any men he knew. She couldn't be bullshitted. They both knew how high the stakes were for Hunt. They needed to warn him.

"What were you trying to do just now?" Carter asked. "You have a way to get in touch with Pierce?"

"It's old school," Anna said. "But it's easy and it works."

"What is it?"

"We share an email address, and we communicate by leaving messages for each other in the drafts folder."

Carter had heard of this somewhat clandestine method of communication. It worked most of the time, but the users needed to make sure they weren't using a device or a network that was being monitored by people hostile to them. If the Wi-Fi network was compromised or the device used to log in to the account had been hacked, it would allow unwanted persons unrestricted access to their communications.

"We only use it for emergencies," Anna said. "When I checked this morning, there were no messages."

"What are you gonna tell him?"

179

"I'll attach the photo of Max Oswald and tell him Max is one of the men responsible for the ambush on his mother's vehicle."

"Don't use names or—"

"For Chrissakes already! I know what I'm doing, Simon."

Carter let her type her message and waited for her to be done. Then he'd call Dorothy Triggs and tell her his findings. Even if Hunt didn't trust her unequivocally, the woman deserved to know that it was her son who had betrayed her. That said, since Carter had no undeniable proof that Triggs wasn't involved, he'd call someone else too. And there was only one person in a position to help who Carter trusted entirely for situations such as these.

Tom Hauer.

CHAPTER THIRTY-NINE

Milan, Italy

Hunt had allowed himself to drift off, his hand faithfully wrapped around a Glock. When he awoke, he had no idea how long he'd been sleeping, but knowing that someone at the DEA was keeping watch had given him the assurance he'd needed to let his anxieties go for a few hours. Even though the curtains were drawn, he could tell it was still dark outside, not yet morning. He gazed at the red numerals on the clock on the nightstand.

Yep—3:05 a.m.

Hunt threw back the covers and swung his legs out from under the blankets. He got up and stretched, only to realize that his range of motion was brutally reduced. His fight with Jorge Ramirez and the two Swiss police officers had taken its toll. His whole body was stiff, sore in the most random places.

Nothing that a long, hot shower can't fix, Hunt thought, heading into the walk-in shower alcove. He turned on the water and waited for it to warm up—it didn't. Hunt cursed at the unfairness of it all. He let the water run for a few more minutes and used the time to brush his teeth and shave. As he was doing so, he looked in the mirror. Hunt not only felt older than his thirty-nine years but was starting to look it too. His usually bright-blue eyes were bloodshot and swollen, his face drawn and pale. While the hair on his head remained brown, traces of gray and white had started to sneak into his beard. Anna thought it was sexy, so there was that. Hunt wondered how old he would look in ten years if he kept going at this pace. At six feet two and just a touch under two hundred pounds, Hunt was still in better shape than most men half his age.

But I do need my shower to get warm, he thought. Seeing no moisture on the glass panes of the walk-in shower wasn't a good sign. He extended his hand to touch the water. Cold.

How was it possible that the sink had hot water but not the shower? With a deep and resigned sigh, Hunt walked into the cold water.

———

The incessant ringing of the satellite phone on the nightstand forced him to end his shower sooner than he wanted to. The cold water had energized and invigorated him more than a hot shower ever could. Hunt wrapped a towel around his midsection and walked back to the bedroom. He grabbed the offending satellite phone from the nightstand.

"You slept well?" This was Tom Hauer.

Hunt cleared his throat. "I did. What's up?"

"Dante and Abigail are only a few hours away. They'll be there by morning," Hauer said. "I've given them directions to the safe house and your phone number."

"That's good news, but how did you manage that?" Hunt asked. When Hauer had told him the night before that Dante and Abigail were on standby, Hunt had expected to see them a day or two later, not twelve hours.

"It just happened that they were in Croatia. Split, to be exact."

In addition to their help when searching for his daughter, Hunt had also been able to count on the two ex–DEA special agents' support going after Ramirez during his last mission. But Hunt's friendship with Dante dated back to their time in the military. Dante, a former Black Hawk pilot, had been shot down on his fifty-third combat mission by a surface-to-air missile that had found its way into his Black Hawk engine's exhaust above a small town just south of Baghdad. He'd succeeded in crash-landing his helicopter on a sand dune despite multiple hydraulic system failures. Hunt and six other Rangers who'd been operating not far from the crash site had seen the chopper go down. With enemies dangerously close to the downed Black Hawk, Hunt and his men had provided suppressive fire to pin them down—allowing Dante and the rest of his crew to escape.

"I can't thank you enough, Tom," Hunt said, meaning it. "I'll let you know when they're here. Is there something else?"

"I'm afraid there is," Hauer replied. "And it's not good news this time."

Hunt, who had put the satellite phone on the bed and in speaker mode so he could dry himself and get dressed while talking, picked up the phone and pressed it against his ear.

"What kind of bad news?"

"A few hours ago, while you were asleep, I received a call from Simon Carter—"

"Is Simon okay?" Hunt asked, immediately alarmed. "What about Anna and the girls?"

"Yes, Simon's fine, Pierce. Everybody's fine," Hauer said.

Hunt felt a big weight lift off his shoulders. During the last few days, he hadn't had much time to think about Anna and the girls. And for that he felt bad. These three human beings should always be his top priority. The mirror in the bathroom hadn't lied. He wasn't getting any younger. But if he didn't let go of this life completely, there would always be a new target to go after. A terrorist to be taken down or a drug dealer to be put behind bars. Maybe it was time for him to step aside. For good.

Hauer's voice suddenly broke through his thoughts. "Did you hear what I said, Pierce?"

"Sorry, I was somewhere else for an instant," Hunt said. "What did my friend Simon have to say?"

"Before I get into this, I need to tell you that Dorothy Triggs hired Simon to investigate what happened in the Bahamas. Either she didn't trust the FBI to report back their findings to Langley—and why should they, since it isn't in their mandate?—or she didn't want to wait for them to do so. I really don't know, and at this point I don't care. What I do know is that Simon did as he was told and—"

"And he found something, didn't he?"

"He did. Triggs's son, Max Oswald, is alive."

Hunt was about to say that this was good news, but something in Hauer's tone suggested otherwise. "Okay," he said noncommittally.

"He killed the four Bahamian police officers who raced to Triggs's rescue."

Hunt couldn't believe what he was hearing. His mind kicked into overdrive. What did he know about Max Oswald? He'd met him only briefly when Triggs had visited his townhome. Even at Langley, before and after the initial briefing, Triggs had only spoken vaguely about her son. Hunt hadn't pushed for more details, not wanting to deepen her grief over his death. The little he had learned about the man was good, though—a former infantry officer who'd then gained undercover experience with the CIA, even taught a bit at the Farm, before joining his mother at the Directorate of Operations, most certainly so she could groom him for an important role one day.

Something had gone wrong along the way.

"I guess you wouldn't tell me that if you weren't one hundred percent sure, right?" Hunt asked.

"Actually, it's not only Simon who's sure. It's Anna too."

"Anna? Don't tell me Triggs recruited her too." Hunt entered the weapons vault looking for one of the military-grade Toughbooks he had seen earlier. He wanted to check if Anna had left him a message on their shared email address. Thinking she was having fun with friends and family, he hadn't even thought about checking the drafts folder.

"She has nothing to do with this. She simply helped Simon analyze the intel he secured in Nassau."

"Which was?" Hunt asked as he powered up the laptop.

"The dashcam footage from the cars the officers were driving when Max Oswald killed them," Hauer said. "I'm not sure how she did it, Pierce, but Anna really came through. She managed to isolate the image of Max Oswald and enhance its quality. There's no doubt about his identity."

Now logged in to his and Anna's shared account, Hunt saw there was a message waiting for him in the drafts folder. He clicked on it. It was a photo of Max Oswald from the dashcam footage and a couple of lines of text from Anna wondering if he was okay. She was worried and wanted to hear back from him as soon as possible.

"We'll have to think this through, Tom," Hunt said while typing his reply. "We need to figure out who's the biggest threat. Ramirez or Max Oswald."

"Why? I think both deserve to be caught," Hauer said. "Don't you agree?"

"It's not that I disagree, but we don't have the resources to go after both at the same time," Hunt replied. "I think Max should be our biggest concern at the moment. But what are we supposed to tell Triggs? That her son is a killer? I'll let you make that decision, but if it was me, I wouldn't share anything with her."

"That option has come and gone, I'm afraid. Prior to calling me, Simon had already contacted Triggs."

"Shit! What was he thinking?"

"She hired him, remember? And from what I can see, the poor woman had no idea. Simon made the right call."

"Then I respectfully disagree," Hunt said. "Do you really expect Triggs to stay put now?"

"We don't," Hauer said. "I had a quick chat with Linda Ramer about this just before I called you, and we came to the same conclusion.

The instant you and I hang up, I'm going straight to the attorney general with this."

Hunt sighed loudly.

"You disagree with that too?" Hauer asked. Hunt had a feeling that he had ticked him off.

"Is there anything I could say that would convince you to give me, Dante, and Abigail a couple of days to hunt Max down by ourselves?" Hunt asked.

Hauer didn't reply immediately. Hunt couldn't blame Hauer for following protocol, though he would have appreciated a forty-eight-hour head start before Hauer informed the AG. Once he was made aware of the situation, the FBI would launch a major investigation and make it almost impossible for Hunt to successfully chase down Max Oswald.

"My official response to your request is absolutely not," Hauer said. "I'll write the attorney general a thorough report about the situation and will send it to his office as soon as I'm done."

"And usually, how long does it take you to write a full briefing for the attorney general?" Hunt asked.

"No more than twenty-four hours," Hauer replied.

"I see." Twenty-four hours wasn't much, but it was better than nothing. With Dante and Abigail on their way, things would start happening fast. It pained him to forgo his pursuit of Jorge Ramirez for the moment, but Hunt didn't have the manpower to chase down two rabbits at the same time.

"One more thing, Pierce. I think you'll be happy to know that Simon is on his way to you," Hauer said before hanging up.

Hunt allowed a small smile to crack his face. The next twenty-four hours were going to be interesting.

CHAPTER FORTY

Somewhere in Turkey

Charlie Henican didn't feel good. His health was deteriorating fast. His coughing fits were only getting worse and more frequent. There was now a thick, phlegm-like sound behind every cough. The chilly, damp weather left him feeling cold all the time.

At least his captors had stopped beating him, and he was now given a cup of water every three or four hours, but he was in need of serious medical attention. Henican tried to haul himself up off the cold cement floor but found it almost impossible. The metal bars of his cell whirled before his eyes as he tried to push away the tremendous pain. Usually his captors gave him five to ten minutes to slurp his soup and drink his tea before they took his spoon and bowl away. Henican had no idea what the Turks had planned for him, but he didn't intend on sticking around to find out.

He was going to escape.

If he failed, the consequences would be grave. He wasn't a soldier operating in a theater of war anymore; he was a spy, and as such, he couldn't expect anyone to come after him. And Henican being Henican, he wasn't about to sit in his cell and wait for his captors to kill him. If he was going to get out of this shithole alive, he'd have to think things through logically—which was almost impossible in his current state.

The only silver lining was his location. He was pretty sure he was still in Istanbul. When they had picked him up from his hotel and shoved him in the SUV, they had traveled for less than ten minutes. The fact that he was being kept captive in a former swimming facility told him that he wasn't in an official military prison. The guards weren't military either. The only time he'd seen a real Turkish official after his initial capture was when the man dressed in civilian clothes and a balaclava had interrogated him. There was a small chance that if he could get past the two guards, he'd be able to escape the facility. And if he was still in Istanbul, he wasn't too far from the American consulate.

I have to do this, Henican thought. *Because if I don't, I'll die in this cell.*

The possibility that he'd never see Harriet Jacobs again solidified his will to escape.

You're in love, Charlie, Henican thought. *For the first time in your life, you're actually in love.* Whatever he needed to do to escape, he would do. Then he would marry Jacobs—if she was brave enough to say yes—and retire. He had just enough money saved up to start that fishing charter business in the Keys he'd always dreamed about.

Yeah, Henican thought. *I'm getting out of here.*

———

It was another two hours before the guards came. This time they brought some solid food. The guards, as usual, weren't carrying any firearms. It was possible they were leaving their firearms outside the area he was in, but Henican doubted it. The two men carried police batons and stun guns. In any other circumstances, Henican would be able to neutralize them in seconds. But in his present condition, he wasn't so sure.

As the two guards approached the door of his cell, he started having second thoughts—not something he was used to. His heart rate skyrocketed.

Focus.

The door opened, and the two Turks entered. One was tall and thin, while the other was short, with a stocky fighter's build. Summoning what reserves of strength he had left, Henican lunged. His shoulder slammed into the first guard, and the man staggered backward until he ran into the wall. The guard had already dropped the tiny cup of water destined for him and replaced it with a stun gun. Henican grabbed the guard's wrist and yanked the arm toward him while turning and throwing the guard over his shoulder. For the brief moment the guard was on top of him, Henican twisted the man's wrist away from the direction of the fall, forcing him to drop the stun gun. As the guard's back slammed into the concrete floor, Henican dropped his knee into the man's ribs, the loud crack of shattering bones reverberating off the walls of his cell.

The second guard jumped on Henican's back with both his arms around his neck. He pulled and twisted, trying to bring Henican down by kneeing him in the back. Henican reached up and grabbed the guard by the hair. He then bent his legs and dived forward while tucking in his head. The guard flipped above him, and Henican let himself fall on top of him. Henican punched the man in the throat. Unable to breathe, the guard lay still, his eyes and tongue bulging out.

Henican grabbed the guard's stun gun and baton and frisked him for the keys. Once he had found the keys, he exited the cell and closed the door behind him, locking it.

CHAPTER FORTY-ONE

Henican stared down a long, brightly lit corridor. Except for the hum of a poor ventilation system, there was no noise, no sign of activity. Stun gun in hand, Henican walked down the hallway, inspecting the layout of the interior, trying to find a clue that would confirm his location. He listened for noises that would suggest the presence of other guards. Barefoot, he didn't make a sound as he walked on the cold concrete floor.

A series of cells like the one he had been kept in lined the right side of the hallway. They were all unoccupied. The subdued sound of a door opening and closing came from behind him. Henican flattened himself against the wall but had no place to hide. At the opposite end of the hallway, a guard turned the corner and headed toward his cell. The guard's eyes were fixed on his phone, but it was only a matter of seconds before the guard would realize what Henican had done to his colleagues. Henican didn't want to be around when that happened. Since he was going to be seen whether he waited to be discovered or not, he bolted toward the set of double doors at the end of the hallway, betting they weren't locked. He hadn't seen an access card on either of the guards.

Someone shouted something in Turkish behind him, but Henican ignored it. The end of the hallway was fast approaching, and he forced himself to run faster. Just as he was about to crash into the doors, two guards opened the doors from the outside. One of them, the smaller of the two, stared at Henican in disbelief. Henican didn't think. He rammed the smaller man with all his force, tackling him and slamming him through the doorway and onto the floor in a small storage space, the kind used to store pool equipment and chemicals. Henican had the time to deliver two punches to the man's face before the other guard grabbed him, wrapping his beefy arms around Henican's neck. Within seconds, Henican lost access to oxygen, and everything became blurry.

He swung his head back as hard as he could, shattering the guard's nose. The man groaned but didn't let go. Instead of loosening his choke hold, he jumped on Henican's back and wrapped his legs around his waist, making it virtually impossible for Henican to head strike him again. Henican, his vision swimming, took a few involuntary steps back before stumbling on a piece of rusted chain. Knowing the wall was only a few feet behind him, he let himself go backward and slammed the guard against the wall. Henican then threw himself forward, twisting to his right while bending his left knee. The guard flew over the top of him and crashed to the floor.

Using the last of his energy, Henican got up, but before he could take a full step, a hand wrapped around his left ankle. In midstride, Henican fell forward onto his knees. With his right foot, he kicked at the guard's already-bloodied face as viciously as he could. The guard's head snapped back, and his hand released Henican's ankle.

Henican sucked in a deep breath and pushed himself up off the floor. Then something slammed into his back, and he fell face-first onto the floor.

Shit. The third guard, Henican thought.

Henican twisted to one side and brought his elbow backward into the guard's face, allowing him to wedge a knee underneath himself and roll both of them over. The guard was the first to rise, and he drew a collapsible baton from his belt. The guard took a swing just as Henican struggled to his feet. The baton connected with Henican's already-broken ribs.

Henican cried out and collapsed to the floor, holding his side. The chain he had tripped over only moments ago was between him and the guard. As the guard swung his baton down, Henican rolled to his right, grabbed the chain, and delivered a hammer fist into the man's groin. His fist connected squarely with a sickening thump.

The guard dropped his baton and almost folded forward but ended up taking a few steps back, holding his crotch. The distance allowed Henican to stand up. The guard was still wobbly on his feet. Henican seized the moment to swing the chain at his face with all his might. The rusted chain hit the guard across his right cheek, drawing blood and breaking teeth. The guard spun around, and Henican leaped on his back and wrapped the chain around his throat.

The guard fell over backward, slamming Henican to the floor. But Henican didn't let go; he kept maximum tension on the chain. The guard's feet were kicking frantically, his nails digging into Henican's forearms. The guard's body was now thrashing wildly in a last attempt to break free. And he almost succeeded. Henican's muscles, battered from numerous beatings, were burning from exhaustion. He couldn't hold on much longer. He only had to tough it out longer than the other guy.

And he did.

The guard finally stopped moving. Henican kept the hold for another ten seconds before letting go. Then he pushed the guard off him and lay there panting, only able to breathe in short, painful gasps.

Get up! Get up! You need to move. Henican willed himself up. He felt a dull throbbing all over his body, but all his limbs seemed to work. He frisked the guard and found five hundred Turkish lira, a mobile phone, and a set of keys. The phone was locked. He placed it in front of the guard's face, but it didn't unlock.

Shit! He remembered that the older model didn't have facial recognition and needed the user's fingerprint to unlock. Henican lifted the man's hand and pressed his thumb against the phone.

Henican breathed a sigh of relief when it worked.

Resting his back against the wall, he dialed a number he had learned a long time ago but had never had to use until now.

An automated voice picked up on the first ring and asked him to enter his personal number. With a shaky hand, Henican entered his sixteen-digit personal identification number. As he waited for the number to clear the CIA's computers, he took in his surroundings amid a coughing fit that left him breathless.

Old pool-cleaning equipment and stacks of lounge chairs occupied most of the space. His eyes stopped on a single folding table at the other end of the storage building. On it was a coffee machine and a lone computer. Behind the table was an emergency exit door. On the opposite wall, up high, a single dirty window let in a narrow stream of light.

Morning, Henican thought. The rest of the light was from fluorescent tubes hanging from the ceiling. A human voice took over the line at the other end.

"Can I have your six-letter identification code?"

Henican had been given different codes for distinctive scenarios. He had to take a moment to remember the right one. He fought the urge to simply let the person know what was going on and that he needed immediate assistance. That would be counterproductive. The person at the other end would simply hang up and expunge his number from the system.

"Sierra-Charlie-Oscar-Oscar-Hotel-Oscar."

"One moment, please."

Despite the situation, Henican chuckled. Had they just put him on hold? The chuckle led to a coughing fit, which brought blood to his lips. He spat in between his legs, and a tooth fell out.

A male voice he didn't recognize came on the line. "My line is secure. Is your line secure?"

"No," Henican said. Then he heard a series of clicks.

"Hello?" Henican asked, afraid they had hung up on him. "Hello!"

"Henican, is that you?"

Henican sighed. *Thank God.* "Yes. Yes, it's me."

"Can you confirm your exact location?"

"I can't. I—"

"The city, maybe?"

"Istanbul, I think," Hauer replied.

"Confirmed," the man said. "Are you injured?"

"Yeah."

"Are you ambulatory?"

"As long as I don't have to go too far," Henican said, slowly and painfully getting up.

"I have your location pinged at about three miles south of the American consulate in Istanbul," the man said. "Can you hold your position for twenty minutes?"

"Negative."

"Wait one."

Henican, holding his side, slowly made his way to the closest door. Dizziness was taking over, and he had difficulty walking in a straight line, needing to lean on the wall to remain standing. Then his breathing became shallow and beads of sweat materialized on his forehead as he slipped into a semiconscious state.

Punctured lung, Henican thought. That was the worst possible scenario for him. The last baton strike had probably caused the most damage. Henican didn't panic, but he was conscious that at least one of his lungs was slowly but surely filling up with blood.

One more step, he kept repeating to himself. *Just one more step.*

He was only a few feet from the exit door when he fell to his knees, giving in to exhaustion. His hand left his side as he tried to reach for the door, but he only managed to fall on his face.

Henican had no idea how long he lay motionless on the floor. It could have been ten minutes or an hour. He didn't even care. He was done. He had nothing left to give. The man he had called at the emergency number never returned. The CIA had abandoned him to his fate.

When the same men who had arrested him six days ago stormed the building five minutes later, Henican had already stopped breathing.

CHAPTER FORTY-TWO

CIA headquarters
Arlington, Virginia

Triggs was still shaken by Simon Carter's revelation. At first, like any sane person who loved her son more than anything in the world, she hadn't believed Carter. She'd argued that he had botched the investigation and had no real evidence Max had shot at the police officers in the Bahamas. When, minutes later, Carter had forwarded her the enhanced video stills he and Anna Garcia had worked on, she still hadn't believed him.

Why would her son do that? It didn't make sense. Then she'd remembered Doru Kazak's claim that she had a leak in her office. He had even insinuated that the leak could be *her*. Now his words made total sense. She had trusted Max with everything. Read him in on every current covert operation. It had been against protocol to do so, but she had justified it by thinking she was grooming him for higher office within the agency. She wanted him to learn from the best.

Her. His mother.

———

Triggs nodded at the director of the CIA's secretary and walked right into his office. It was an impressive space. Floor-to-ceiling windows, rich dark carpeting, and a large conference table with twelve chairs.

There were two large retracting screens next to the table and a meeting area with two comfortable-looking couches and three dark leather club chairs.

"What's so damn urgent, Dorothy?" Walter Helms asked from behind his mahogany desk.

Helms was necessarily as much a politician as he was a spymaster. Everything that came out of his mouth was weighed carefully. He was respected by both sides of the aisle and had President Reilly's ear. Even though Helms wasn't a warm-and-fuzzy man, he'd been affected by Max's disappearance too. Helms's son, an army pilot, had lost his life when his Apache helicopter had crashed close to Kabul while flying a combat mission in support of ground troops. Though Helms and Max hadn't been friends per se, they had respected each other's opinions.

"My son's alive, Walter," Triggs said.

Helms closed the file he had been working on and removed his reading glasses. He came out from behind his desk and leaned against it, crossing his arms over his chest. He was tall and lean, with the shape of an Olympic swimmer, which he was. Helms was as much at ease chatting with senators as he was playing with his grandkids at Disneyland.

"That's great news," he said, forcing a smile. "But where's this coming from? The FBI haven't even begun their investigation."

"About that—"

"Simon Carter?" he asked, raising an eyebrow.

"So you knew about it?"

"I'm the director of the most powerful intelligence agency in the world. Of course I knew. Have you lost your touch, Dorothy?"

Triggs scratched her head, messing up her blonde hair. "Apparently so. I believe Max hacked my entire communication network. He played me like a fool."

That was clearly not the answer he had expected. Helms motioned for her to sit. "Want something to drink?" he asked, walking toward the small bar next to his desk.

"I need to think clearly," she replied, "but you might want to pour yourself a stiff one."

Helms let go of the bottle of single malt and instead picked up two bottles of mineral water. He threw one at her, and she caught it on the fly.

"That bad, huh?" he asked.

"Worse."

CHAPTER FORTY-THREE

Milan, Italy

Hunt opened the door of the safe house. Dante and Abigail Castillo were standing on the porch, smiling. "You ordered a pizza?" Dante asked.

"What took you so long?" Hunt said, letting them in.

"It's good to see you, Pierce," Abigail said as Hunt kicked the door shut with his foot.

"I'm so glad to see you," Hunt replied, giving her a big hug. Just like her husband had done, Abigail had risked her life and her career with the DEA to help Hunt rescue Leila and Sophia from a merciless Mexican drug cartel.

Hunt put his hand out to Dante, but his friend wrapped his arms around him.

"I missed you, brother," Dante said. "How have you been? Man, you look tired."

"I am," Hunt replied honestly. "It's been a tough few days."

"We heard. Hauer briefed us," Abigail said, lifting Hunt's hands and inspecting his gashed knuckles. "That's from your fight with Ramirez?"

Hunt looked at his hands. "I hadn't even noticed, to tell the truth. The master's mine, but there's another bedroom upstairs with an en suite," he continued. "Why don't you drop your go bags and come back down in ten. I'll cook you guys breakfast. How does that sound?"

"Perfect," Dante said, walking past the dining table, on which Hunt had displayed an impressive selection of ready-to-eat meals—MREs.

"Really? That's breakfast?" Abigail asked, looking at the MREs. "Maybe coming here was a bad idea after all."

———

Hunt looked at Dante, who was finishing up his second serving of Menu Item No. 4, the cheese-and-veggie omelet. "You kind of forget how good these are, right?" Dante asked.

Abigail shook her head in disgust.

"He's the only guy I know who loves this rectangular slab of yellowish food matter," Hunt said.

"I can't even stand the smell," Abigail said, playing with the real piece of bacon Hunt had fried for her.

"That's because they stopped making it in 2009, Abi," Hunt said. He added, pointing at Dante's plate, "That thing your husband is putting in his mouth is at least eleven years old."

Her eyes grew wide. "You're kidding, right? Tell me that's not true."

"Sorry, no can do," Hunt said, but he was smiling. "Did you know what we used to call Menu Item Number Four?"

"I don't want to know," Abigail said, sipping her glass of orange juice.

"Vomelet," Hunt said.

Abigail laughed so hard some orange juice came out of her nose.

Dante gave him a look. "Was that really necessary? She'll never look at me the same now."

"She deserved to know, brother. I'm sorry."

Dante gave him the finger but kept eating. Fifteen minutes later, once the plates were cleared and the dishes done, they sat at the table. Hunt placed a map before them.

"I'll walk you through exactly what happened," Hunt said. "If you have any questions, just ask them on the fly. Got it?"

Abigail and Dante nodded. They each had a notepad, and during the next two hours they took pages and pages of notes as Hunt went through the entire sequence twice. From Triggs's visit to the Bahamas to his arrival at the DEA safe house in Milan, he didn't leave anything out. Dante and Abigail each asked a couple of questions, then went upstairs to the weapons vault to kit up.

Hunt had done his best not to show it, but it had been difficult to talk about Harriet Jacobs. He hadn't known her well, but she'd been a good operator, and knowing that Henican had liked her made him feel like shit. During the last twelve hours, he had thought almost nonstop about the firefight that had ended her life. It was too late to change anything now, but he couldn't help thinking that if Jacobs hadn't been there, he would have been the one with two bullet holes in his chest. And every time he thought about *his* death, his mind automatically went back to Leila. How many times had his daughter pleaded with him to do something else with his life? How many times had Leila told him that he had done enough, that he should step down and let others do the heavy lifting? And how many more times would she need to ask him before he finally listened to her?

The satellite phone vibrated next to the map. It was Tom Hauer.

"Don't you ever sleep, Tom?" Hunt asked, knowing that it was five hours earlier in Virginia.

"Is this really your biggest concern, Pierce?" Hauer replied.

"Sorry. What's up?"

"A lot," Hauer said.

"Give me a minute. I'll get the others."

A minute later, Hunt placed the satellite phone on speaker as Abigail and Dante sat with him at the table.

"We're all here," Hunt told Hauer.

"Have any of you heard about Operation Familia?" Hauer asked.

"I have," Hunt said. "It was a major operation coordinated by the DEA and Europol. Didn't they just seize a ton of cocaine in Switzerland?"

"Yes, they did, and they arrested sixteen people and seized two million euros in cash. We teamed up with Europol and went after a Balkan organized crime family we suspected of bringing large amounts of cocaine into Europe."

"Yeah," Abigail said. "I read that in the newspaper while we were in Croatia. That was a big deal over there."

"It certainly was," Hauer admitted. "The cocaine came from South America, and the Balkan gangsters were using private planes to import it."

"Is there a link between Operation Familia and our current assignment?" Hunt asked.

"Only indirectly," Hauer replied. "This operation allowed us to forge strong partnerships with other agencies, especially with the Swiss police and the folks at Europol."

Hunt had a sense of where Hauer was going with this, but he didn't dare say it out loud, so he let the DEA administrator continue. "Even though his involvement in the overall investigation was limited, DEA Special Agent Kleiner's role was key to its success."

Hunt wasn't surprised. Hunt and Carter had spent a few hours with him when they had returned from their last mission. Kleiner was quick on his feet and had proved himself invaluable during the firefight that had saved Anna from a professional hitman working for Jorge Ramirez.

"I've kept in touch with him," Hunt said.

"So you know he's now assigned to Europol headquarters at The Hague, right?"

"I do," Hunt replied.

"What you probably don't know is that he's presently in Zurich assisting the Swiss police with their court documents for Operation Familia. Linda Ramer contacted him earlier, and she confirmed that Special Agent Kleiner will be waiting for all of you in Lugano."

"You want us to go to Lugano, sir?" Abigail asked. "Why?"

"The Swiss police recovered multiple bodies and are in the process of identifying them. There's a high probability that Ramirez is still in Switzerland. Special Agent Kleiner's presence will open doors that would be otherwise closed for regular DEA special agents like you."

Hunt agreed with Hauer. He had a feeling that Ramirez was still in Switzerland, doing his best to keep a low profile until the dust settled. One thing confused him, though. He was about to ask Hauer for clarification, but Dante beat him to the punch.

"What do you mean by 'special agent,' sir?"

"Linda Ramer suggested that the three of you be reinstated as special agents—at least temporarily," Hauer replied. "I was initially reticent about the idea, but it makes sense for you to have official status if you're to work with Kleiner and Europol. So what do you say?" he added.

Hunt hadn't expected that. He looked over at Abigail and Dante. They each gave Hunt a thumbs-up. When Hauer had forced him and Carter out of the DEA, he'd never expected he'd be given a badge again. But as much as Hunt wanted it, he wasn't sure Hauer had the authority to give it back. He wasn't convinced Anna would be thrilled either.

"I mean no disrespect, Tom," Hunt said, "but I'm not sure how the attorney general would feel about that."

"Let me worry about my boss, Pierce."

"So we get salaries, and we keep our pensions too?" Abigail asked.

"Absolutely. I'm not expecting you to work for free."

Hunt was excited about the idea, and he wasn't the only one. Abigail and Dante looked at him expectantly. They wanted back in the game too.

"This is a legitimate offer," Hauer added. "You'd be working under the authority of the DEA Special Operational Detachment, Europe."

Hunt's eyes narrowed. "I've never heard of this unit."

"I just made it up," Hauer replied. "And you're the special agent in charge, by the way."

CHAPTER FORTY-FOUR

Just north of Lugano, Switzerland

Ramirez passed the razor under the hot water of the faucet, flushing away the shaving cream and accumulated stubble. With a lot more effort than it should have required, Ramirez looked at the face in the mirror before him. It wasn't a pretty sight. His right eye was swollen shut. His bottom lip was cracked, and he had nasty bruises under both cheeks. His beaten face belonged to a man who had been humiliated, not to a former Venezuelan special forces soldier. The Swiss cop had completely owned him. Ramirez didn't remember ever taking such a beating. He was usually the one giving it or ordering it.

Ramirez unconsciously lifted the razor. As he eased it across his chin, he found himself wondering where he had gone wrong. Unless he hadn't. Maybe none of this was his fault.

Max Oswald had given him an exit strategy. As he dried his face, he wondered if he should take Max's offer or keep looking for something better—and in doing so risk losing his life.

He had a decision to make, but deep down he'd already made it. Max Oswald was a persuasive man. Ramirez would go as far as saying that he was a man with a vision. Of course, the fact that Max would probably execute him if he declined his less-than-fair offer played a significant part in his decision-making process.

Following their discussion, Max had ordered the guard to remove the handcuffs and shackles and allow him free movement within his room. He wasn't allowed outside without prior approval from one of the guards. The rules were simple. And the consequences of breaking them equally simple.

He'd be shot.

The door of his room opened. Max entered but remained in the doorframe, leaning against it. "So?" he asked, bringing the coffee mug to his lips.

"Okay," Ramirez said.

"Where is it?"

Ramirez was about to take the longest and most dangerous leap of faith of his life. Because once he gave the information to Max, he'd lose his leverage.

"Transfer the funds like you promised, and I'll tell you," Ramirez said.

"Fair enough," Max said. "Follow me."

The only time Ramirez had been outside his room was when they had first brought him into the house. They had parked the SUV inside the humongous garage and walked him directly to his room. The property was nice and bright, and as he climbed the stairs to the second level, he noticed the stunning views of the surrounding mountains. Ramirez was glad he had picked this option. There were a lot more guards than he had thought—four plus Max and his two friends. There was no way he could have escaped this place.

"Have a seat," Max said, inviting him to the table. Max's friends were already there, enjoying a copious breakfast.

Ramirez's stomach growled.

"Would you like something to eat?" Max asked. "We have cereal, eggs, bacon, toast, and grapefruit juice. Grab whatever you like."

"Thank you," Ramirez said, taking a seat.

Max made the introductions. "This is Aidan Wood, formerly with the New Zealand Special Air Service, and Thomas DeLarue, a French Legionnaire. Gentlemen, this is Jorge Ramirez."

"Former drug dealer, right, mate?" Wood said, his eyes fixed on Ramirez.

Ramirez returned his stare. "You and I aren't much different, you know?" Ramirez said.

"I think we have nothing in common with you," Wood replied.

"But you're wrong," Ramirez said, grabbing a piece of toast. "Do you care to know why?"

Wood shrugged, but DeLarue smiled. "Enlighten me."

———

Max only partly listened to Ramirez's story. He had heard it the day before. In fact, he had used Ramirez's own story to convince him that it was worth joining forces with them. Yes, there was the million-and-a-half payment, but the cause was just too. Since Ramirez was a former paratrooper, he surely understood what they were trying to accomplish. Max had taken the time to explain why he felt compelled to provide financial assistance to the families of special forces operators who had died on clandestine missions but whose deaths had never been properly and fairly compensated. How important it was for these families to be able to live in dignity—instead of on food stamps.

Ramirez's response had surprised him. Since Ramirez had taken the time to listen to Max's story, he had returned the favor. Even though Ramirez had chosen a different path, he'd always fought for the well-being of his countrymen. He had first done so by joining the army and then by doing everything in his power to bring in hard currencies to his country. It was only when the former president's plan had collapsed that Ramirez had sought something for himself.

From the look on Wood's and DeLarue's faces, it appeared that Ramirez was saying the right words. The man was a natural. Either he was sincere, or he was the best actor Max had ever seen.

Max logged into his offshore bank account. His trusted associate had recommended a bank either in the Cayman Islands or in Andorra. Max had selected the Caribbean nation because it had offered him a higher interest rate, and the minimum balance to maintain this rate was much lower than the Andorran banks had offered.

He waited for Ramirez to finish his story, then asked for his bank information. Ramirez angled the laptop toward himself and typed his information in. Max had called in earlier to let the bank know he was about to transfer an important sum of money. The bank manager had promised there would be no hiccups.

Max entered the number he had promised Ramirez: €1,500,000. He showed him for his approval. Ramirez looked at the number, then shook his head. He pressed the delete key and removed one zero. He pushed the laptop back to Max.

Max smiled. "You sure about that? I'm ready to hold up my end of the bargain."

"Nah, I'm good. If we get the amount you talked about, then yes. If not, let's help as many families as we can."

"We?" Max asked, curious about what was pushing Ramirez to join him.

"What choice do I have? My mentors are behind bars, and I'm persona non grata in my own country. Without you, Aidan, and Thomas, I'd be in a Swiss jail by now. I'll tag along for a while, but I do have one question."

"What is it?"

"I'm curious. Who took a shot at me at the hotel?"

DeLarue raised his hand. "C'est moi! But I missed on purpose."

"From a small motorboat about four hundred yards out?"

"How did you know?"

Ramirez smiled at him.

Max looked at Wood and DeLarue. "You guys good with that?" They both gave the thumbs-up.

"All right, then, it's settled," Max said, shaking hands with Ramirez.

They toasted their newly formed alliance by clinking their glasses of grapefruit juice.

"I put everything I have on Queen Bee on a thumb drive," Ramirez said. "It's at the railway station. It's only a two-minute walk from Ristorante AnaCapri. We could go now, but I don't recommend it."

Max thought about it for a moment. "I agree. The Swiss police will have watchers in every public space for the next few days. I don't think I or my men have been spotted or identified, but why take the chance? As for you, we have no idea if you were caught on camera or if the police have your description."

"You could give the instructions to the South Africans," DeLarue suggested.

Max turned to Ramirez. "Are you okay with that?"

Ramirez shrugged. "Fine by me."

Max went to pour himself another cup of coffee. "I have a call to make, then we'll brief the South Africans."

CHAPTER FORTY-FIVE

Lugano, Switzerland

Hunt saw the benefits of partnering with Europol the moment he and his team set foot in the downtown heliport. A black Europol EC145 helicopter was waiting for them as they walked onto the tarmac. Leaning against the helicopter was DEA Special Agent Kleiner. He was dressed in blue jeans, with a dark red polo shirt. His gold DEA badge was clipped to the left side of his belt, next to the two spare magazines for his DEA-issued Glock 22.

Hunt shook Kleiner's hand and made the introductions. They loaded the equipment into the chopper. Two minutes later, they were on their way to Lugano.

Kleiner gave everyone a pair of headphones so they could communicate above the noise. The last time Hunt had climbed aboard a chopper with Carter, Abigail, and Dante, they had been shot down by an RPG. Hunt hoped they'd have more luck this time around.

"Welcome back to the fold, lady and gentlemen," Kleiner said, handing each of them a packet.

Hunt opened his and looked inside. He hadn't expected this. "How did you manage to get that done so fast?" he asked, pulling out his newly minted DEA badge and credentials.

"When the big boss wants something done fast, it gets done. What can I say?"

Abigail and Dante were smiling too. "How long before we get to Lugano?"

"Flight time is approximately twenty minutes," Kleiner said. "That's two-zero minutes."

"Have they identified the bodies they found at the TOC and the apartment?" Hunt asked.

"Two cops were killed yesterday, so everything went into overdrive. So yes, they've already identified the bodies."

"What about Jacobs?" Hunt asked. He felt bad about what he had said to the Swiss police officer when he'd left Jacobs's body behind at the apartment. That was another thing he hated about the CIA. The nonstop secrecy. He understood why she couldn't be identified, but it sucked nonetheless. Jacobs deserved better.

"I took care of her, and Hauer will take care of repatriating her body. Same goes for Pike's and Crawford's," Kleiner said. "It will be done discreetly, of course."

"Means a lot. Thanks," Hunt said. *And thank you, Tom Hauer,* he thought. *From the bottom of my heart.*

"Sorry about your loss," Kleiner said. "You two were close?"

"A friend of mine was," Hunt replied, thinking about Henican. "The men who shot her," he said, changing the subject. "Known criminals?"

"Yes, most of them," Kleiner replied. "Mercenaries. Three of them were former Russian army. I've already sent Hauer everything the Swiss police have found. We should know more by the time we land."

Hunt couldn't believe the difference it made partnering with top law enforcement agencies like Europol and the Swiss police. Compared to the bureaucratic nightmare he'd experienced in Mexico and Afghanistan—where almost all officials needed to be bribed just to pick up a pencil and do their job—the Swiss didn't need to be told twice what to do. Furthermore, when they did something, they did it right the first time.

———

They landed in Lugano exactly twenty-three minutes after takeoff. Hunt was the first to disembark. He grabbed his load-out bag and walked toward a waiting Alfa Romeo Stelvio. The driver's door of the SUV opened, and Simon Carter climbed out. He waved at Hunt and headed toward him.

He took Hunt in his arms and squeezed him in a bear hug.

"Nice to see you too, big guy," Hunt said. "I know I told you we were going fishing this week, but Switzerland isn't half-bad either, right?"

"It's good to see you, brother. Did you get yours?" Carter pointed at the DEA badge clipped to his belt.

"We all did," Hunt replied.

Carter opened the tailgate of the Alfa Romeo SUV and loaded Hunt's bag into the cargo space. He did the same for Abigail's and Dante's bags before handing Hunt an envelope.

"From Anna," he said.

Hunt tore the envelope open. He reached inside and pulled out a handwritten note.

You are the center of my life. You're my happy place.
Be careful. I love you. We love you.

Hunt took a deep breath and smiled.

"All good?" Carter asked.

Hunt nodded.

"Then we should go," Carter said. "There's been a development."

CHAPTER FORTY-SIX

Istanbul Hospital
Istanbul, Turkey

Charlie Henican's eyelids flickered and then snapped open. He tried to focus, but his vision was blurred. His senses were coming back to him slowly, one at a time, like a laptop booting up programs after a shutdown. He tried to move, but the pain in his chest was too much. His limbs were heavy, as if weighted down. He lay on his back, staring up at the ceiling, his brain trying to remember where he was.

"Ha! You're back, Charlie. I'm relieved," a man said to his left.

Henican tried to swallow, but his mouth was too dry. He turned his head toward the voice. The fog in his eyes began to clear. The voice belonged to a medium-height balding man with a dark mustache on a leather-tanned face.

"At one point we were afraid we had lost you," the man said, his voice familiar somehow. "You're lucky that the best surgeon in Turkey was on shift. You weren't breathing when we rescued you."

I'm still in Turkey? Oh shit, Henican thought, wishing they had let him die. He looked down at his hands. They hadn't handcuffed him to his bed. Maybe that was a good sign?

"I'm afraid you'll have to extend your stay in our beautiful country for a few more days," the man said. "You're in no shape to fly."

Simon Gervais

Henican spotted a bottle of water next to the TV set. He pointed at it. The man took the bottle and opened it. He poured some water into a plastic cup and held it so Henican could drink from the straw.

"Thanks," Henican croaked out.

"How are you feeling?"

With the exception of the pain in his chest, he felt numb and heavy. Henican figured they must have him on the good drugs.

"You've done quite a good job, Charlie," the man said. "You killed one of the terrorists who kidnapped you and critically injured two others."

Terrorists? What was the man talking about? He hadn't been kidnapped. He'd been arrested. Major difference between the two, one would think.

Henican cleared his throat and gestured for more water, which the man provided.

"Who are you?" Henican asked.

"You know exactly who I am, Charlie. Don't play games. You were hired to kill Jorge Ramirez. You must have known it was me he was meeting, yes? But since we haven't been formally introduced, I'll play along. My name is Doru Kazak. I'm with the Turkish General Directorate of Security."

Henican had been given a potential time and a place to take care of Ramirez, but he'd never heard the name Doru Kazak before. But it was obvious that Kazak was more than a mere investigator. Men dressed in black battle dress uniforms with no insignia of any kind—just like the men who had arrested him at his hotel and the ones who had accompanied the man wearing the balaclava inside his cell—were standing outside his private hospital room.

That's where I've heard his voice before, Henican thought. *He's the man with the balaclava.* Something in the back of Henican's mind warned him that he'd better keep this piece of newfound intel to himself.

212

"Am I free to go?" Henican asked, his eyes moving to the men standing guard outside his room.

"These men aren't here to restrain you, my friend," Kazak said. "They're here to protect you."

Henican forced a weak smile. "Really? So these aren't the men who dragged me out of my hotel room?"

Doru Kazak stared right at him, face set like stone. He waved a finger at Henican the way one did when warning a child that what he was doing could become perilous. "Don't you want to go home?"

Time to keep your mouth shut. Don't say anything stupid you might regret, Henican thought.

"Of course," he said. "I'd love to go home."

Kazak's features softened again. "You owe Dorothy Triggs a big debt of gratitude."

Now that wasn't something he'd expected to hear. Dorothy Triggs? As far as Henican was concerned, the CIA had left him to die.

Kazak pulled the only chair in the room up to the bed and sat next to Henican.

"You were betrayed by one of your own, Charlie," Kazak said. "And please don't start with the denials. I'm short on time."

Betrayal. That was something he had considered while being beaten almost to death by the two brutes. For the first time in his career, he was being tackled by the ugly side of the business: the possibility that he had become a liability. And in Henican's line of work, liabilities had the tendency to be erased from the equation. Permanently. Henican couldn't think of anything worse than being betrayed by someone he worked with or worked for.

But abandoned? Absolutely. That was part of the game. That was exactly what he'd thought had happened at the storage facility after he had called the emergency number and nobody had shown up. It was also possible that Kazak was playing with his psyche.

"What do you want?" Henican asked.

"I want you to get better, and fast," Kazak replied. "The minute we can move you safely, we'll take you to the US Consulate General."

"Why are you doing this?"

Kazak seemed surprised and maybe even a bit offended by the question. "Why not? That's what your question should have been, Charlie. Why not?"

Kazak paused for a few moments, then said, "We're allies, Charlie. Our countries have fought side by side since World War II. Did you know that?"

Henican nodded. He didn't think that now would be the appropriate time to highlight the fact that Turkey had only joined the war in February 1945, seven months before the end of hostilities.

"How do you know I was betrayed?" Henican asked.

Kazak seemed to consider the question, then said, "What I'm about to tell you, I've learned from the terrorists you locked in your cell."

There were a lot of things that crossed Henican's mind, but since he didn't feel like being a smart-ass, he said, "I understand."

"The leader received a detailed message from Dorothy Triggs's office," Kazak started. "It indicated at which hotel you were staying, the room number, and other interesting pieces of intelligence."

"Interesting pieces of intelligence about what? Jorge Ramirez?"

Kazak shook his head. "You've got it all wrong, Charlie. The intelligence was about you killing our president."

"Intentions you're well aware I never had."

Kazak shrugged and stood up. He put the chair back where it had come from and looked at Henican.

"Someone will need to put your house in order and probably add a new coat of paint too. Because it isn't what it once was. Public opinion in Turkey about the United States isn't favorable. If we are to remain strategic partners, we need to be able to trust each other. We could have taken care of Jorge Ramirez for you. There was no need for you to come to Turkey."

Henican doubted that. Men like Kazak were driven by money and not much else. You couldn't count on them to always do the right thing.

Kazak lit a cigarette and blew his smoke toward the ceiling. "The last thing I'll tell you is this, Charlie. I don't know who leaked your information, but it wasn't Dorothy Triggs."

That got Henican curious. "What makes you so sure?"

Kazak beamed. "Because she's paying me half a million dollars to get you out of here in one piece."

CHAPTER FORTY-SEVEN

Lugano, Switzerland

Hunt's Italian was nonexistent. He'd always wanted to learn the language but seemed to continually find a reason not to. Kleiner, though, was fluent, and Hunt—not for the first time—found himself impressed with the younger special agent. Entering the police station, Kleiner waved at no fewer than half a dozen officers. Whatever Kleiner had done during Operation Familia had impressed a whole lot of Swiss officers.

Since the English of the Swiss police officer they were meeting was as good as Hunt's Italian, Kleiner played a pivotal role in the discussion. Switzerland was seated on the European crossroads of Germany, Italy, and France. The strong imprint of topography mirrored how the Swiss spoke. There was no official Swiss language, so it wasn't uncommon that Swiss citizens living in the Italian-speaking part didn't speak German or French, and vice versa.

"That was interesting," Kleiner said, once the Swiss officer had returned to his desk.

"What did he say?"

"The Russians entered Switzerland through Zurich five days ago."

"Okay. What else?" Hunt asked, sitting behind a desk the local police had set up for him and his team.

"The rest wasn't related to the case," Kleiner said, sitting on a green swivel chair.

"What? You guys spoke nonstop for five minutes! What the hell did you talk about if it wasn't about the case?"

"His sister saw me on TV during the press conference regarding Operation Familia, and she thought I was cute," Kleiner replied.

Hunt laughed. "Really? That's what you guys talked about?"

"Yeah, why? Don't look so surprised."

"I'm not. Good for you. Hope she's hot."

"Oh, she is," Kleiner replied, a big smile on his face. "We've been out together twice already. Her brother doesn't know."

Hunt shook his head. "Be nice with the lady's brother, Kleiner. I'm telling you."

"Anything from Hauer yet?" Kleiner asked, plugging the power cord of a laptop into the wall.

"I'm sure he or Ramer will call as soon as they have something new to report."

The rest of the team came back with sandwiches and coffee. The office space the police had graciously given Hunt's team consisted of several empty filing cabinets and five metal desks with swivel chairs of different colors. There was a computer terminal on Hunt's desk, but he didn't know the password. It seemed that nobody else knew it, either, so he opened his laptop and waited for it to securely connect to the main DEA server.

He was halfway through his second sandwich when his satellite phone rang. Hunt placed the phone on his desk and put the call on speaker.

"Everything okay in Lugano?" Hauer asked.

"We're all here, Tom," Hunt said. "Do you have something for us?"

"I'll let Linda take over, if you don't mind. She's more familiar with this stuff than I'll ever be."

Another reason Hunt enjoyed working for Hauer so much. The man knew how to surround himself with top-quality people and let them do their jobs without too much interference. Hauer's job was to make sure his subordinates had everything they needed to complete their tasks, and he was very good at it.

"Hi, everyone," Ramer said. "I'll start by saying that I wasn't able to get everything I wanted and that I'm still waiting for some answers to my questions.

"We've run all the names of the dead Russians through all our internal and partners' databases. There were several matches. The three Russians that took part in the attack against Pierce in Lugano were former soldiers. Nothing in their military careers is worth mentioning, but they are suspected of working for an arms dealer based in France—someone who's done business with us in the past, I'm afraid to say."

"If the DEA has had dealings with that particular arms dealer, I can assure you the CIA has done the same," Hunt said.

"You have someone in mind, Pierce?" Carter asked. "Someone at the Directorate of Operations, maybe?"

As hard as he tried, Hunt couldn't fathom why Max would need to hire Russian mercenaries. "I'm not sure," he said between sips of coffee. "We're still missing a few pieces of the puzzle."

"Maybe the French arms dealer holds some of these pieces," Abigail suggested. "He'd be a good guy for us to question."

"Agreed, but men like him don't keep an updated website," Carter said. "Is he in France now?"

"We're not sure. The guy moves around a lot. Ireland, Corsica, and Monaco are his places of choice, but he could be anywhere," Ramer replied. "I'll keep digging, and I'll get back to you."

After she hung up, everybody turned to Hunt. "What's wrong?" Carter asked.

Hunt stood behind his desk, leaning forward with the heels of his palms on the edge of the desk. He looked at Carter. "Nothing's wrong, but hear me out for a second."

"Of course," Dante said. "What's on your mind, Pierce?"

"Listen, I'm not saying we shouldn't pursue the arms dealer, but I don't think this should be our primary focus." Already he could see Abigail fidgeting in her chair. "You disagree, Abi?"

"I think it's a great place to start our investigation. The Russians were his mercenaries. I'm sure he knows who hired them."

"And how are you planning on making him talk to us?" Hunt countered. "Men like him have an army of lawyers to take care of folks like us. If we had the money, the manpower, and were playing the long game against him, then sure. We'd end up building a strong case against him, and we'd use it as leverage."

"That's how police work is done," Abigail said.

"You're absolutely right, Abi," Hunt replied. "That would be the way to go if our objective was to send the man to prison or if we wanted to use the intel he'd give us in exchange for his freedom to build a case against someone else."

"I was under the impression that was exactly what we were supposed to do," Kleiner said.

Carter laughed, his fingers laced behind his head. "If that's what you think, you haven't been around him long enough," he said, using his right elbow to point at Hunt.

"What are you proposing?" Kleiner asked.

"I want us to think outside the box. I know I said that Max Oswald represents a bigger threat to our national security than Ramirez. I still think that, but let's not forget that Ramirez isn't a choirboy either. He's an important target too."

"I don't think any of us disagree with you on that," Dante said. "But what do you suggest we do? I thought the arms dealer was a nice starting point too."

Hunt smiled. "I think Ramirez is still in Lugano, hiding somewhere. Waiting for the dust to settle."

"What makes you say that?" Kleiner asked.

"Because that's what I'd do if I was in his shoes. There's probably a safe house in Lugano, or within a fifteen-minute drive of the city center, that the Russians used as their base of operations."

"Are there any doubts that Ramirez is working with the Russians?" Carter asked.

Hunt shook his head from side to side. "Ramirez was right there with the Russians when they surprised us at the apartment. If we find the Russians, we find Ramirez."

"And how do you intend to find the Russians' safe house?" Kleiner asked.

"Watch and learn, Kleiner. Watch and learn."

CHAPTER FORTY-EIGHT

Palm Cay Marina
New Providence, Commonwealth of the Bahamas

Anna Garcia had only a couple of pages left to read in her book when her phone began to vibrate. It vibrated for a couple of seconds, then stopped. Then started again. She closed her Kindle e-reader and picked up her phone.

"Who's this?"

"Good morning, baby," Hunt said. "How are you?"

Just the sound of his voice was enough to make her smile. He had been gone for less than a week, and already she missed him.

"You got my note?"

"I did, and it warmed my heart."

"When are you coming back? Me and the girls miss you, and I know Chris and Jasmine won't leave before you take Chris out to the Exumas on the boat."

"Believe me, I can't wait to be back. The sooner the better," he replied. "Do you think you could help me speed up the process?"

Anna sat up straighter in her lounge chair. "What do you need?"

"Where are you? At home?"

"Yes, I was reading on the beach," she said. "Everybody else is still sleeping."

"I need you to hack a couple of servers for me," Hunt said.

"Anything sexy?" she asked, swinging her legs off the lounge chair.

"Not really," Hunt replied. "Just a few home-rental websites."

Anna sat on the terrace and powered up her laptop. "Thinking about hacking your way to a cheap vacation?" she asked, pushing her hair away from her face with her sunglasses and adjusting them on top of her head.

"I wish it was that," Hunt replied.

"What's it about, then?"

"I believe Jorge Ramirez is still in Lugano. I need you to see if you can find a rental property that fits the description me and the team came up with."

Anna opened a new Word document and started to write down all the websites she knew that provided this type of service. "Understood. What are the features you want me to cross-reference with the listings?"

"The property needs to be at least three thousand square feet, indoor garage spaces for at least two large vehicles, and within twenty minutes' drive of Lugano."

Anna typed all the information into the Word document. She would enter all the criteria into an algorithm later. "What else?"

"The property needs at least four bedrooms and two bathrooms."

"Got it. What about the dates? Any minimum or maximum length of stay?"

Hunt gave her the dates and told her she should look for stays with a minimum of five nights but no longer than six weeks.

"Any specific instructions about payment methods?" Anna asked.

"No credit cards," Hunt replied. "We need properties that accept cash, prepaid credit, or cryptocurrencies."

"That should shrink the results nicely," she said.

"How long do you need, babe?"

"Depends how long it takes me to get into the different websites," she said, already attacking the first server on her list.

"Give me an estimate."

"For a lot of the things you asked for, I won't need access to the servers. I simply need to use a cross-reference program compatible with the different websites and run the parameters. That should take me less than thirty minutes."

"You're the absolute best," Hunt said. "And next time I ask you to do this, I promise it'll be so we can take that vacation in Bora Bora."

CHAPTER FORTY-NINE

CIA headquarters
Langley, Virginia

Dorothy Triggs closed her laptop just in time to see CIA director Walter Helms stride into her office, briefcase in hand.

"Good morning," Helms said as he placed his briefcase on her desk. He flipped the catches and opened it.

"Is it?" Triggs asked.

"I told you I'd take care of the leak for you," Helms said, dropping a yellow folder in front of her. "This came overnight from the Office of Information Technology. Take a look, read it through, and let me know what you want to do about it."

"Okay."

Helms closed his briefcase and walked out of her office, closing the door behind him.

Triggs looked across her desk at the folder. Had Helms already found the leak? She had first spoken to him about it the night before. Everything was easier when you were the D/CIA. As powerful as she was within the Directorate of Operations, she had very little control over what was going on in the other four directorates. For example, the Office of Information Technology reported to the Directorate of Support and wouldn't entertain a work order from her if the official request wasn't initiated from their own directorate.

She reached across the desk and pulled the folder toward her. With a sigh she opened it. Her heart sank as she read the report over. She felt as if she'd just fallen from a tall building. At least she knew who else had betrayed her.

Andrew Collings.

Collings was one of the two analysts who had worked on the Swiss operation. He was a real tech whiz, a longtime analyst she'd trusted. Why had he betrayed her?

She continued reading, sick to her stomach.

Collings's brother Kirk, a father of four and an air force pararescueman with the Twenty-Fourth Special Operations Wing, had been killed during a combat search and rescue mission in Afghanistan less than six months ago. Kirk's wife, Elizabeth, had been paid the $100,000 death gratuity she was entitled to receive but had lost it all in a scam run by remorseless assholes based in India. Desperate and about to lose the family home, she had turned to Andrew for help. Unwilling to say no to his brother's grieving wife, Andrew had hacked the Department of Defense mainframe and issued a second $100,000 payment to Elizabeth. He had left no bread crumbs behind. He had cleaned every system log and program he'd used to complete the transaction. The only thing Andrew hadn't planned for was a surprise polygraph test less than thirty days after his crime.

Holy shit! How the fuck did I miss this? Triggs got her answer a few paragraphs later.

It seemed that the polygraph examiner had reported the inconsistencies in Andrew's test to Max. Max had told the examiner that the office of the deputy director would take it from there, but there was no record of Max taking the appropriate steps to fire Andrew. And more money had gone missing after that—$10 million this time, from a CIA black ops fund. The rest was easy to conclude. Triggs's son had been an expert at recruiting sources in Turkey as a NOC; she was sure he'd had no difficulty convincing Andrew to help him steal more money in exchange for his silence.

Triggs was floored. Had Max arranged the ambush in the Bahamas so he could escape with the stolen funds? But why had they tanked the Swiss operation? Why had they betrayed Henican and made it look like it had come from her office?

It tore her apart to know she'd never see Max again. What had begun as a growing suspicion had become an unshakable conviction. With what he had done, there was no way he had any intention of coming back.

What she still couldn't wrap her head around was the why. But now, thanks to Walter Helms, she knew who to ask. Triggs opened the bottom drawer of her desk and grabbed the Taurus 856 UltraLite .38 compact revolver. She balanced it in her hand. It had been a while since she'd last fired it, but for what she had in mind, she didn't need to be a sharpshooter. She opened the cylinder and checked that the revolver was unloaded. She grabbed six bullets from the same drawer and loaded them into the cylinder before she snapped it back in place.

She put the .38 in her purse and left her office, waving at her secretary as she walked past her desk.

CHAPTER FIFTY

Lugano, Switzerland

Max Oswald closed the door behind him and punched a long-distance number into a phone he used only to call one person, a mentor who'd helped him from the beginning. Who'd even planted the seed for Max's plan by first calling his attention to the country's deeply unfair treatment of its special ops veterans.

His associate replied on the first ring. "How's it going?"

"After a few initial hiccups, we're back on track."

Max heard a sigh of relief. "I'm happy to hear that. For a while I was wondering if you were going to pull this off."

Me too, thought Max. But he kept his opinion to himself. "We're not done yet, but I should have the thumb drive within the hour."

"You think he's bluffing? You think there's another thumb drive hidden somewhere? Did he threaten you by saying that if anything happened to him—"

"No!" Max interrupted. "He's joined us. He understands what we're doing and why."

"He's a loose end, Max."

The words cut him off at the knees. Max clenched the phone so tightly that his knuckles blanched. "What are you saying?" he asked.

"Kill him," his associate said before cutting the line.

Max shook his head in disgust. He was so tired of this shit. He had always known there would be collateral damage, but never had he imagined it would be so much. They were supposed to help the families of fallen soldiers, not create more grief.

Fuck!

His associate didn't seem to understand that, and Max was starting to wonder if he wasn't being used for another purpose. But what could that purpose be? His mentor had lost someone, too, just like Max had lost his Zehra—it was one of the things they had in common. Was Max about to be double-crossed? That wasn't something he was ready to accept.

Or forgive.

Max cursed out loud and threw his phone across the room with all his strength. It shattered on impact, littering the hardwood floor with sharp pieces of plastic.

"Fuck!" he yelled, louder than he had intended. He had shaken Ramirez's hand. They had agreed on something. Max had given him his word. And now he was supposed to kill him? To what end? What would it accomplish?

And what about me? Max thought. Would he become a loose end too? And Wood? And DeLarue?

Goddamn it!

"Everything okay?" someone said behind him.

Max turned. It was Wood, his eyes on the broken phone.

"What happened?" he asked. "Who the hell were you talking with to get so mad?"

Caught off guard, Max didn't know what to answer. Wood took a step toward him. "Who were you talking to, mate?"

"It was the broker I dealt with for the Russians," Max lied. "He screwed me."

"What did he say?"

"No discount," Max replied. "And he wanted me to compensate him because they're all dead and said he'll never again be able to make money off them."

"Piece of shit," Wood said. "Screw him."

"That's what I told him," Max said, sidestepping Wood. "C'mon, Aidan, let's get out of here."

CHAPTER FIFTY-ONE

Lugano, Switzerland

For the third time in the last hour, Hunt used a laser pointer to indicate on the wall map where he wanted each member of his team to be and repeated precisely what was expected from them.

Anna had come back to him with six likely homes that matched the characteristics he had given her. Using the Swiss police and Europol resources, Hunt had narrowed down the choices to only two properties. Like most high-end rental homes, the owners had given their properties exciting names—one was named Eagle Nest, while the second one was called Mountain Heaven—so that the people who were renting them could use the names on social media, offering the owners free publicity. Hunt had been about to order the team to conduct surveillance on both properties when Abigail had notified the team that someone had just posted a story on Instagram with the hashtag #MountainHeaven. The photos showed action shots of a happy multigenerational family reunion. In some of the photos, the property was clearly visible.

Having only one property to stake out made Hunt's life much easier. Kleiner had asked for and received authorization to conduct a surveillance operation in the canton of Ticino.

"I know we've been through this twice already, but I want to make sure everybody understands their assignment. Any questions?" Hunt asked.

There were none.

"Okay, then. Let's go grab our gear and meet at the vehicles in ten," Hunt said.

CHAPTER FIFTY-TWO

Lugano, Switzerland

Max called a general meeting in the living room. The only two people not attending were the South African mercenaries assigned to the exterior patrol and CCTV monitors.

"This will be an easy get-in, get-out scenario," Max started. "You'll take two SUVs and head down to the train station, where Jorge has secured the thumb drive we need. I'll be keeping a bird's-eye view of the situation with real-time drone footage."

Max pointed to one of the mercenaries and said, "You'll get out of the vehicle two blocks away and take the rest on foot. You'll look for police officers—uniformed or plainclothes—and call me back with updates. Depending on the situation, you'll either return to the vehicle or enter the train station. If I give you the go-ahead, you'll once again be my eyes and ears inside the terminal. Go get a coffee or a piece of cake and take your time. Anything suspicious, you let me know. Understood?"

"Yes, sir."

"At that time, if nothing's sketchy, Jorge will disembark, get the thumb drive from his locker. The rest of you will stay in the vehicles and will only come out if there's a problem.

"Before you leave," Max continued, "I want you to read your packets about your personal exit strategy. Make sure you have all your documents in case everything turns to shit. You get me?"

Everybody did. Even Ramirez gave him a thumbs-up.

CHAPTER FIFTY-THREE

Lugano, Switzerland

Hunt had divided the team into three groups. He and Carter were on foot and had taken position about five hundred meters from Eagle Nest. They were on the southwestern side of the house, just in from the tree line, giving them an uninterrupted view of the front of the property and its underground-garage access door. Abigail and Dante were deployed on the northeastern side of the property, using small bushes and tall trees to conceal themselves from view.

Kleiner was in the Alfa Romeo, ready to follow a vehicle if needed in order to identify its occupants.

It hadn't taken long for Hunt to confirm that it was the right house—or at least that something suspicious and worth investigating was happening there. The lone guard walking the grounds made it easy. Hunt couldn't say for sure if the guard was armed. No bulges were noticeable from his position. He brought his long-lens camera up to his eye, making sure the camouflage material was over the lens so it wouldn't reflect light and alert anyone who might be looking in their direction, and took a number of shots of the guard. The pictures were automatically uploaded to a special cloud accessible to the TOC back at DEA headquarters in Virginia.

Linda Ramer's voice cracked in his earbud. "Delta-One, this is Nimitz, over."

"Go ahead for Delta-One."

"Pictures received, Delta-One. We've identified the guard as South African. He served with the One Parachute Battalion."

"Anything else?"

"He has a rap sheet in the US. Fifty-one years old. Was arrested in Atlanta two years ago for carrying a concealed weapon during a sporting event. He served fifteen days in jail and paid a one-thousand-dollar fine."

"Delta-One copy."

Hunt made sure his team had received the information. They all had.

They had been in position for just over two hours when the front door of the property opened. Hunt took more photos that were beamed directly to the TOC for analysis. It took less than three minutes for the DEA's facial recognition and data mining programs to begin returning hits. The second guard was also from South Africa and had served with the same parachute battalion. Hunt was certain that the guards were mercenaries. That brought up more questions: Who had hired them, and why? What was their mission?

"All Delta call signs, this is Delta-One for a message, over." Hunt waited five seconds, then said, "We're now facing an unknown number of South African mercenaries. They're most probably armed and dangerous."

"Delta-Five copy," Kleiner came in. "I'll advise the Swiss police and The Hague."

As much as Hunt wanted to keep the operation low profile, he had to keep their partner agencies in the loop. This wasn't a covert mission. If something bad happened to a civilian because his team hadn't communicated essential intelligence to their partners, Hunt and his team could face criminal charges. Switzerland wasn't known for giving foreign agents a lot of wiggle room when operating inside its borders. They'd been lucky—thanks to Kleiner—to obtain permission to

conduct surveillance. The last thing Hunt wanted was to get his team pulled from the operation because of his lack of transparency.

Thirty minutes later, the garage door leading to the underground garage opened.

"Are you seeing that?" Carter asked.

Hunt brought his camera to his eye and zoomed in on the garage door. Out of the garage, the driveway was a straight line leading to the street, allowing Hunt to see clearly inside the vehicles through their windshields, which weren't tinted like the rest of the SUVs' windows. Hunt took more than two dozen pictures before the first SUV was even out of the garage. To his right, Carter was warning the rest of the team.

"Delta-Five from Delta-Two, over," Carter said.

"Go ahead for Delta-Five."

"Be advised that two dark-colored BMW SUVs are on their way to you."

"Delta-Five copy."

Since the second SUV was following the first one so closely, Hunt had only half a second to take pictures of its occupants before it turned at the end of the driveway. Even though he was only able to snap one sequence of three photos, he knew he had hit the jackpot.

CHAPTER FIFTY-FOUR

CIA headquarters
Langley, Virginia

Triggs had tempered her anger by the time she walked into Andrew Collings's office space. The analyst's cubicle was at the end of an open-floor office space where dozens of gray cubicles lined the walls.

Analysts got far less fanfare than the case officers most people imagined were the face of the CIA. For every Charlie Henican and Pierce Hunt, there were two dozen analysts like Andrew Collings. No movies were ever made about a middle-aged man with two PhDs sitting in an office cubicle reading and creating reports. Triggs didn't see that movie ever becoming a blockbuster either. But in many ways, it was the analysts who did the most important work for the agency. In fact, the good ones—and there were many of them—gathered strands of information, vetted them, then put them together to form the true picture of a given situation. This was the picture the operators in the field needed to succeed. Triggs had always compared the work of a CIA analyst to building a forest from the descriptions of individual trees observed in a deserted field. The very best of them provided not just an arrangement of information but also the context within which said forest needed to be viewed.

She didn't know why Andrew and Max had betrayed Henican and the agents on the Swiss operation, but she was going to find out.

When Triggs arrived at Andrew's cubicle, the analyst was gone, and for a brief moment she panicked. Had he somehow seen the report Helms had prepared for her? She walked to the next cubicle and asked the woman there if she'd seen him today.

"He was called to the seventh floor," the analyst said, not bothering to look up from the transcript she was reading. "He was escorted by security officers."

Damn it! Walter Helms had told Triggs she could decide how she wanted to handle the report. Instead, he'd sent for Andrew before she could talk to him. It was certainly Helms's prerogative to do so as D/CIA, and if she was honest, she understood why he'd done it. He didn't trust her not to be emotional when her son was involved. The weight of the .38 in her purse forced her to admit he was right.

Still, she wished he had given her some one-on-one with Andrew, who was undoubtedly already calling his lawyers and clamming up. With Andrew under arrest and inaccessible, never knowing what had happened to Max was a real possibility.

And she wasn't ready to accept that just yet.

CHAPTER FIFTY-FIVE

Lugano, Switzerland

Hunt considered the overall situation and decided there was no point staying put. There was a real possibility that Jorge Ramirez wouldn't be returning to his safe house. In addition to Ramirez, Hunt had counted two more men in the second SUV and four men in the first.

"Delta-One, this is Delta-Five, over."

"Go ahead for One."

"Vehicle One and Vehicle Two just passed my position. They're headed toward Lugano. I'll give them plenty of room to maneuver."

"Delta-One copy," said Hunt, slowly backing up toward the tree line. To his right, Simon Carter was doing the same.

"One, this is Five. One more thing," Kleiner came in. "Swiss police have been advised, and numerous plainclothes officers are being deployed within the city limits."

"This is One, good copy."

There wasn't much else that Hunt could do. He wished the Swiss police could have stayed back and simply acted in reserve, but that wasn't a realistic expectation. Two of their own had been killed in the line of duty the day before—the rest of them wanted revenge.

"Delta-Three and Four from One," Hunt said.

"Go ahead," Abigail replied.

"One and Two are going back to the vehicle and will head toward Lugano."

"Three and Four copy. Where do you want us?"

"Four, stay put. Three, come to my position," Hunt replied. "Nimitz, did you copy our last?"

"Delta-One, this is Nimitz. We copy."

This way Hunt would keep eyes on the residence while also having a presence in the city.

Once they were twenty feet into the tree line, Hunt packed his camera equipment in his bag while Carter covered him with his M4.

They double-timed back to the Alfa Romeo. A minute later, they were in the SUV and on their way to Lugano.

CHAPTER FIFTY-SIX

Lugano, Switzerland

Jorge Ramirez was in the back seat of the BMW X5, a Sig SG 551 assault rifle at his feet—just in case trouble found them. Even closer, holstered on his right hip, was a Glock 17 with three spare magazines. One of the mercenaries was driving, and Aidan Wood occupied the front passenger seat. The men were quarreling about who had the best rugby team, South Africa or New Zealand. Wood kept repeating the fact that in head-to-head matches, the All Blacks had won more often, a point the South African mercenary conceded. That said, he was trying to convince a stoic Wood that the Springboks had won the most important game of all time when they had captured the attention of the world in 1995 with Joel Stransky's extra-time drop goal, which had secured South Africa their first Rugby World Cup.

Ramirez was only half listening to their debate; his eyes scanned the streets for possible threats. So far, Ramirez hadn't seen a greater police presence than usual, which was a relief. He was surprised how much he wanted to get the thumb drive out of the train station terminal. Max Oswald, a former CIA officer and someone he hardly knew, inspired him. Ramirez believed that Max was fighting for a just cause but remained cognizant that their odds of success weren't high. That was fine with him. He had faced worse odds than this before.

And I'm still here, Ramirez thought.

"We're almost there, mate," Wood told him. A couple hundred yards later, the driver parked the SUV.

"They've deployed the drone," Wood said, pulling his phone from his jeans pocket. He played with it for a minute, then showed the display to Ramirez.

"That's the drone footage?" Ramirez asked.

"Yeah. Max is flying it from the safe house. My phone serves as a booster. That means he can control it from pretty much anywhere in the world, as long as our phones are connected."

Ramirez didn't care much about the specifications. He was most interested in the two black sedans that had just entered the drone's field of view.

———

A few seconds after the first vehicle launched the drone, Max took over its commands with the controller, with his phone serving as a display. He brought the DJI Mavic 2 Pro to an altitude of three hundred meters and assessed the comings and goings around the train station. The terminal was quite busy, which was both a blessing and a curse. It was a blessing because it would be easier for Ramirez to blend in with the crowd and a curse because this was also true for plainclothes police officers.

The Mavic 2 Pro might have been more costly than its competitors, but Max had convinced himself it was worth the extra money for its wind-resistant software. Even with a wind speed of twenty-five knots, he didn't need to constantly adjust the controls. Without any input from Max, the drone could stay in a static position until it ran out of battery life. The only drawback was its actual flight time. Despite the thirty-minute flight time claimed by the manufacturer, Max had never been able to fly the drone for longer than twenty-two minutes before he'd been required to change the battery.

Using his iPad, Max sent a text message to DeLarue asking him to give the go-ahead to the South African mercenary tasked with the initial reconnaissance of the train station. Moments later, Max was tracking the mercenary's progress with the drone. At the bottom of his screen, he noticed two dark sedans slowly driving through the area. One of the sedans found a parking spot, but the other kept driving around. No one climbed out of the sedan, but from its position the sedan's occupants could easily see the east entrance of the train station.

Surveillance? Could be. They expected it, and Max wasn't overly concerned. The second sedan had finally found a place to park a couple of blocks away. Two men climbed out—the driver and a passenger. One man went south and the other north.

Max sent a message to Wood and DeLarue, letting them know about the two sedans and the two possible plainclothes officers. He was about to return his attention to the mercenary, who had reached the terminal, when he noticed more men converging on the train station.

Then the blood in his veins ran cold.

Should he call off the operation? If he did it now, there was still a chance for Ramirez and his men to get out of the X. If he waited longer, their odds of escaping would be greatly diminished.

Damn it! He dialed Wood's number and waited for him to pick up. Every second counted. Why wasn't he picking up? He tried again. Same results. He punched in DeLarue's number.

"Qu'est-ce qui se passe? Everything okay?" asked DeLarue.

"I'm calling it off," replied Max, looking at the display. "Get out of there now!"

"Merde! What about the thumb drive?"

"Just go! We'll figure something out."

There was a moment of silence at the other end. And then the firefight began.

CHAPTER FIFTY-SEVEN

Lugano, Switzerland

Hunt knew something was about to go down when Kleiner couldn't get through to the Swiss police. They had used Hunt and his team to identify the target, then cut them out of the loop. Hunt wasn't mad. He understood. Two of their own had been assassinated in broad daylight.

Hunt had parked the Alfa Romeo on a side street close to the train station terminal. "Delta-Five, this is One. Do you know where they are?" he asked for the third time.

"Sorry, One. I was on the phone with my local contact. The Swiss police are taking them down. The two BMWs are parked at the Lugano train terminal. Do you know where it is?"

Hunt and Carter looked at each other. "We're close to the train station. Can you be more specific?"

"Sorry, guys, I can't. That's all I know. I'm making my way there too."

Hunt turned off the engine, and both men climbed out of the SUV and walked back around the car. Hunt opened the tailgate, grabbed two specially marked DEA bulletproof vests, and handed one to Carter. Hunt fastened the Velcro straps around his body and put a blue DEA jacket on top. He fetched his HK416 rifle from his load-out bag and grabbed two extra magazines and put them in his jacket's pockets.

"All set?" he asked Carter.

In response, Carter held out his fist. Hunt gave him a bump.

Hunt's DEA jacket made him a target for Ramirez and his men, but it also identified him as a police officer to the Swiss police.

"Delta-Five from One. What's your twenty?" Hunt said over the radio.

"One . . . this is Five. I'm on foot and two minutes out," Kleiner replied, slightly out of breath, as if he'd been running. "I'm coming in from the lower platform."

"Copy that, Delta-Five. Also, I know they might not respond to you, but let the Swiss police know that three armed DEA agents are in the area," Hunt said.

"Already done."

Hunt and Carter were just walking past the front bumper of the Alfa Romeo when the first shots rang out. Hunt dropped to one knee, his rifle scanning for threats. The shots hadn't been directed at them. A few pedestrians, not knowing what the sounds were or what they meant, had simply stopped walking. Hunt yelled at them to take cover behind the vehicles.

Carter tapped on his shoulder, letting Hunt know that he was ready to go. Hunt stood up and, with Carter behind him, methodically combat walked toward the train station.

CHAPTER FIFTY-EIGHT

Lugano, Switzerland

Ramirez tensed at the unexpected sound of gunfire, and his hand automatically moved to his pistol. He pulled it out of his holster and pressed it against his thigh.

The mercenary restarted the BMW just as two police cars raced past them. Ramirez figured they were going after the other vehicle. The mercenary looked at Wood for instructions, but it was Ramirez who told him what to do.

"Get me to the train station. I'll get the thumb drive."

"Are you crazy, mate?" Wood asked him. "They've made us."

"I don't think they have. Are you seeing anyone shooting at us? Go!"

The mercenary pulled out of the parking spot and sped toward the train station. As they drove past the street where the other BMW X5 was parked, Ramirez saw that three police cars had boxed in the German SUV.

Wood had seen it, too, because Ramirez heard him swear. Ten seconds later, the driver slammed on the brakes, and the BMW came to a stop a few steps away from the main terminal door. "If I'm not back in sixty seconds, leave," Ramirez told the driver as he rushed out of the SUV. He had left the rifle on the floor of the BMW and was only

carrying his pistol inside the train station. He pulled his shirt over his holster, hoping not to attract undue attention. Ramirez walked fast but didn't run, trying to keep his pace even and casual. His heart beat faster, and he forced himself to breathe deeply. Every fiber in his body told him to run, and for an instant, he considered dumping the pistol in a garbage bin and taking the next train to Milan. He had shaken Max's hand, but had he done so during a moment of weakness? He didn't owe anything to anyone.

Out of the main corridor, he turned left toward the escalators up ahead and saw three uniformed police officers standing next to them, their ears pressed against their radios. Ramirez assumed their dispatcher was notifying them of the shooting and hoped they'd be running outside to assist their colleagues. That didn't happen. Instead, they stayed there and sized up everyone who came up or down the escalators. Ramirez fought the urge to turn around. He put his hands in his pockets, hoping that would hide the bulge of his pistol. The officers were thirty or forty paces away now and were scrutinizing everyone walking by. But so far Ramirez hadn't seen them stop or talk to anyone.

Twenty paces now. One of the officers was looking straight at him, but Ramirez didn't make eye contact. He could feel the man's eyes scanning his body up and down. Ramirez was conscious of his pistol and the extra magazines on his hip and wondered if the officers could sense it.

Ramirez was now shoulder to shoulder with the first officer. Another few steps and he'd be past them and on his way to the lower floor to retrieve the thumb drive.

"Signore?" one of the officers said.

Ramirez kept walking, pretending he hadn't heard.

"Mi scusi, signore!" This time the voice was much louder. Ramirez couldn't pretend he hadn't heard the officer.

He stopped only a few steps from the escalator. He turned around. Ramirez saw the adrenaline rush in the officer's eyes as he recognized

him. The officer's mouth opened, surprise flickering in his eyes, and his hand moved to his holster. By the time the officer's finger pressed the release mechanism of his holster, Ramirez had already drawn his pistol.

He shot the Swiss officer in the mouth once, then angled his pistol to the officer to the immediate right. He squeezed the trigger again. His round struck the officer in the side of the head, and he sank to the floor. The third officer, though, was much faster. Instead of reaching for his firearm, the man rushed the five or six feet between himself and Ramirez. By the time Ramirez moved his gun toward him, the officer was already on him. The officer's right shoulder rammed Ramirez just above his navel. Ramirez was driven backward into the partition between the two escalators. He struck the officer between the shoulder blades with his left elbow with all his might. The man's knees buckled, giving Ramirez the chance to aim his pistol at the man's back.

Ramirez fired. The bullet came out of the gun off angle and hit the officer in the lower back. His legs collapsed and he fell on his ass. Ramirez kicked him hard under the chin, knocking him unconscious. All of this had taken less than ten seconds. All around him people had stopped walking. Children were pointing in his direction. A young man, no more than fifteen by Ramirez's estimate, snapped a photo of him and gave him a thumbs-up. For some reason, that made Ramirez very sad.

A woman screamed. The scream found an echo, then another. And suddenly the whole terminal was filled with fear.

Then someone tackled Ramirez from behind.

Ramirez was hit so hard that his head whipped back and smacked into the head of his attacker. His pistol flew from his hand. Ramirez landed face-first on the ground, his attacker on top of him. Ramirez felt every last bit of air leave his lungs. Then he was viciously punched behind the head, and almost immediately, his right arm was painfully brought to his back, then his left.

Ramirez turned his head. The man on top of him was wearing a blue jacket. The letters *DEA* were clearly visible.

"Jorge Ramirez, you're under arrest for murder," the DEA special agent said as he closed the cuff around Ramirez's right wrist.

Then three shots rang out in quick succession. Something warm hit him on his cheek. The next thing he knew, the DEA agent fell to the floor at his side.

CHAPTER FIFTY-NINE

Lugano, Switzerland

Hunt saw where the initial shots had come from. As he and Carter were crossing the last intersection before reaching the train station, he saw that three police cars had boxed in a BMW X5. Officers had taken cover behind their vehicles and had fired on someone. That person now sprawled in the street halfway between the police cars and the BMW.

One of the officers, armed with a megaphone, was giving instructions to at least two other people who had barricaded themselves in the BMW. Hunt made the decision to keep going toward the train station since the cops seemed to have gained control of the situation.

"Are you hearing this?" Carter asked him.

Hunt paid close attention but didn't hear anything suspicious. Thanks to too many gunfights, his hearing wasn't as good as it used to be.

"There it is again," Carter said.

Carter pointed. Hunt looked up but didn't see it right away. There was indeed a quiet whooshing sound. Then he saw it. A small drone. It was zipping back and forth between the terminal and the BMW. As they approached the train station terminal, the whooshing grew closer, and Hunt heard a chirp. He looked up again, and there was the drone.

Hunt had a feeling that he and Carter were going to make the evening news. Suddenly, people rushed out of the train station, their faces twisted with alarm.

Something had spooked them.

"Delta-One from Five. Shots fired inside the train station. Shots fired!"

Kleiner's words were like a double shot of adrenaline. Hunt led the way toward the east entrance of the train station. Freaked-out people were running past him and Carter without paying them much attention— which surprised Hunt since they were scanning left and right with their rifles up. Then, amid the chaos surrounding them, Hunt noticed the idling black BMW parked in front of the main entrance. His eyes moved to its license plate.

"This is one of Ramirez's vehicles," Hunt said, approaching the vehicle from behind.

"Roger that."

Since the sun was up and in front of the vehicle, the brightness it brought into the vehicle's interior allowed Hunt to scan inside despite the tinted windows. It took him an extra half second to realize the driver was aiming a pistol at him.

"Gun!" Hunt shouted, ducking behind the SUV just as the rear windshield exploded.

Hunt heard the driver's door open and rolled to his left in time to see one of the South African mercenaries climb out of the SUV, his pistol pointing toward the rear of the vehicle.

Hunt fired twice, both rounds slamming into the mercenary's chest. He dropped like a stone. Hunt got up and approached. A large red stain covered the mercenary's chest. His breathing was slow and shallow, but his eyes were open. Dimples appeared as a devilish smile flashed across his face. Then he stopped breathing.

Hunt joined Carter, who'd already cleared the vehicle. Hunt tapped him on the shoulder, and they entered the terminal just as three quick shots were fired.

CHAPTER SIXTY

Just north of Lugano, Switzerland

Max couldn't believe what he was seeing with the drone. DeLarue and one of the mercenaries were in custody, while the driver of the other BMW had been killed by Pierce Hunt. Max had been so close to—but at the same time so far from—his objective. There was so much more work to do. He longed for Wood and Ramirez to use their heads and the exfiltration plan he'd given them and leave with the thumb drive. Max sure hoped they weren't thinking about coming back to the safe house, because if they did, they would be by themselves. He'd be long gone.

He feared that his safe house had been compromised, despite the precautions he'd taken. How else could the police have found them so quickly? They had locked in on them the minute they'd reached Lugano. Max wondered if the Swiss police were on their way to arrest him. Maybe. If that was the case, he wouldn't resist.

But there was one more thing he wanted to do. One more person to apologize to.

His mother.

CHAPTER SIXTY-ONE

CIA headquarters
Langley, Virginia

Triggs didn't even bother acknowledging Walter Helms's secretary as she barged into his office.

"What is this?" she shouted.

In Helms's office were two CIA uniformed police officers and the analyst Andrew Collings—who was crying.

Helms looked at her. The director was angry, furious. "What are you doing here?" he barked.

"Well, excuse me if I forgot to make an appointment, but I hope you understand how pissed I am right now. What's this microbe doing here?" Triggs pointed her finger at Andrew.

Helms looked at the two police officers. "Please leave us, gentlemen," he said. "And be kind enough to ask my secretary to lock the door. I don't want to be disturbed."

Without a word, the two officers left Helms's office, nodding at Triggs on the way.

"Care to explain?" Triggs asked. "And what is he doing without handcuffs? What the hell is he doing here? Why bring him to your office?"

Helms sighed and looked at his watch.

"You have somewhere else you'd rather be? For Chrissakes, Walter!"

"Have a seat, Dorothy," Helms said, walking to his small bar.

"No, I'm not going to sit down, Walter."

"As you wish," Helms said, pouring himself a glass of orange juice and making it a point not to offer her one. "Things are a bit murkier than we thought."

"What does that even mean?" Triggs asked, her voice rising and her anger finally boiling over. "Max hacked my entire—"

"But that's not entirely true, is it, Dorothy?" cut in Helms, stepping toward her. His face had turned red, and a vein had begun to pulsate near his left eye. "He didn't *hack* your system; you gave him all your goddamn passwords and access codes."

"Are you accusing me of something, Walter?"

"How long did you know your son was still alive? That he'd betrayed his country?" Helms asked.

For a fleeting moment, Triggs thought about shooting the prick. How dare he accuse her of any wrongdoing? But escalating to the point of no return wasn't the solution; she needed to understand the situation.

"I came to you the moment I learned Max was alive. You know that."

"Do I?"

"Damn it, Walter! I've read the entire file you dropped on my desk. There's nothing complicated about this," Triggs said, fuming. "We know the how. Max sold us out, with Andrew's help. What I want to know is why. Why did he order the killing at the TOC? Why did he want to kill Hunt and Jacobs? I wasn't even aware that ten million dollars had disappeared from the black budget before I read the last page of your report."

Triggs was a volcano ready to erupt. In fact, she wanted to explode. But Helms seemed entirely uninterested in what she was saying. "The first report I gave you this morning was incomplete. My apologies, Dorothy. I should have waited until I had all the facts. We made a mistake about who was ultimately responsible."

Helms's last words hit her: *made a mistake about who was ultimately responsible.*

"Are you telling me Max and Andrew aren't behind all of this?" she asked.

Andrew had started to cry again, mumbling stuff that didn't make sense. It was driving Triggs nuts. "Are you kidding me? Why are you crying, you goddamn misfit?"

She only got more sobbing from Andrew in response.

"If not him or Max, then who? I read the whole report, and there's no mention of anyone else."

"We've revised the report with our new findings."

"New findings? What new findings? You're making no sense, Walter."

"Feel free to read the revised version. I'm sure you'll find it intriguing. It's on my desk." Helms pointed to a document. "Go read it."

Triggs gave him a look of pure scorn.

"You'd be an excellent stage actress, Dorothy. Anyone else ever told you that?"

She grabbed the document and flipped it open. *Why's my picture attached to the top page?*

She read the first two pages in less than three minutes. She felt nauseated. Whoever had written the report had done his very best to make it look like she'd been working with her son all along. That *she* had been the architect of it all. That *she* had stolen over $10 million from the CIA black budget fund. The second page of the report included the time and date of all the communications she'd supposedly had with her son and a bunch of Russian mercenaries who had murdered the CIA officers in Switzerland. It was all bullshit.

She suddenly felt an enormous pressure building up in her chest. Her knees shook under her, and Triggs thought she was going to swoon. She steadied herself by holding the edge of the desk with one hand. She looked at Helms, who was now standing in front of her across the desk.

"What the fuck is this? Did you write this?" Triggs asked, holding the report in her free hand.

"Keep reading, Dorothy. It gets even more interesting toward the end," Helms said. "The evidence against you is overwhelming."

This isn't happening, Triggs thought.

Before she could turn the page, her personal cell phone rang. She thought about letting it go to voicemail but changed her mind. Rushing to retrieve it out of her purse before the call went to voicemail, she knocked her purse to its side, her small revolver sliding out onto Helms's table. She quickly pushed it back into her purse, but it was too late: Helms had seen it and was staring at her in disapproval. She ignored him and looked at the call display.

Maximus Oswald.

No. It can't be. Her legs became wobbly, and she had to sit down. She sat in Helms's chair. She put the phone to her ear, her heart thumping in her chest.

"Hello? Max?"

CHAPTER SIXTY-TWO

Lugano, Switzerland

Hunt and Carter moved in unison. Years of kicking down doors down-range together allowed them to communicate without the need to talk. The terminal was deserted by now. Someone had activated the fire alarm; its noise was deafening. Hunt forced himself to ignore it, but it was easier said than done.

As they walked down the terminal toward the escalators, Hunt's head was on a swivel.

"Delta-Five, this is One, over," Hunt called for the fifth time.

No response. *Shit.*

Hunt got a sickening feeling in the pit of his stomach.

Despite the cool weather, Hunt could feel the sweat forming on his skin as the adrenaline dumped into his bloodstream.

"Escalators to the right," Carter called.

They made the turn, both in a combat crouch. Hunt was the first to see him. His heart sank. They continued to move down the hallway at a steady pace. Three more Swiss officers were sprawled on the floor next to Kleiner, who was easily recognizable because of his DEA jacket.

"Kleiner! Kleiner!" Hunt called.

Fuck! Please, God, no.

The closer they got, the sicker Hunt felt.

"I got him," Carter called, dropping to a knee next to Kleiner.

"Covering," Hunt replied. It took everything he had not to look down at Kleiner and the three downed Swiss officers. Hunt scanned left and right, then moved closer to Carter so he could cover his friend with his body while he worked on Kleiner.

Hunt had just pivoted 180 degrees to scan their rear when he saw two men turn the same corner he and Carter had turned twenty seconds earlier. The men, leading with their pistols, were advancing toward them in a combat crouch. Hunt hesitated. It took a fraction of a second too long to identify one of the South African mercenaries. The man on his right, tall and thin with a narrow mustache, Hunt had never seen. The mercenary was the first to fire.

Hunt heard Carter grunt just as he pulled the trigger twice, dropping the South African where he stood. Then Hunt had the sensation of being hit in the chest twice in quick succession by a jackhammer. He was pushed backward and tripped over Carter as more bullets flew above him. Despite falling and the immense pain he was in, Hunt's muscle memory kicked in. His hands let go of the HK416, and he drew his HK45 Tactical. He fired six shots the instant his back hit the floor. He had no idea how many of his rounds had found their mark, but the last one had taken off the top of the second shooter's head.

Hunt wrestled with the vest until he was able to slide his hands under to assess the damage. The bullets hadn't gone through. He'd be all right. Even though he was only able to gulp air in short, painful gasps, he wanted to check on Carter.

Carter had been shot in his side, just below his armpit. Hunt looked for an exit wound but didn't find one. His friend's face and skin were pale, deathly pale. Carter's breath was coming in shallow gasps. In between breaths, his lips trembled.

But at least he's breathing, Hunt thought.

———

Simon Carter knew he'd been hit bad. He had difficulty breathing, and the pain was unbearable. He had no idea where his rifle was. He'd seen Hunt fall too. He had painfully managed to pull his pistol from his holster, but it had drained him of all his strength. Since then, he had been unable to open his eyes.

His thoughts, though, weren't for him. They were about Emma and how pissed she'd be if he didn't make it home. She didn't know he knew, but she had planned a surprise for their upcoming anniversary: a marvelous month-long cruise aboard a luxury ocean liner. A once-in-a-lifetime experience.

As his body began to shut down, he could feel Emma's warm, kind hands holding his hand on her cheek. He felt a wetness roll down his face.

And then nothing.

———

Jorge Ramirez was out of options. The police were everywhere, and they had cordoned off the entire area. He had been supposed to meet up with Wood after he and the South African mercenary had taken care of Pierce Hunt. Their plan had been to leave the dead DEA agent next to the escalator so that he would be easily seen and identifiable by the other American agents. Wood had said it would be their best chance to take them all down. But now Ramirez had a feeling that neither the New Zealander nor the mercenary had made it past Hunt.

He'd have to take care of Hunt himself. Hunt would never stop chasing him. Wherever he was in the world, he'd have to look over his shoulder. He was done running.

With what he had in his pocket, there was a whole lot of freedom he could negotiate. But he had to get out of Switzerland first. The Swiss authorities wouldn't much care about his thumb drive and the intelligence it had on it. Colonel Arteaga would, though. Maybe Ramirez could find a way to negotiate directly with Venezuela's new president? And who cared if Arteaga didn't pay much? This *new* him wasn't greedy. A small place by the water, a small boat, a fishing rod. That wasn't too much to ask, was it?

As long as Pierce Hunt was dead, he'd be smiling.

Ramirez, playing the scared traveler, retraced his steps and went up the escalator.

CHAPTER SIXTY-THREE

CIA headquarters
Langley, Virginia

Dorothy Triggs didn't know if she was happy, sad, angry, or just over-whelmed by Max's call. She sat in Walter Helms's chair, trying to clear her thoughts. In the background, Andrew Collings sobbed.

"Where are you?" she asked Max. Tears were already welling up in her eyes. As much as she hated what he had done to her, he was still her little boy, a man who had lost his wife and unborn child to a terrorist. Somehow, she felt as if she were the one who had failed him. Maybe she had.

"It doesn't matter where I am, Mom. You and I both know I can never come home."

Triggs remained silent. Max was right. What he had done was beyond reprehensible. He had committed treason. Maybe it was indeed better that he didn't share his location with her.

"Who have you been working with, Max?" she asked, her hand slowly moving toward her purse.

There was an audible sigh at the other end of the line. "I never thought I'd be the cause of so much mayhem, Mom. You have to know this."

"I do, Max."

"Watch your back around Walter Helms. He . . . he's a devious bastard. I thought he was one of the good ones, but he played me like a fiddle. Be careful around him."

Her breath caught in her throat. *It's too late for that,* she thought. She looked at Walter Helms, who had moved nearer the table, a small pistol in his hand. There was no way she could get to her revolver without him shooting her first.

"Just wanted to call to let you know how sorry I am, Mom, and that I love you very much."

Tears were freely rolling down her cheeks. She tried to speak but choked on the words she wanted to say.

"I love you too," she managed to whisper, but Max had already hung up.

Was this what the experts called *closure*?

Triggs threw her phone at Helms's head with all her strength and went for her revolver.

———

Helms ducked, and the phone flew over his head. He fired twice at Triggs's heart just as her hand reached the interior of her purse. The impacts pushed her backward into the chair.

Helms knew he had to be fast. The instant after he fired his second shot, he pulled Triggs's revolver from her purse and turned toward Andrew Collings. Andrew screamed. Helms shot him three times center mass with Triggs's revolver. He then wiped the revolver with his handkerchief and placed the gun in Triggs's hand.

Helms took two deep breaths. Once his heartbeat had returned to normal, he picked up his phone and, after reassuring his secretary that he was okay, asked her to unlock the door and call security.

CHAPTER SIXTY-FOUR

Lugano, Switzerland

What's taking so long?

Hunt didn't understand why it was taking so long for the other first responders to come inside the terminal. He and Carter had already been inside the train station for almost three minutes now. Carter needed immediate surgery, or he was going to die. It was that simple. If the paramedics didn't show up in the next sixty seconds, he'd take Carter to the hospital himself. He was cutting away Carter's bulletproof vest when he caught movement to his left.

In that one fleeting moment, Hunt couldn't believe what he was seeing.

Jorge Ramirez.

———

Ramirez squatted on the escalator to make sure he wouldn't be seen by someone standing next to the top until it was too late. After Wood had saved his life, he'd taken the pistol of one of the police officers he had killed. It was this gun that he kept tight against his leg as he willed the escalator to go up faster.

Then everything happened in slow motion. Ramirez's first action was to scan for other potential threats as his head crested the escalator, particularly police officers since they were armed. Firefighters and paramedics—they were easy targets. Hunt was less than seven feet away to the left near the top of the escalator, tending to someone. Maybe it was because his arm wasn't fast enough, or he wasn't as fluid as he used to be because of the beatings he had received in the last couple of days. Or it could have simply been bad luck. But Hunt turned and saw him before he had time to aim. Hunt was lightning fast, and surprising Ramirez, he rolled toward him. Ramirez hadn't even started to adjust his aim when Hunt stabbed him in the leg.

———

For Hunt, it was as if everything slowed down. The moment he saw Ramirez, it was immediately clear to him that he wouldn't have the time to draw his pistol and that his only chance was to close the distance and to do it fast. As Hunt sprang to his left and rolled once to his side, images of Pike, Crawford, and Jacobs all burst into his mind. Either he was about to join them, or he'd be sending their killer to hell. At the apex of the roll, Hunt let out a guttural scream as he drove his knife down. He felt the blade pierce flesh and then hit bone. Ramirez's long yell of agony was a bonus.

Leaving the knife embedded in Ramirez's thigh, Hunt moved with blinding speed and reached up with his free hand to grab hold of the back of Ramirez's neck. Using his own body weight, Hunt pulled Ramirez toward the floor. At the same time, he jerked his knife free and thrust it upward, slicing through the soft flesh of Ramirez's neck and severing a carotid artery and his windpipe.

Hunt held Ramirez close and his knife deep as he watched the life slowly leave his eyes.

"This is for Jack Cameron and all the other young, innocent lives you took, you goddamn cockroach," Hunt said. "Leila Hunt sends her regards."

A soft murmur of plea escaped Ramirez's lips, but then his eyes blinked for the last time, and Hunt dropped him to the floor with a thud.

CHAPTER SIXTY-FIVE

Just north of Lugano, Switzerland

Max Oswald strapped on his helmet and mounted his motorcycle. The two South African mercenaries did the same. There was nothing left for him to do in Lugano. He had lost a battle, but he was still in the fight. It might take him months, even a year or two, to truly get back on his feet, but he owed it to his fallen comrades to keep fighting for what was right.

"You guys know what to do," Max said to the two mercenaries, giving them each an envelope filled with Swiss francs and euros.

Both men nodded.

Max started his bike, and the mercenaries did the same. The roar of the bikes' engines inside the garage was earsplitting. Max used the garage door remote to open it. He and the two mercenaries would take different routes in case the house was under surveillance. If the Swiss police had limited resources, they wouldn't be able to track all three of them. Max had four different license plates for the bike and hoped to drive it as far as Lucerne, where he planned to stay for a while, or at least until he figured out what to do next. One of his top priorities would be to deal with Pierce Hunt. Even though he didn't know Hunt on a personal level, he understood better than most how the former Army Ranger operated. He knew that the deaths of Colleen Crawford, Barry

Pike, and Harriet Jacobs would be hard on Hunt and that he would go to the moon and back to get justice for them.

And I'll be his number one target, Max thought. Which wasn't a good thing. Not that he owed Hunt anything, because he didn't, but for some reason Max felt he had to set the record straight. He'd never in a million years thought things would get so screwed up so fast. Deep down, he felt like he'd been betrayed by his mentor. Walter Helms had drawn him close with what now seemed like empty promises. Had Helms ever truly planned on helping the families of fallen special operations soldiers? Or had he used his son's death and Max's pain over Zehra's death to enrich himself?

Max fully intended on finding out. He wouldn't rest until he did. But in the meantime, he'd find a way to contact Hunt and make amends. Max didn't want Hunt hot on his trail.

Once the garage door had fully opened, Max closed his helmet visor, gunned the powerful bike's engine, and raced out of the garage.

CHAPTER SIXTY-SIX

Ten weeks later
Palm Cay Marina
Nassau, New Providence, Commonwealth of the Bahamas

Pierce Hunt couldn't stop laughing. It might have been the big hug his daughter had just given him, or the beers, or the wine, or simply the good company. He didn't care. He was happy. And by the looks on everyone's faces tonight, he wasn't the only one who felt this way.

"Dad, can Sophia and I go to Maya's?" Leila asked.

Hunt made a show of looking at his watch. "Only if you're home by midnight. Deal?"

Leila fist-bumped him and left with her friends. Anna took a break from the conversation she was having with their neighbor Marguerite and placed her hand on his forearm.

"What did the girls want?" she asked, but before Hunt could say a word, she said, "Let me guess. They want to go to Maya's?"

"How did you know?"

Anna chuckled. "You know who Maya's neighbor is?"

"Should I know?"

"He's a former FC Barcelona player, and his son, Lorenzo . . . well, he thinks Leila's the prettiest girl in the world."

Hunt wasn't sure if he should like Lorenzo or not. On the one hand, he agreed with him that Leila was the prettiest girl in the world.

But on the other hand, Hunt wasn't happy that Lorenzo thought that Leila was the prettiest girl in the world.

"You know what she told Lorenzo?" Anna asked, smiling at him.

"Please enlighten me, my love," Hunt replied.

"She told him that her father didn't want her to date until she's eighteen."

"I never—"

Again Anna interrupted him by placing her finger on his lips. "It doesn't matter what you said or didn't say, tough guy," she replied. "The point is that Lorenzo was super sweet with her. You want to know what he said?"

"Sure."

"He said, 'It's okay. I'll wait for you.'"

Hunt sighed. It *was* sweet. Maybe that Lorenzo guy wasn't so bad after all.

"Just thought you'd like to know, baby," Anna said, squeezing his hand.

Hunt looked around, his feet happy in the cool evening sand. Their setup on the beach was exceptional. Twenty good friends and neighbors seated at five tables they had put together to enjoy a sensational dinner by the ocean. A dozen Tiki torches illuminated the night, adding to the enchantment of the culinary experience they had all loved. Chris Moon and a friend who was an offensive tackle for the Kansas City Chiefs had taken care of everything that needed grilling. Never in a lifetime had Hunt imagined that the two of them could prepare such a succulent grilled-chicken dish. Hunt had literally licked his fingers—despite Anna's chastising eyes.

Simon Carter's health was improving every day, which made Hunt very happy. Hunt had yet to forgive himself for not shooting the South African mercenary a tad sooner. Not that Carter ever complained, but Hunt knew his best friend was still in pain. Following a three-week stay at a state-of-the-art Swiss hospital, the doctors had given Carter permission to travel back to the United States. Since his return, Carter had done a lot of physio and, if Hunt was to believe Emma, a lot of TV binge-watching. A couple of weeks ago, Carter had had a long discussion with Tom Hauer, and it had been mutually agreed that Simon Carter's career in the field, to Emma's delight, was officially over. He'd receive a DEA medical pension for life, but Hauer had told Hunt that Carter had agreed to do some consulting work once in a while.

Dante and Abigail had returned to Croatia, once again exchanging their DEA badges and guns for a glass of wine and a good book. Hunt kept in touch with them and planned on bringing Anna and the girls to the Dalmatian coast for a visit soon. Dante had apologized a number of times for being unable to intercept the three motorcycles that had departed the house north of Lugano, but Hunt had assured him it wasn't his or Abi's fault. The Swiss police had been too overwhelmed with all the action that had taken place at the train station to respond quickly.

As for Charlie Henican, he had yet to fully recuperate from his ordeal. His body was fine, but the emotional scars of losing Harriet Jacobs were still fresh and would probably remain so for a very long time. Hunt knew he'd have to keep a close eye on his friend and was in the process of convincing Henican to purchase a small house not too far from his and Anna's place.

"And you'll be close to our marina, brother," Hunt had told him. "It's the perfect spot to start that one-boat chartering company of yours."

A few weeks ago, Henican had said to Hunt that he didn't believe for even a second that Dorothy Triggs had betrayed either of them. He'd even told Hunt he had proof that it was Helms who had killed Triggs first before killing Andrew Collings. One of the security officers who'd been present on the seventh floor that day had confided in Henican that there had been two pistol shots followed by three more. Not the other way around, like the official report had claimed. If the security officer's version of events was the right one, it would indeed mean that Triggs had been shot first.

Hunt understood the implications and what it could mean for Helms if it ever came out, but he wasn't holding his breath. After Triggs's death, not only had Walter Helms solidified his reign at the CIA, he had also been hailed as a national hero by President Reilly. The man was untouchable. Hunt had retrieved the thumb drive from Ramirez's pocket, and even though the intelligence it contained was deeply incriminating, it mostly implicated Colonel Arteaga and Dorothy Triggs. The evidence against Helms was razor thin, and it wouldn't be enough to bring him down. Not by a long shot.

Then had come Max Oswald's letter. At first, Hunt hadn't known what to think of it. He had shown it to Carter, Henican, and Anna. Max had carefully explained the reasoning behind his actions, and even though Hunt couldn't agree with the path Max had chosen—couldn't forgive Max for manipulating him into killing Aram Diljen—he understood what the man had wanted to accomplish. Max's written apology looked sincere, and his version of events was compelling and added veracity to the security officer's claim about the sequence of the Langley shooting.

Between the lines, Hunt understood that Max had taken on his shoulders the burden of not just Diljen but all the CIA and police officers killed in Switzerland and in the Bahamas and had vowed to find a way to make it right.

Hunt had no idea how Max would achieve this. It was a tall order.

Hunt finished his Barolo and whispered something in Anna's ear that made her giggle. He kissed her on the head and walked toward Jasmine, who was standing alone on the beach, her feet in the warm ocean.

"Can I see it?" Hunt asked.

Jasmine showed him the ring Moon had given her ahead of their vow renewal. Hunt wasn't really into jewelry, but this was spectacular. He'd never seen such a big diamond before.

"Wow." That was all he managed to say.

His ex-wife turned to him. Her eyes were filled with tears.

"Oh shit. Did I say something wrong?" he asked her, immediately worried that "wow" wasn't the proper thing to say.

She shook her head and wiped her tears with the back of her hand. "Actually, I have no idea why I'm crying. I'm just so happy, I guess. I have a fantastic, healthy daughter, an ex-husband who's not too bad, and I'm married to the guy of my dreams. What more can a girl ask for?"

Hunt was relieved that everything was okay. He loved Jasmine very much. She was a fantastic mother. She deserved to be happy. "I'm glad about you and Chris. I'm happy for you both."

"Thanks, Pierce. Believe it or not, that means a lot to me. Chris is the best man I've ever met. Present company included," she said, gently punching him in the chest.

They spent a few moments in silence, enjoying the warm breeze coming from the ocean.

"You're okay with being Chris's best man?" Jasmine asked.

"Yes and no, to be honest," Hunt said. "It will really depend on how you answer my question."

Jasmine's eyes widened. This was clearly not the answer she had expected. But now that the can of worms had been opened, she was ready to listen. "Okay," she said. "What's wrong?"

Hunt sighed heavily. "It's the suit," he said after a moment.

Jasmine snapped her head in his direction. "What are you talking about?"

Hunt shrugged. "I don't wear them. Would it be okay if I wear shorts to your ceremony?"

EPILOGUE

One year later
Orlando, Florida

Max Oswald watched D/CIA Walter Helms order vanilla cones for his two tween grandkids at the amusement park stand. After Helms paid for the ice creams, he signaled the two members of his protective detail that he was going to use the washroom.

It had been a long day, but it was finally winding down. The sun had completed its descent behind the horizon hours ago, and most people had already left the theme park or were in the process of doing so.

That gave Max the opportunity he'd been waiting for.

Even if one of Helms's bodyguards might have known or seen Max in the past, they'd never recognize him now. His beard was long, and he had gained approximately twenty-five pounds of muscle since he'd left the CIA. He had purchased colored contact lenses just in case, but he was sure it was overkill. He was dressed in a pair of jeans and a polo shirt but was also wearing a light windbreaker to hide his imposing stature. And to hide the Glock at the small of his back. And the suppressor he was carrying in his right pocket.

One of the bodyguards accompanied Helms inside while the other stood guard outside the washroom facilities. The kids were seated at a picnic table partly hidden from view, licking away at their humongous ice cream cones while watching videos on their phones.

Max scanned the area one more time. Satisfied there was no one else in the immediate vicinity, he nonchalantly walked toward the washroom, inserting AirPods in his ears. He wasn't listening to anything, but having something in his ears would justify his not obeying the bodyguard's upcoming commands. Max knew exactly what was going to happen. He almost felt sorry for Helms.

He'd never see it coming.

"Sorry, sir, it's presently occupied," the bodyguard said when Max was still fifteen feet away. "Please come back in five minutes."

Max kept walking. To his credit, the bodyguard realized that something was wrong and sidestepped to his left to block access to the door. But he didn't pull his weapon out.

Big mistake.

By the time the bodyguard realized his error in judgment, it was too late. Max was already on him. The bodyguard's first move was to lash out with a kick to create some distance between him and Max in order to get to his weapon. The bodyguard knew how to throw a kick, but Max was faster. He grabbed the man's foot midair and violently twisted his ankle. The man yelled in pain and landed face-first on the cement. Max stepped over him and delivered a powerful punch to the base of the man's neck. The door of the bathroom opened to reveal the second bodyguard. He'd heard his colleague scream and come out to investigate. His hand was on his holster, but the pistol was still secured. Max sprang to his feet and delivered a searing knee strike to the man's groin. As Max had predicted, the bodyguard doubled over in agony. But Max wasn't done. He crashed his left elbow down between the man's shoulder blades. The man dropped to the floor.

The whole fight had lasted less than ten seconds.

"Dewey?" Helms asked from one of the bathroom stalls. "Everything okay?"

Max attached the silencer to his pistol and hurried toward the stall where Helms was busy doing his business. He didn't want to give the man a chance to react.

Max kicked the stall door, snapping the lock.

A look of pure hatred appeared on Helms's face.

"Hi, Walter."

"Hi, Max."

"Why?"

"Why what, Max?"

Max fired. His round shattered Helms's right knee. Max took three strides and struck Helms on the side of the head with his pistol. With his left hand, Max squeezed Helms's throat so he wouldn't scream. Helms's mouth opened in an attempt to gulp some air, and Max took the opportunity to shove his pistol deep into it, breaking a tooth or two in the process.

"Listen, Walter," Max said, "it's over for you. You know it. I know it. What you can do, though, is save the lives of your two grandkids and these two officers. You decide."

Feeling that Helms was about to be sick, Max pulled his pistol from Helms's mouth.

Helms laughed, or at least tried to, but there were tears of pain in the corners of his eyes. "I think you broke my jaw, Max."

"Why? Why did you frame me?" Max said.

"I lost my only son to a stupid war, Max. Me and my wife deserved to be compensated for his sacrifice. What else?"

"You selfish bastard," Max said, slamming the butt of his pistol into Helms's nose. "You took ten million for yourself when that money could have gone to other families."

Helms yelled in pain, but Max quickly thrust his pistol back into his mouth to silence him. Helms's blood dripped from his nose into his mouth.

"Why kill Pike and Crawford?" Max asked once he was sure Helms would stay quiet. He removed the pistol from Helms's mouth.

Helms spat blood and another tooth. "Fuck!"

"Why kill Pike and—"

"Pike found out, goddamn it! While he was tracing the leak, he found out I took money out of the black budget, okay?"

Max shook his head. "What's wrong with you? We had a dream, Walter. We were supposed to do this together. Or was it all a lie to you?"

"Do what you have to do, Max, and fuck off! You'll never understand what my wife and I went through."

Max didn't see the point in reminding Helms that he had lost his wife to a terrorist.

"Why did you kill my mother?" he asked instead.

Helms smirked. "I needed someone to take the fall. Someone who had the same access I did to the black budget. Your mother was the perfect patsy. She was—"

Max shot him twice in the heart.

"Goodbye, Walter."

ACKNOWLEDGMENTS

As always, the first thank-you goes to my readers. Whether *Time to Hunt* is the first book you read in my Pierce Hunt series or you've been with me since *Hunt Them Down*, I thank you for your support. I hope you enjoyed the ride.

I'm so happy with my Thomas & Mercer family. I'd like to thank my sagacious editor, Liz Pearsons, for taking a chance on me when she bought *Hunt Them Down* back in 2018. Her continuous support means the world to me. Enormous gratitude to Gracie Doyle, Sarah Shaw, Caitlin Alexander, and the rest of my team at Amazon Publishing for doing an amazing job in a tough market. You're doing everything right! Without you, none of this would be possible. I'm greatly indebted to you all.

Thanks to my dear agent, Eric Myers of Myers Literary Management. Eric has been with me from the very beginning, and for that I'll always be grateful.

Thanks, too, to my friends in the literary world: Marc Cameron, James Hankins, K. J. Howe, Jack Carr, Mark Greaney, RIP Rawlings, Ryan Steck—a.k.a. the Real Book Spy—Joshua Hood, Lee Goldberg, Brian Andrews, Jeff Wilson, Don Bentley, Slaven Tomasi, Matthew Farrell, Chad Zunker, and the guys over at *The Crew Reviews* (Mike, Eric, Sean, and Chris).

Finally, I must say thank you to my wonderful family. To Gabriel and Florence: I adore you. You two are the reason I wake up with a smile in the morning. To my divine wife, Lisane, who puts up with so, so much while juggling being an endodontist, a businesswoman, a wife, and a mother to our two awesome kids: you inspire me, and after twenty years together, you still take my breath away.